—*Where Fear Lives In The Shadows Of The Soul*—

Destination-Fate!

Order this book online at www.trafford.com/07-2197
or email orders@trafford.com

Most Trafford titles are also available at major online book retailers.

Note for Librarians: A cataloguing record for this book is available from Library and Archives Canada at www.collectionscanada.ca/amicus/index-e.html

ISBN: 978-1-4251-5053-2

We at Trafford believe that it is the responsibility of us all, as both individuals and corporations, to make choices that are environmentally and socially sound. You, in turn, are supporting this responsible conduct each time you purchase a Trafford book, or make use of our publishing services. To find out how you are helping, please visit www.trafford.com/responsiblepublishing.html

Our mission is to efficiently provide the world's finest, most comprehensive book publishing service, enabling every author to experience success. To find out how to publish your book, your way, and have it available worldwide, visit us online at www.trafford.com/10510

www.trafford.com

North America & international
toll-free: 1 888 232 4444 (USA & Canada)
phone: 250 383 6864 • fax: 250 383 6804 • email: info@trafford.com

The United Kingdom & Europe
phone: +44 (0)1865 722 113 • local rate: 0845 230 9601
facsimile: +44 (0)1865 722 868 • email: info.uk@trafford.com

10 9 8 7 6 5 4 3 2 1

Contents

Chapter 1

JOHNNY NASH LOOKED upon the imposing structure of Warlock Inn from a distance with a mixture of exuberance and trepidation. He had wanted to do a series of articles and essays about the history of the large house. The opportunity had at last come to him.

His fascination with the huge two-story Queen Anne style frame house went back to his early childhood in Seville. He grew up in the nearby neighbourhood. The little town located just south of St. Augustine was his world until his teen years.

With the arrival of October, the inn was at the minimal occupancy rate of the year during this part of the off season. Business would not pick up again until later in November as the holidays began gaining momentum.

The final burst of summer trade ended in late August. The busiest time after that was generally between Thanksgiving and Christmas followed by spring breaks when some of the college crowd heading south around Easter elected to remain north as it was generally less raucous than Daytona.

Despite the close humidity and the fast-moving grey clouds coming from the southwest indicating the first line of showers in advance of an early autumn cold front, Johnny continued to observe the imposing structure seemingly oblivious of the weather or anything else.

The house had an ambience about it. On one hand, it felt foreboding and ominous. But on the other hand, it had an inviting and warm appeal. For the average tourist, the place was just a typical old inn such as you might come across in towns like Savannah or Charleston. To those who knew something about the history of the house, Warlock Inn was far more than just an ordinary old house that had been converted into a southern inn.

The house was built in the late 1860's by an unscrupulous northern carpetbagger, Jonas Van Gilder. He came down from somewhere up in New York around 1866 during the period of military occupation that followed the civil war.

Van Gilder was a cruel, hard man as he proceeded to plunder Seville and the surrounding countryside, bleeding the populace of their money and their land. He amassed millions for himself in his scurrilous appetite for wealth.

Van Gilder had the house built at the time he met a southern belle from an old prominent family in Savannah on one of his numerous trips to that elegant city which epitomized southern charm and graciousness. The lady's name was Jeanine O'Rourke. The family had a huge cotton plantation and a small fleet of sailing ships. After the war, the O'Rourkes lost much of their fortune and assets.

When Jonas took a fancy to Jeanine, she reluctantly agreed to marry him after he offered to invest a good deal of capital into the O'Rourke shipping line and promised to assist in reactivating the plantation and cotton gins for her father, Douglas O'Rourke.

The building of the house was completed in late 1868. Jeanine and Jonas were married shortly after and tool occupancy of the great house after returning from their honeymoon in Paris.

There was far more to Jonas Van Gilder's dark reputation than just his cold, calculating cruelty when it came to business. Rumour constantly circulated in Seville concerning the belief by many that the man was a practitioner of witchcraft and was in fact a Satanist.

He was known to keep company from time to time with several notorious witches in the region. They would even come to the house at various times of the years for sabbats and to perform the blasphemous Black Mass. Infants, children and virginal young girls disappeared at these times and were not seen again. There was also the bizarre manner in which many of Van Gilder's enemies would suddenly be stricken and cut down by some peculiar malady and then ebb away before dying; men and women that had been shortly before the picture of health. These phenomena always seem to occur after a particularly strong confrontation with Van Gilder over business matters or accusation of witchcraft had been made on the part of the person struck down with the fatal malady.

After five unbearable years as Van Gilder's wife, Jeanine died suddenly of a massive stroke following a debilitating bout of yellow fever. It was apparent to the citizenry of Seville that the poor woman could not endure life with the tyrant any longer. There was talk that she was on the verge of leaving him when she was struck down with the yellow fever.

Things finally came to an inevitable head in 1873 when a servant girl witnessed a gruesome sacrifice on the night of February 1, which was known by the apostates of Satanism as Candlemass Eve. The girl managed to get out of the house and relay what she seen to the military authorities in St. Augustine. The murder had taken place in the cellar of the house. The house was unique in that it sat on high enough ground to permit for a large cellar, which had been used as a Black Chapel by Van Gilder and the two women.

A detachment of soldiers was sent out to bring Van Gilder into St. Augustine on a charge of murder and witchcraft. The apprehension of the two female cohorts came shortly after his arraignment. The women were caught at Cowford, which was also known as the city of Jacksonville and named for the first territorial governor of Florida, Andrew Jackson.

An extensive search was made of the house and grounds following Van Gilder's arrest. Numerous bones identified as both animal and human were found along with the remains of half decayed bodies identified as children and young girls just past the age of puberty.

A trail was held shortly afterward. The courtroom was filled to capacity with spectators from all over the north Florida area wanting a glimpse of the hated Satanist and the two witches. Van Gilder was found guilty of mass murder and witchcraft along with the women. He was taken over to Fort Matanzas near the coast and hung. His body was cremated afterward and his ashes were buried in unconsecrated ground in a secret location that no historian or any other interested person had been able to unearth right up to the present day. The two women were burned at the stake just outside of St. Augustine.

In 1874, a nephew of Jonas Van Gilder arrived in Seville with his young bride. His name was Nathaniel Van Gilder. His wife was a sweet young thing named Mimsy. Nathaniel was as different from Jonas as day is from night. He was a devoutly religious and likeable young man and went out of his way to help people in the area and do good works mostly out of a need to atone for his black-hearted uncle's blasphemies.

At first, the local populace was extremely weary of the young man and his lady. But little by little, they got to know the couple and accepted them into the community graciously.

For the first couple of years, things went well for Nathaniel and Mimsy. Then strange inexplicable things began to happen such as unearthly noises which came from the cellar. Articles of furniture began to levitate in the air followed by small objects and kitchen utensils suddenly being hurtled across the kitchen in poltergeist fashion. This all culminated with Mimsy contracting a severe case of yellow fever much in the same manner as Jonas's poor wife had and dying shortly after being struck down with the illness.

Mimsy's death devastated Nathaniel. He left with her body and returned to New York State for burial vowing never to come back to Seville or that damned house again.

The house remained unoccupied and allowed to fall into a state of disarray and deterioration until 1887. A wealthy businessman from Atlanta, Stephen Cartier, purchased the property and had it extensively renovated.

The house was used as a private retreat for the Cartier family until 1895. Cartier was lucrative opportunities in the property and proceeded to turn the house into a vacation retreat. He took notice of the wave of wealthy northerners vacationing in Florida particularly during the harshest part of the winter season. The house became a regal breakfast and bed inn. Cartier successfully lured tourists away from the St. Augustine area because of the houses close proximity to fine scenic beaches nearby.

The house was just on the outskirts of Seville. The main commuter line of the North Florida Railroad ran right through Seville. It did not take that long a time to go from Seville up to St. Augustine for a day of sightseeing.

The inn was originally named Cartier Retreat. It remained in the Cartier family until the death of Stephen Cartier in 1900.

The house was purchased by Lockwood Realty Properties shortly after Cartier's estate was settled. Just before the First World War, it received an extensive renovation, It was at that time that the large observation tower was added onto the front end of the house.

The inn was never able to escape its sinister origin and history. In a daring move on the part of the Lockwood management, it was decided that they would capitalize on the origin of the house. The Lockwood people renamed it Warlock Inn, as old Jonas was a male witch or warlock.

The master bedroom, which Jonas occupied during his time in the house, achieved a rather bizarre reputation through the years on account of the wallpaper design depicting numerous fairy tale creatures in a macabre manner such as elves, fairies, gremlins, and impish demons. The color of the wallpaper was a deep shade of amber. It contrasted sharply with the scarlet red coloring of the oriental carpet, which covered hardwood floor.

The master bedroom became the famous number 207. Through the years, the room attracted many an eccentric to the inn. In more recent times, college students and historians of local history such as himself along with the just plain curious requested the room for a night or two mainly to see for themselves if the room was haunted by the ghost of old Jonas as a local legend would have it.

He felt both a shudder and a great thrill as he speculated on that aspect of the famous number 207. he hoped to get to the truth of that particular legend and a great many other things while occupying the room during the time he would spend researching the series of articles on the curious history of the place for his magazine, the Florida Historical and Cultural Journal.

As a child, his buddies and he, which included Billy Barber, Terry Williams and Barney Soretto, would sneak into the inn and search for the bogeyman that was said to haunt the house. On each of their incursions, they found the cellar door barred and padlocked. They then sneaked upstairs to room 207. They were determined that they were going to learn for themselves the truth of the legend about the room being haunted by the spirit of old Jonas.

They were discovered on several occasions by either a cleaning woman or a wiseass bellboy and taken to the manager. He would give them a stern lecture and warn them about carrying on like that would get them into bad trouble. He would let them go after the lecture.

The last time they tried such a stunt, Mr. Valance, the manager of the inn back then, was ready for them. He his in the large closet in room 207 after being informed by one of the bellboys that he had seen the boys in the back of the inn snooping around. Old Valance instructed the bellboy to get under the covers of the large bed. He was to first put on a large, grotesque-looking ape mask that a guest had left behind. When they sneaked into the room, Mr. Valance whispered from inside the closet that the bogeyman lived in the room and was going to snatch their soul away. The bellboy pulled the covers down and jumped up yelling like a screaming banshee. When they say the glowing ape mask, they hauled ass out of there like the very devil himself was after them. They never tried sneaking into the inn after that.

Johnny's fascination with Warlock Inn and the sinister origin of the house did not end with childhood. Through the years, the aura surrounding Warlock Inn became an all consuming obsession even when the family moved up to Jacksonville when his father landed a position with the Seaboard Coastline Railroad at their headquarters. He was fifteen at the time.

Upon graduating Parker High, he was accepted into the school of journalism and communications a Florida State University. After receiving his BA for FSU, he interned as a cub reporter at the Tampa Tribune. He stayed with the paper for three years and then took a post as the crime reporter for the Fort Lauderdale Sun. After a year and a half at the Sun, he became assistant editor and field reporter for the Florida Historical and Cultural Journal out of Winter Haven. The magazine was a bimonthly dealing primarily with the architecture and little known aspects of culture and history which is distinctive of the Florida scene.

Upon taking up his duties at the magazine, he began hawking the idea of doing a series of articles on the inn to his senior editor, Ted Mathius. Ted turned thumbs down on the idea for more than a year. Johnny continued to push it. Ted finally caved into him and gave him the go-ahead several months ago.

Preliminary arrangements were struck with the current owners of the property, the Magnolia Corporation, and he was sent over on assignment at this time to do a fast article which would appear in the November issue, telling about Jonas Van Gilder and the bizarre history of room 207 through the years relating to a number of guests that had met with unusual fates while occupying the room and why that room seemed to draw so many people t it as if they dared to tempt fate while residing in it. "Play up the jinxed and cursed angle," as Ted put it.

Johnny continued to gaze at the house and wondered if he was like that, wanting to tempt fate and even flirt with it. He had to finally know the real reason why the house has consumed him all these years. He had to know why room 207 had claimed the lives of a number of people, as it seemed to him and number of Seville's citizens. And he was finally going down into that cellar and see the place where Van Gilder murdered so much innocence in the name of Satan. He was going to look into that old cistern well down there and see for himself if there was anything in it as the legend persisted through the years in Seville stating that there was such a thing down there.

The owners of the inn placed the cellar off limits to him. He was determined though that he was going down into the underbelly of the house with or without the blessing of the management.

He considered himself fortunate that he was able to persuade Miranda Spencer to come up from Deland for the next several day. She was a good friend with a genuine gift of psychic abilities. He had personally observed her talent like the time she assisted the Fort Myers police in locating the body of the missing Fairfax tobacco heiress, Wanda Paige, after the authorities virtually gave up on finding her. Miranda's special talent, as he came to regard her keen psychic powers, was instrumental in determining that Wanda's brother, Vinton Paige, murdered her so that he would be the sole heir to the estate after their father, Ridley Paige, and his new wife were killed a short time before in a private plane crash near Columbus, South Carolina.

Johnny had witnessed other examples of Miranda's telepathic empathy with numerous people and institutions seeking her assistance. Miranda was genuine. He was sure of her beyond a shadow of a doubt. She really did have a sixth sense. A strong feeling for whatever was out there that could not be explained away with normal everyday logic.

He first met Miranda while a student at Florida State. He realized right from the first of their special friendship that she was a special human being, someone with a very special gift.

They dated regularly. He soon found himself just a little bit in love with her. Miranda made it clear to him that their relationship would have to be that of two very good friends and little else. Her special gift consumed her to such an overwhelming degree that she had no room for a serious personal relationship. He found himself wishing at times that she did not possess such a talent. But he knew that form her perspective, it was better this was. He had seen her completely drained after one of her deep trances to the point of mental and physical collapse.

Miranda made her basic living as a freelance commercial artist. She was very good at what she did and earned a comfortable living. She refused any money offered to her by the various people she had been able to help. She only took money to cover her basic expenses such as food, gas for her Porsche, and lodging, Her special gift was from God and it would be wrong for her to try and reap financial reward from such an ability was the way she always answered him when he suggested that she ought to get more for what she had been able to render. Miranda was a very principled woman. It was one of her qualities that endeared her to him.

He called her a week ago, asking her to come up and assist him. He wanted her to try and pick up any psychic scarring to the atmosphere in room 207. Through Miranda, he hoped to learn the special relationship between those people that had stayed in the room and met with fateful experiences and even death as a result of their occupancy in the famous number 207. He ultimately hoped to lean of the inn itself had taken on aspects of the evil nature of the original owner.

His thoughts were cut short at that point as sharp flashes of lightening showed in the south western sky followed by the ominous sound of rolling thunder. He made a dash in the direction of the carnation pink Queen Anne house as the rain suddenly came down a near torrential downpour.

Chapter 2

THE PORSCHE CRUISED slowly down the narrow drive. As the dominant line of Warlock Inn came into view, Miranda Spencer once more had the strong negative reaction she had when John got in touch with he rang asked her to come up and assist him on the first article about the inn that he was doing for his magazine.

The morning air was cool, crisp, and clear with the passage of one of the early cold fronts of the season. It certainly was a welcomed change from the heat and humidity which clung cloyingly in the air during the past week. There was just the hint of the salty ocean scent coming off the Atlantic.

The verdant green St. Augustine grass along with the various tall palms, cypress, and live oaks adorning the grounds were feast for the eyes.

Although the grounds surrounding Warlock Inn was a pleasant sight for the eye, Miranda's negative mood increased markedly as the house clearly came into sight. She sensed immediately the evil that was part and parcel of the large and rambling structure.

As she pulled up to the close proximity of the large L-shaped veranda by the front entrance, she spotted John at the top of the steps that led down to the short cobblestone walkway. He smiled at her and waved. She waved at him as she brought the handsome light beige Porsche to a slow halt.

John quickly came down the steps and up to t he car as Miranda opened the door and stepped out. They embraced warmly. He kissed her lightly on the right cheek that was his custom when they had not seen each other for a period of time. "Great to see you, again. I'm glad you took me up on my offer," he said in a pleasingly exuberant manner.

Miranda forced herself to smile pleasantly. "It's good to see you too John." And it was good to see him once more and to be with him. She was very fond of John Nash probably more so that any other man she had ever known. That was the only reason why she agreed to come up and help him in his research in learning why the history of the house and the very aura of it had proven to be such an obsession with him through the years. Whenever they were together, this fixation on Warlock Inn would invariably come up going back to their early days at the university when they first began to date. That was when she thought she wanted to b an elementary school teacher. But her need to express herself more creatively became paramount. She was a really good artist and had a very strong artistic learning as far back as her early childhood. She transferred out of FSU in order to study at the Art Institute in Orlando. After she left the university, they stayed in close touch with each other through the years. Their affection for one another remained unerring.

John smiled and told her to get back inside. He was going to drive her around back to the large visitor's parking lot.

She went around to the passenger side and got in as he got in behind the wheel. They quickly zipped around the side of the house to the expansive parking lot in the rear. John pulled up in a spot marked "Guest" closest to the back entrance of the inn.

He looked over at her and smiled broadly. "Hey! Thanks again. This means a great deal to me, Miranda. Your very special gift may prove invaluable to my research."

She smiled somewhat uneasily as she replied, "I know John. I have to be truthful with you though. I have very bad vibes about this project. I had them when your first asked for my help. And I still have them. Just driving up here to this house, I got a strong impression of something evil."

He frowned slightly at her but quickly switched on that winning smile of his which she loved so much. He was fully aware of her feelings and there probably were good reasons for them. She did have the gift. But to finally have the opportunity to come to terms with Warlock Inn and his admitted nearly pathological obsession with the house was too good to pass up. If he did not finally learn what it was about the house which had so affected him through the years, then he wasn't sure as to whether he could ever find any real peace or satisfaction for whatever span of life he may have left on this earth.

"I know," he said. "And I love you all the more for honouring my request. I'll got your luggage," she smiled and nodded as he got out of the car and went around to the rear to open the trunk. He got out her overnight bag and patent leather valise and came around to the passenger door. He was as amiable as ever she thought as he put the overnight bag down on the blacktop surface of the lot long enough to open the door for her. She felt instantly invigorated as she stepped out of the car and felt the full impact of the cool, dry morning air which cut right through her light cream-colored silken pants and light cotton blouse.

Her long silky strands of blond hair whipped all about her trip shoulders as the northeast breeze coming off of the Atlantic began to gust very strongly.

John instructed her to follow him. They went along the walkway around the side to the short cobblestone walk to the step leading up to the large veranda at the front entrance.

A cheerful young man in his late teens dressed in the traditional uniform of a bellboy was waiting for them at the top of the steps. John quickly gave the bag and valise to the bellboy. He smiled and offered her a hearty welcome to Warlock Inn and asked her to follow him.

He proceeded to escort them through he large front doors hewn from the finest quality cypress wood. They proceeded down the short hallway of the lobby up to the front desk where an equally pleasant looking swarthy complexioned an in his early forties dressed in a traditional grey pin-striped business suit stood just behind the desk. He smiled at them. "Ah, Mr. Nash. I take it that this is your lovely colleague who will assist you in your journalistic endeavours during your time with us." His voice was well modulated with a slight accent suggesting that he came fro the Mediterranean part of southern Europe.

"Yes, indeed, Mr. Stavolous. I was recently on Mysteries of the Mind," she volunteered.

He threw up his hands in recognition and smiled. "Of course… you are the psychic who worked with the Miami police in capturing the thieves that stole the very expensive Renoir painting form the famous Romero mansion.

"Yes, That's right," she acknowledged.

"Well, it is indeed a pleasure to meet you, Ms. Spencer. I'm sure that you will be a great help to Mr. Nash as he writes about our rather famous establishment. I must say that the officers of the Magnolia Corporation consider this to be a fine bit of publicity considering the rather peculiar history of room 207."

Nate Stavolous was very courteous in Old World Greek manner. She thanked him once again and assured him that she would do her best to assist John. She concluded by asking him to thank the Magnolia people for allowing her to stay at the inn free of charge.

He smiled broadly, It is our pleasure, dear lady. I hope your stay here will be a pleasant one.

Miranda smiled at him once again before turning to follow the bellboy up the elegant stairs to the second floor landing. She glanced back down at the exquisite lobby with its plethora of exotic potted plants and large crystal chandelier that was suspended from the unique marble inlaid ceiling.

They proceeded along the north end hallway that had a pleasant Mediterranean feel due to the design of the hallway runner and the various articles of small furniture and statuary that lined the walls of the corridor. They stopped about halfway down the hall in front of her room which was directly across from room 207. The bellboy quickly took the key and opened the door.

She thanked him as John took out a five-dollar bill and gave it to him. The bellboy grinned broadly and delivered the usual spill about calling him anytime he was on duty for assistance.

John thanked him and told him that he would take her luggage. As he got the overnight bag and valise, she went into the room and was immediately struck by the pleasant old world atmosphere which the room readily conveyed from the sturdy hardwood floor to the large antique four poster bed with its large fringed overhead canopy. The amber colored wallpaper had a pleasing floral design. An elegant antique Spanish style dressing table with a large oval shaped mirror stood across the room from the large bed. There was a large intricately carved Mediterranean designed cypress wood chest of drawers in one corner of the room. Several large, comfortable easy chairs were placed on either side of a highly polished cherry wood round table that was off to the side of the bed.

A large antique wooden clothing cupboard was placed against the wall nearest the large bay window that had an excellent view of the grounds surrounding the inn.

John placed the bag and valise on the bed. He smiled, "I hope it's to your liking, Ms. Spencer."

She giggled slightly. "It's very nice, Mr. Nash." "I'm so glad, dear lady," he said with a slight giggle also.

The only concessions to the modern n the room consisted of a large reading lamp on the nightstand next to the bed and a 19 inch cable ready Panasonic TV which stood in front of the bay window. There was also a small wood grain finish radio on the nightstand along with an extension touch-tone phone.

The room was immaculately kept and had a cozy mood about it. But the inviting sensation, which the room initially conveyed, did not take away from the undercurrent of evil, which she continued to very strongly sense.

John walked over to her and slipped his arms around her and kissed her lightly on the lips. She pulled away. He sighed, as he knew that her basic attitude had not changed.

He welcomed her assistance and her ability. But there were times when he cursed it and wished with all his heart that she did not have the gift. He wanted her so much.

If he were to ever settle down, Miranda Spencer would be the woman he wanted to spend the rest of his life with in a sharing relationship. But he knew that as long as she had the gift, it would not be like that. She told him on many occasions that her life could not be her own… not as long as she had such powerful psychic abilities. She would be compelled to make use of them when she was called on to do so.

She had been instrumental in saving more than one life as a result of her visions. She had helped to fine more than one body of a missing or murdered victim. The gift first manifested itself in her early teens when a boy in her high school class died while scuba diving in a series of underwater limestone caves down in south Florida. She saw it happen in a dramatic vision. She was able to help the authorities in locating her friend's body. She nearly had a nervous breakdown as a result of that first experience.

The gift had drained her emotionally after every major encounter. As a result, she could not think of a committed relationship. "It just wouldn't be fair to that special someone," she told him on more than one occasion.

It hurt not to be with her except for an occasional weekend and the like. They had made love on several occasions and he took some comfort in knowing that he was the only man she had known physically and perhaps romantically.

He continued to hope that someday Miranda might come to feel more comfortable about the gift and decide that she could share her life hopefully with him.

His attention swung back to the reason for her being here. "I have to warn you Miranda that my room, the famous 207, is just a little bit disconcerting when you first see it." He was as pleasantly diplomatic as he could be knowing the way certain houses and rooms in particular had affected her in the past when she picked up strong vibes of psychic residue in areas where violence and death had occurred.

Miranda smiled uneasily as she answered. "Thanks for the warning." She paused then. Her expression became very serious. "John, I wish I could talk you out of this. I wish you would consider leaving this place right now."

He was stunned for a moment. He thought that had all been settled between them. "You know I can't Miranda. I've just got to do this."

She nodded dutifully. "I know, I think I understand. But I wish it wasn't so." Her soft voice quivered slightly as she once more felt a disturbance come on her.

He smiled and said cheerfully, "Well, I'll leave you to get settled in. Meet you in the dining room at noon. We'll have lunch before I introduce you to number 207."

She smiled back at him. "All right. That sounds good."

He left the room. She shuddered slightly after he was gone. She felt very cold for a moment just before she began to unpack.

Chapter 3

JOHNNY SAT AT the table closest to the entrance of the dining room. Only three other people were in the room besides himself, a middle-aged couple sat at the table closest to the large bay front window which overlooked the veranda and an elderly gentleman sat three tables down from where he sat busily scanning the late morning edition of the Jacksonville Times Union while nibbling at a plate of broiled sea trout.

Miranda came into the dining room a few minutes past the noon hour. She wore a fetching combination of tight hip hugging designer jeans and striped red, blue and white blouse. He was struck once again by her desirable, lovely and natural appearance.

That old longing and need wailed up inside of him as it so often had when they were together. He wanted to sweep her off of her feet and take her upstairs and have her and hope that she would want it as much as he did. "Down boy," he told himself. Even if Miranda was in the right frame of mind, this was not the time or the place. After the first session was ended this evening or early tomorrow morning and the proper notes were recorded and arranged, then perhaps they would have the time for each other, and only after Miranda had recovered sufficiently from the deep trance state which always consumed so much of her energy and strength. Her physical and mental exhaustion would be overwhelming.

Miranda smiles as he got up and proceeded to extend a chair away from the table for her and motioned for one of the two waiters to come over to their table with the noon time menu. She seated herself as the waiter handed them two menus and suggested the special of the day which was broiled sea trout marinated in butter sauce. Miranda said that the special would be fine. John ordered the same. The waiter smiles as he took the menus and disappeared through the entrance of the spacious dining room heading back to the kitchen toward the read of the inn.

John Nash smiled warmly as he took her white slender hands into his own. "It is so good to be with you again, Miranda. Thank you. You have no idea how much this means to me."

She smiled guardedly as she gently disengaged her hands from his and studied him closely. "You mean a great deal to me John Nash and I do realize how important this is to you. But I still feel that it isn't in your best interest. I can't put it into proper words. I just know that this place is not right. I told you that when you got in touch with me about this project. That feeling had been reinforced since I saw the inn for the first time this morning. There is something profoundly wrong with Warlock Inn, something that is intangibly evil. It's in the walls of the house itself just waiting for God knows what."

He felt that uneasy sensation as she made clear her opposition again. He had to go through with this. There wasn't anything that was going to stop him now even if it meant facing the possibility of some intangible danger. Warlock Inn was his mountain, which he had to surmount and conquer. He just prayed that he was not placing Miranda in any kind of jeopardy.

He came armed with some elements of protection which he hoped would be enough, such as the small crucifix he purchased in the gift shop on the old historical mission grounds in St. Augustine where it is generally believed the first white men sat foot on the soil of the present day continental United States. In addition, he had with him several plastic vials that contained holy water drawn from the baptismal font of the old cathedral in the historic downtown of the old city. He also had vials of mercury and salt as a number of books he had studied indicated that these elements offered some measure of protection from negative influences and spirits.

He smiled reassuringly as the waiter returned with an urn filled with a piping hot fresh brew of coffee and placed it on the table which was already decked out with turned down coffee cups and place napkins with the silverware wrapped inside. The waiter informed them that their orders would be ready in a few minutes. Johnny thanked him as he left to attend another table.

"I'll promise you this Miranda. Once I'm finished with this assignment and ready to go to the press, I'll never set foot in this place again if you tell me not to."

Miranda smiled approvingly as she turned up the fine china cup in the saucer and poured herself a cup of the heady brew. "I'm glad to hear you say that John Nash. If I can safely assist you in getting this house out of your system and that's the end of it. I'll be more than satisfied. But that still doesn't take away from the very strong negative feeling I have. I still wish you wouldn't do this."

He nodded. "I know."

He poured himself a cup of the hot brew and added some cram and a Sweet 'n Low. He leaned over the table, holding the cup firmly between both hands, and taking a large sip. "You always call me John and everybody else has always called me Johnny. I never asked before, but why?"

She put her cup down and looked at him with a quizzical expression as she thought about it. "I don't know really. To me, you will always be John just like when we began dating in college," she answered.

John mused over her reply as she asked curiously, "When do you want to begin?"

"Tonight. Do you want to see the room before then?" he asked in a straightforward fashion.

"No," she replied firmly. "I realize that you would like for me to get used to it first. But it's better if I go into the room when we're ready to begin the trance state phase. I don't want to be disturbed by preconceived reactions to the atmosphere in the room before then. It's been my experience that when I enter someplace where the vary air has been seared by negative influences over a great many years that it can so unnerve me to the point of possibly disrupting the trance state."

This took him back some since he thought she would like to see the room first. He nodded affirmatively, "Understood. We'll meet in the room shortly before midnight and continue until you tell me that enough is enough."

"I'll bring my things with me at that time… say five or ten minutes till midnight," she said.

"I want to warn you once more Miranda to be prepared if you do go into a transmigratory state that the ill-fated people who stayed in 207 met with bizarre and even rather frightening fates," he said with a dead-on firmness.

She nervously gulped down most of the coffee before answering him. "I already picked up on that just by being in such close proximity of the room. I don't mind telling you John Nash that I will be damned glad when it's all over."

"I just wish that Stavolous would let me go into the cellar where old Jonas did his nasty deeds. Stories have floated around Seville for decades about Jonas having a gateway actually leading to hell down there and that a monstrous demon resides down there in the old cistern well."

From Edgar Allan Poe's *The Haunted Palace*:

And travelers now, within that valley,
Through the red-litten windows see
Vast forms, that move fantastically
To a discordant melody,
While, like a ghastly rapid river,
Through the pale door
A hideous throng rush out forever
And laugh — but smile no more.

From Edgar Allan Poe's *A Dream Within a Dream*:

All that we see or seem
Is but a dream within a dream.

Destination-Fate!

1st Trance

Hurricane Schizm

Chapter 4

FRANCIS EXAMINED HER body and wondered what had happened to her in the nearly two years since her commitment to this place. For instance, what had happened to the fullness of her bosom? She had been so proud of her breasts when she observed them in the past. Why did her figure appear so straight and lean? Why were these people so cruel to her and insisted that she wear a man's simple white linen shirt and loose baggy trousers held up by a pair of ugly suspenders.

She found herself wondering more about these things with every passing day. When she gazed at herself now, she felt frightened, confused, and perplexed. Why was Dr. Lauten so insistent in his persistent attempts at making her try to believe she was a young man named Franklin rather than who she really was? Her name was Francis not Franklin.

She got up from her small cot that was her bed and looked about the dismal room. She walked over to the small mirror on the wall on the other side of the cramped room that was her prison and looked at her face. Tears flowed down her cheeks as the features of a delicate young man stared back at her. She could not believe what they had done to her. Her beautiful hair was short and cut very close and parted neatly down the middle.

She managed to take some comfort. They had not been entirely successful in their cruel program to erase all of her feminine attributes. Her complexion was still creamy and smooth. Her features still had the soft qualities of a woman of some gentility. But they had managed somehow to stimulate the growth of hair on her face. Her inner sense of womanhood was completely outraged at this development.

One of the orderlies came in every day in the late afternoon and insisted upon her shaving or he would do it himself. At first she hated it. After it continued like that over a period of some time, she actually came to look forward to that daily removal of ugly male stubble from her face.

"Why did the courts make her come to this horrible place." She asked herself over and over again. She was thankful for one thins. Dr. Lauten allowed her to wear regular issue clothing. So many of the really patients were forced to wear nightshirts all day long. They were never allowed to leave certain areas of the huge house that served as the primary building in this forlorn institution.

She sighed as she slowly began to walk over to the narrow window of her prison. She peered out between the grey iron bars that covered the front of the window, preventing her from entertaining any thoughts of escape from this awful place.

The sky was grey and overcast. There had been a slow drizzle for most of the morning. She judged by the rumble of thunder off in the distance, there was a good chance that another furious thunderstorm was coming in again for the afternoon.

The change in the weather a few days ago proved a most welcome one. The area had been in the grip of an oppressive heat wave for the past several weeks. It was so hot during the past few days that she found it hard to get her breath. The air seemed to seer her lungs. She had wanted desperately to strip off these clothes and lie down on the small cot completely naked, wanting some small measure of relief from the oppressive heat. But she would not have done such a thing even if they had let her. She could not bring herself to look down at that thing they somehow had grafted onto her body in their obsessive need to make her think she was a man. Neither did she want to look at that full, large, obscene sack between her legs where her vagina should rightfully be.

The thought of it was enough to drive her into frenzy. Whenever she had to engage in her toilet activities, she would sit down every single time. She was not going to give them the satisfaction of seeing some sign of acceptance on her part just to satisfy their insane need to make her think that she was male and that her name was really Franklin and not Francis.

Assaults on her emotions and intellect occurred almost daily. She was told that papa took his revolver one morning and fatally shot mama and then put the gun to his temple and blew out his brains. The impact of that tragedy had so affected her that she had thought about doing away with herself if the opportunity should come. But she did not want to give them even that kind of satisfaction.

She wished ardently at times that she could better control her temper. If only she hadn't gotten so violently upset when Ted Butler tried to come onto her the way he did. Something inside her snapped when he undid her blouse and attempted to fondle her breasts and then began taunting her and laughing at her and then puller at her hair which he claimed came off in his hands. He called her all kinds of names and accused her of being a boy.

She couldn't help herself. The little penknife was right there on papa's desk in the parlour within easy reach of the sofa. Something just snapped inside and she stabbed him with it over and over again. She could not allow him to get away with that sin of debased humiliation directed against her. He deserved to be punished.

When her rage subsided, panic and fear overtook her when she though that she might have killed him. Mama came into the parlour and could not stop screaming. She found that Ted was still alive barely and immediately called for an ambulance. That was when the police came and took her away and put her in jail.

She was forced to share a cell with vile and leering, despicable men. They taunted her and threatened her.

There was a court hearing and that horrible old wrinkled man they called the judge had her committed to Lakeshore because of her so called mental disorder.

She wondered why in heavens name did she allow that awful Butler boy to make such obscene advances. Always before, she found complete satisfaction by putting her fingers down there in the moist, warm walls of her sex and masturbating until her excitement built to a thrilling climax and quietly died away. The idea of having relationships with boys or men had always frightened her before that evening.

She met Ted on that Saturday afternoon at the Ritz theatre during a Charlie Chaplin movie. She rather liked him. He seemed like a nice boy. They met again a few day later at the Emporium Ice Cream Parlour. He told her that he liked her a lot and wanted to get to know her better. That was the first time a young man made her feel all warm and tingly.

Papa was out of town seeing about a piece of property his real estate firm was representing. Mama had gone to visit her best riend Viola at her house for a game of bridge.

When Ted arrived, he was very nice and polite at first. Then he started kissing her and pawing at her and tried first to put his hand down there under her blue cotton dress. She told him not to do that. But he kept pawing her. When he undid her blouse and felt her breasts and ripped open her blouse and cursed her and slapped her and called her those wicked names as he laughed at her… she closed her eyes and tried to block out the memory of her rage. She could still see all that blood. Mama was so right when she told her to never allow a by to become intimate with her.

She lowered her head as a dull emptiness settled over her. She walked back over to the cot, cringing from the grating sound of the creaky wooden floorboards. She sat back down on the edge of the cot and began humming a lullaby her Aunt Meg used to sing to her when she was a very small child.

Aunt Meg would come over and stay with them whenever mama would go into one of her bad spells and started slapping her around. That was when mama started calling her Franklin instead of Francis. She would slap her and curse her and lock her in her room and tell her that she should have died and not Franklin. But she was Francis. Franklin died of spinal meningitis when he was three years old. Her brother was dead. It was she who survived and not he.

Mama just sort of went a little mad at times and thought she was Franklin instead of Francis. But she was alive and Franklin was dead and had long since rotted in the grave.

Mama grew worse as the years went by. It was as much her fault as it was her own when daddy went off the deep end after that bad thing happened with Ted Butler and he killed mama and then himself.

She was thankful for one thing since first having to come to this awful place; the solace which cousin Thaddeus offered her when he visited her. He would bring her little things such as her favorite periodicals and sweet-smelling soaps and the stereoscope which she enjoyed so much, viewing the different pictures of all those far-off places from all over the world on bright sunny days when she could hold it up to the window and see those wonderful sights clearly. She particularly enjoyed the photos of old Vienna and Niagara Falls.

She and cousin Thaddeus had always been very close. He was one of the good things in her otherwise wretched existence. He would visit her at least three or four times a week. He tried his best to humor her although he would occasionally give into dr. Lauten and try to convince her she was really her dead brother Franklin' that she died and not Franklin.

It hurt her deeply when he did as Dr. Lauten demanded. He would stop though when it became clear how much pain it caused her. He would do his best to console her and cheer her up.

She never allowed it to come between them. That was the doctor and the staff not her dear cousin. She loved him so much and was thankful for his affection and support.

On his last visit, he told her that he would come over about ten tonight. He had something very important planned when he got there. She tried to get him to tell her more about it. Thad's only reply was that he had big plans for her. That she might shortly begin a new life.

She prayed desperately that Thaddeus had at last convinced the doctors that she posed no danger to society like that horrible old judge had said about her. She wanted desperately to by free of this dingy prison.

She lay back down on the cot as the rain began to pelt hard against the window of her room. Vivid flashed of lightening illuminated the cramped confines followed by the crackling rumble of thunder.

She closed her eyes and dreamed again of being free.

Chapter 5

THE STEADY DOWNPOUR drummed into Thaddeus Philbin's brain. He felt a numbing ache at the temples as he pulled up alongside the front gate leading into the drive up to the large converted English style manor house, which served as the main building of Lakeshore Resthome for the Mentally Disordered.

He had been on edge for the better part of the day as he hurriedly made final preparations. This night would not only mark a major turning point in Frank's life. It was an irreversible turning point for himself as well.

He had always felt very close to Frank. He seemed like a sad, misunderstood brother since early childhood. He would often come to visit at the family homestead on weekends.

Frank needed his company and the understanding of mom and dad most when poor Aunt Tiffany was having one of her bad depressions. She even threatened Frank with bodily harm during several of those episodes. Frank had been terribly hurt and confused most of his young life and sought what comfort he could from Thaddeus, as he had no other real friends.

His mom and dad did their best to render Frank as much affection and understanding as they could. His dad in particular fount it excruciatingly difficult indulging Frank's delusion when he insisted that he was Francis and that Frank was his long dead brother and the she had never known him.

Thaddeus' father became increasingly antagonistic as Frank grew older and his sexual identity crises became more acute with every passing year. He entertained notions of going before the court and asking that Frank be taken away from Uncle Aaron and Aunt Tiffany. He often said that it was nothing short of a crime what his sister had done to her own boy as a result of never really recovering from the death of her small daughter. She had vented so much of her hurt and anger on poor Frank.

Frank's dual personality developed at a relatively young age and grew progressively worse. The alter ego of Francis became more and more dominant as the years passed by. Aunt Tiffany's progressive mental deterioration was the key factor n poor Uncle Aaron killing her and then himself.

Thaddeus well imagined what tremendous pain and inner conflict the poor man bore having to live with it day after day. Undoubtedly, it was the near death of the Butler boy and Frank's institutionalization that sent Aaron over the edge.

Thaddeus did what he could for poor Frank during the years he had been at Lakeshore. He tried to make things as pleasant for Frank as the courts and the staff of Lakeshore would allow. He gave Frank books, magazines, games, toiletry articles and such which made life a little easier for him.

He did not mind paying extra expenses to make sure Frank bathes properly and had acceptable clothing to wear and things like that. But even with the little things he was able to afford Frank, it just wasn't enough.

His gut feeling was that Frank did not belong in this place. The damn doctors and staff just had not been able to get through to Frank. He was no better now than he was the day he came to Lakeshore.

His feelings for Frank had brown more intense recently. They had been so close for most of their lives. He just couldn't see Frank spending what might turn out to be the rest of his life in this institution. He decided to take matters in his own hands. He made the decision to spring Frank from Lakeshore. Once he sat his course, he made it his business to get to know the staff. He easily found out which ones were most susceptible to bribery. He then propositioned them, paying each one involved in the escape plan a thousand each.

George Weatherly arranged to be the main security guard on duty tonight. Nurse Higginbotham and orderly Ralph Dufek were waiting for a signal. He was to turn on the car headlights four times in rapid succession. Weatherly would then open the front gate Nurse Higginbotham would let him in the house. Dufek would then assist Frank and himself in getting safely out of the building and off the grounds.

Thaddeus reached over to the passenger seat and picked up he electric torch and quickly turned on the strong beam of light and then unbuttoned his brown leather riding coat and got out his gold-plated pocket watch, playing the light on the face of the timepiece. It was now a few minutes to midnight.

Thaddeus breathed deeply, hoping that what he was about to do was the right thing for the both of them. It was too late to turn back. He had sold the lumberyard and disposed of his stocks and bonds. He sighed, as things as things did not look all that rosy anymore what with so many banks beginning to fail around the country.

The train tickets were ready fro Frank. He would take the East Coast Special, travelling under an alias to the little town of Seville, which was just south of the St. Augustine area. Reservations had been secured at the large old inn there. The inn had been a favorite summer vacation retreat for the family in his childhood. It seemed like a good place to stay for the time begin. He wanted Frank well away from New Jersey.

He planned on joining Frank in Seville in another week. They would then plan a new life for themselves somewhere else possible in the states or perhaps flee to another country if the authorities chose to pursue them.

Thaddeus got out to the '26 Pontiac and stood on the funning board of the car. He squinted his eyes as he made out the imposing outline of the mina building against the greyish black overcast night sky. Jutting English Jacobean gables speared up into the sky at both ends of the large house and at the central pediment foyer at the front entrance. The lights were on inside the front entrance.

Thaddeus quickly climbed back inside the Pontiac and flashed the headlight beams four times in rapid succession. He got back out and jumped onto the running board again. The lights at the front entrance went on and off four times in response.

The huge cedar wood door opened and a man emerged wearing a large leather raincoat and cap, which was pulled over the forehead. He quickly ran to the front gate.

George Weatherly shouted that he was to drive in close to the front entrance and not to turn on the headlights. Dr. Judson, the chief of staff at Lakeshore, called earlier in the evening, saying that he would arrive something that evening with a new patient. Weatherly quickly unlocked the huge padlock on the gate and opened it wide. Thaddeus got back inside the car and slowly drove along the narrow drive up to the front entrance. He was glad that the heavy downpour which lasted throughout the afternoon into the evening hours had now died down into a heavy drizzle.

Thaddeus got out of the Pontiac as Weatherly ran up the drive to meet him at the front entrance. Weatherly's wrinkled square-jawed demeanor nervously twitched as he yelled under his breath for Thaddeus not to lose a minute of time. They trotted through puddles of oily water standing on the dark pavement of the drive up to the marble walk leading to the huge front door.

The door was quickly opened and Ralph Dufek nervously motioned for the two men to get inside. He slammed the door behind them as soon as they were inside.

Dufek was a wiry man of slight stature. His thin drawn features glared up at Thaddeus. He told Thaddeus to get upstairs and collect his queer cousin and get the hell out of the building as fast as he could. He had just gotten a call from Dr. Judson. He was on his way and would be arriving at any time now.

Weatherly's twitch grew more progressive as he said that he would go back by the front gate and keep a lookout as the two men proceeded along the checkered tiled floor of the hallway and up the curving marble staircase which led to the west wing of the house where Frank's small room was located.

The door of the room was wide open. Frank stood just inside the room a small suitcase in hand. He appeared to be totally bewildered and perplexed as Thaddeus hugged him warmly.

The matronly features of Nurse Higginbotham came into view. She turned off the lights in the small room and ordered Frank to get out in a sharp, condescending manner.

Frank's features became livid with rage. "Don't call me that. My name is Francis Madison." The near screaming voice was that of a woman.

"All right Francis. You've got your things you came here with. You get out of here — and I mean right now. If any of us get linked to this, it will not only mean our jobs… it could well mean a stretch in prison as well. And I don't want any part of prison life. Not for any amount of money."

"Just a minute," Dufek hissed. "The cover story is that I was overpowered by Mr. Philbin here and Nurse Higginbotham was forced to act as a shield until you tow are out of the building. You better throw a few good punches at me. I want it to look convincing for the police."

Thaddeus protested. He had never hit anyone in his life. Dufek then slapped him on the right cheek as hard as he could. The tension of the past few days exploded inside him and he immediately slammed his left fist into the midsection of Dufek's stomach followed by a solid right to the man's jaw. The thin, wiry orderly went down like a collapsing brick wall. A small trickle of blood streamed down from the corner of his mouth. After he regained his breath, Dufek looked up at Thaddeus and grinned. "Thanks," was all he said.

Thaddeus grabbed Frank's free hand and guided him along the hallway to the stairs. They quickly traversed the stairs down to the large hallway leading to the front entrance. Throwing open the large door, Thaddeus directed Frank over to the Pontiac and opened the door on the passenger side, telling Frank to hop in. He was careful to refer to him as Francis. Nurse Higginbotham came out then as he threw the suitcase in the back seat.

"I hope I never lay eyes on the tow of you again," she snapped. "I'll certainly try to honor your request madam," Thaddeus replied with contempt.

Thaddeus quickly got in and cranked up the engine and slowly drove back down the drive up to the front gate with his headlights off as he was instructed. Weatherly gave the all clear signal as he opened the gate wide. Once they were clear, Weatherly speedily slammed it closed.

Frank looked over at Thaddeus as he switched the headlights on and slowly gained speed. "So this is what you meant about tonight," Frank said in that whining feminine voice.

Thaddeus shuddered as he forced a smile. "Yes."

"Thank you, Thad. I don't know how I will ever be able to repay you," Frank replied in the Francis voice.

Thaddeus shuddered again as Frank spoke in that woman's manner. He didn't know whether he would ever get used to the voice of a woman coming from Frank.

As soon as they were settled into a new life somewhere else, he was determined to get Frank professional help from someone skilled enough to actually do some good unlike that staff of incompetents at Lakeshore.

Chapter 6

AS THE RAIN ceased, a light fog began rolling in just as Thaddeus pulled into the driveway beside his wooden bungalow house. Despite his single status, he preferred having a place of his own as opposed to apartment living. He was a quiet man and valued his privacy greatly outside of the social and day to day demands of his lumberyard business.

He deeply regretted that he had not found the right woman and settled down with a family before his mother passed on. The demands of the business had taken up so much of his time. He just couldn't see the possibility of marriage at any time in the foreseeable future. It certainly wouldn't be fair to a wife and any potential offspring. And there was the all-consuming concern he had for Frank through the years. He just could not bring himself to abandon Frank. He was one of the few people Frank could rely on.

Thaddeus sighed as he switched off the motor and motioned for Frank to get out of the car.

A warm, cloying sultriness lay heavy in the fog-shrouded air. In spite of the damp heavy feeling of the evening, Thaddeus experienced an odd chilly sensation as they approached the front door of the bungalow.

Thaddeus fumbled inside the large pocket of his coat and nervously pulled out his key chain that contained the key to the front door. After unlocking the door, he reached inside and turned on the lights and told Frank to come inside quickly.

The small front room was simple yet tastefully furnished in a New England decorative scheme. An exquisite Maplewood secretariat stood in one corner. An inviting sofa and handsome coffee table sat in the center. A handsomely designed gun cabinet made from the finest New England birch stood against the wall closest to the little hall which connected with the bedroom and bath. The wallpaper was a simple light beige floral pattern.

Thaddeus removed his beret and riding coat, hanging them on a coat and hat rack next to the front door. He told Frank, careful to use the name of his long dead sister, to do the same with his coat and hat. He quickly removed the leather gloves he wore this evening and threw them on the coffee table. He needed a drink badly and went over to the small bar to pour himself a straight shot of bourbon. He asked his still dazed cousin if he (she) would like one also. Frank smiled and replied in the Francis voice, "Yes. Thank you dear cousin. That would be wonderful."

Thaddeus turned away and shuddered as he poured the bourbon in a shot glass and handed it to his cousin. He then poured a large one for himself and drank it down. The warmth of the liquor immediately chased away that odd close yet chilly feeling he had for the better part of the evening.

Thaddeus continued to tremble slightly and quickly poured another shot glass full of straight bourbon and then took the empty glass from Frank and poured another glass full. When he handed Frank his glass, he smiled softly and in the Francis voice said, "cheers" as he blinked his eyes like a young girl flirting with her first boyfriend and raised the glass in a toast before taking a sip.

Thaddeus closed his eyes and winced. 'God all mighty, I'll never get used to that voice coming out of Frank's mouth,' he thought. And then forced himself to toast Frank in return before slugging down the bourbon in one long gulp.

Frank handed him the empty glass. "I'm forever in your debt for what you did for me tonight. But won't this put you in a great deal of jeopardy, Thad?" That soft, womanly voice was heavy with concern.

"I'm pulling out of here, Frank," he said without thinking.

"Francis!" he screamed. "Don't ever call me Frank again. Do you hear me? I've had enough of that dreadful place," he shouted in that woman's voice almost at the to of his lungs. His features were flushed in a livid rage.

Thaddeus swallowed hard in a nervous reflex and apologized. He fervently prayed that he could find some real help for Frank and that what he did this evening was not in vain.

Thaddeus proceeded to tell Frank his immediate plan, careful to refer to him as Francis. His cousin would take the 8:30 Miami Special out of Trenton to Jacksonville. At the Jacksonville terminal, Francis, as he was careful to say, would make a connection onto the Florida East Coast Special, which ran from Jacksonville down to Daytona. She would get off at Seville just below St. Augustine where a room had been booked under the alias of T.M. Beacham at Warlock Inn. The train ticket was in that name as well. He would join her in another week.

"But what about your business?" Frank asked in that womanly voice.

"I sold it. It's only a matter of time until the police find out about my part in getting you out of Lakeshore this evening. We'll start a new life somewhere else." There was a definite feeling of finality about his action this evening.

Frank smiled softly again as he walked over to Thaddeus and put his arms around him, kissing him full on the lips. It was a lingering, wet kiss. "Thank you for what you have done for me, cousin. I hope I can make it up to you at some point in the future." Thaddeus found that womanly voice more and more unbearable. But he realized that he would somehow have to learn to life with Frank's dual personality at least for the foreseeable future. He hoped that he could learn to tolerate the Francis in Frank.

Thaddeus went over to the secretariat and pulled out the upper right hand drawer near the bottom and got out a small paper folder that had the train tickets inside. He handed it to his cousin and told him to take the bedroom tonight. He would sleep on the couch. They could leave shortly after sunrise tomorrow for the train depot.

Frank suddenly began staring at him with an annoying pout. "Thad, did you get me those lovely clothes I asked for in case the day came when I could leave Lakeshore? I want so to feel the caress of a garter and corset; to wear fine stockings once more; to feel a brassiere firmly support my breasts; to wear a nice dress and proper hat and a pair of high heels. I've been denied these basic things for so long."

Thaddeus winced again in anguish, recalling the promise he made to his cousin on a Sunday visit about one year ago. He hoped Frank would have forgotten it. The promise was made under a great deal of duress.

Thaddeus signed saying that a dress and ladies undergarments were in several boxes on the closet shelf in his bedroom along with a hatbox and shoes. Frank giggled like a schoolgirl and kissed him on the cheek before disappearing into the bedroom.

A cold and queasy sensation settled over Thaddeus. He began to seriously question whether what he did was the right thing as he went back over to the bar and poured himself this time a double shot of bourbon, quickly downing it.

This round of the booze made him feel very hot and slightly unsteady as he dwelled upon the irrevocable change that he had made in his life. He found himself suffering pangs of tremendous self-torment over his actions this night.

He again poured another large shot of bourbon and downed it as fast as the last one. He began to ponder the future. Could he possibly live with Frank for years on end the way he was? He could barely handle it this evening even for the short time since he busted Frank out of Lakeshore.

Something snapped inside him at that moment. He sent the shot glass smashing against the wall. It shattered upon impact with a splintering thud.

He ran through the small connecting hall and threw open the door to the bedroom. Frank stood by the bed already wearing the light print cotton dress trimmed in lace. The wide-brimmed hat with the black net veil rested on his head at a slight angle. He even had on the black high heel shoes Thaddeus's mother wore on special occasions that Thaddeus kept as a memento of his late mother.

"How do you like me?" Frank asked in that Francis voice as he made a complete turn around like a model in a fashion show for Thaddeus' inspection.

"Take that goddamn stuff off, Frank. This is not right. It is just not right. You're going back to Lakeshore. I can't help you. I know that now. Dr. Lauten is the only one who can possibly do you any good."

Frank literally froze, staring at Thaddeus with an expression of total disbelief. As the initial shock wore off, he exploded in the Francis voice. "I'll never go back to that place. I would just as soon end it all first rather than go back to that living hell." The voice was almost manly for a second.

Thaddeus lunged forward and grabbed Frank. A frantic scuffle followed as Frank spotted a hunting knife on the chest of drawers near the bed. He lunged at Thaddeus who was already off balance and nearly drunk, forcing him against the chest of drawers and managed to free one arm from Thaddeus' drunken grip long enough to get hold of the knife. Before Thaddeus knew what was happening, Frank plunged the cold steel blade into Thaddeus' left side. The sharp blade went into the soft flesh and buried itself into his bowels.

Thaddeus looked down at his side with an incredible expression of surprise. The knife was in him right up to the hilt. A growing blotch of crimson rapidly spread around the area of the wound. At first, he experienced numbness followed by a burning sharp pain. He looked up at an impervious Frank and fell forward onto the hardwood floor. He lay there very still until there was nothing but darkness.

Frank looked down at Thaddeus' still body, as the pool of deep red blood grew larger on the floor. Tears streamed down his cheeks. "I'm truly sorry cousin. But I will never ever go back to that horrid place alive." It was the Francis voice doing the talking.

The suitcase was still in Thaddeus' car. Frank went out to the car and quickly got it and then frantically searched the small bungalow for any money Thaddeus might keep on hand. There was over fifteen hundred dollars stashed in a small wall safe which he was able to open after locating the combination on a piece of paper which he found in Thaddeus' folded wallet after reluctantly searching his body.

The Francis personality was totally free of Frank and dominant. She decided to wait at the station in Trenton for the rest of the night. But first, she would stop someplace and get some lipstick and a makeup kit is she could find one of those all night drugstores along the way.

By the time the police found Thaddeus, she would be well away from here and on her way to planning a new beginning.

Chapter 7

SHE WALKED OUT onto the small wooden platform of the little train depot as the angry orange orb of the sun was just beginning to rise up in the eastern sky. The morning air felt suffocatingly close.

She reached inside the purse which she purchased at the little all night drugstore she found a block down from the train depot in Trenton and got out her favorite brand of lipstick along with a small cosmetic kit containing facial powder and a powder puff and freshened her makeup and applied a fresh cost of lipstick to her full lips. It felt heavenly as it did back in Trenton when she went to the ladies room after having her ticket verified at the check-in counter and her first use of lipstick in years. It made her all tingly and excited. It had been such a long time since she was allowed to express herself in such womanly ways.

The trip down was quiet and uneventful except for one dirty old man in the seat across the aisle from her. He kept giving her the eye and gawked at her very noticeably. She took some satisfaction from his leering peeks toward her. She still had what it took to get a man's attention once she was in a presentable condition. But she was careful not to give the old coot any encouragement. She was considerably relieved when he got off the train in Charleston.

She was able to manage some sleep along the way. She wished Thaddeus had reserved a private berth. It would have been so much more restful.

Her thoughts began to center on Thaddeus. She regretted terribly what he forced her to do. She wished desperately that it have never happened and closed her eyes, praying Thaddeus was at peace in the hereafter.

She put the kit and lipstick back in her purse and got out the lace handkerchief she purchased at the same time she got the lipstick and kit. It would take some considerable period of time before she was used to this hot Florida climate. But she realized that she had to adapt to the heat and sweltering humidity. She might have to remain in Seville for an indefinite period of time while she made plans for the future. She was on her own now. There was no Cousin Thaddeus to rely on anymore.

She waited in the little depot since first arriving at four that morning after first making the transfer up in Jacksonville to the Miami Special earlier that evening a little after two. She grew bored and restless having spent more than three hours already sitting on the uncomfortably hard and brittle bench, getting up to go to the dingy ladies room to relieve herself and stretch her legs once or twice.

She was careful not to let another woman see her. She didn't want to be humiliated by being accused of having a man's awful penis hanging between her legs. She did not have a penis. She had a vagina. Why did people accuse her of having a man's sexual apparatus when it should be plain to anyone that she did not?

Why couldn't people just leave her alone? Her memory wandered back to the horrid things she was forced to endure in school when her classmate, the boys in particular, would get her in a corner and try to beat her. The girls were almost as bad with their abusive and vile digs at her. Why had she been singled out as being so much different from the other girls?

Francis' introspective thoughts were interrupted as a horse drawn carriage with a fringed black canopy pulled up by the entrance of the little depot. The driver, a stockily built elderly, colored man, looked over at her and smiled pleasantly as he asked if she was the guest bound for Warlock Inn. He had a raspy but warm southern drawl.

Francis smiled back warmly and said that she was. He got down from the carriage and introduced himself. "Henry Struthers at your service ma'am. Is your luggage inside the station?"

She told him that she was travelling with only one small suitcase, which was next to the little bench inside the station. He tipped his cap and disappeared inside and returned seconds later with the bag and put it next to the driver's seat in the front of the carriage.

The brown and white spotted mare snorted slightly as he offered her a lift up into the carriage. "Excuse me, ma'am. Sarah is frettin' about her mornin' treat. After I've given it to her, we'll be departin' for the inn." He walked up to the horse and pulled a small burlap sack out of the large pocket of his baggy trousers, which were held up by a pair of extra large suspenders, and proceeded to feed the animal several large lumps of sugar. He then gingerly climbed up into the driver's seat and released the carriage brake and cracked a thin riding whip lightly in the air above the horse's head. The animal slowly began to trot away from the depot out onto the narrow two-lane road. And as the carriage started down the road, a pleasant gusty sea breeze began blowing inland off of the Atlantic as a cluster of low, grey clouds passed swiftly overhead.

She sat back, relaxing as best she could, and enjoyed the passing scenery, particularly the tall pines, live oaks, scrub oaks, and cypress trees which proliferated along the roadway. She particularly enjoyed observing the tall oaks with their billowing strands of Spanish moss hanging from the long, flowing branches, wavering in the wind. It all seemed like something form the days of the antebellum South.

"Signs in the sky tell me that a storm might be brewin' up way out there in that big ocean ma'am. We've had some pretty squally weather in the past few days. And this here is the kind of wind that comes and goes with a spray of rain every now and then like when one of them big ones is a comin'." The old man spoke very thoughtfully as he observed the sky. She detected a hint of trepidation in his tone.

"Big one," she echoed.

"Yes ma'am. Hurricane… that's what I mean ma'am. I have lived in these parts for an awful long time. You get a feel for ole mother natures road signs. Seems to me that a hurricane may be a comin'."

"Oh," she replied with a hint of her own sudden sense of unease.

"Don't threat none ma'am. Chances are that if a hurricane is brewin' up out there in that big ocean… it don't mean that we'll take a big hit. More than likely, we'll just get some of the winds and rain from the lady." The old man made a good effort to keep her from becoming too alarmed by his prognostication.

It took less than a half-hour for them to pass through the little town of Seville going south along the coast road before entering the grounds of the inn. They would encounter an occasional Ford or Chevrolet chugging past them on the coast road. Some of the drivers would honk their horns and the old man would throw up his hand in a friendly gesture of recognition, giving the acknowledging driver in the passing motor car a warm good morning.

Large sand dunes with thick spotty growth of scrub oak, cypress, and squatty palms along with a plethora of sea oats and sea cactus mostly obscured her view of the ocean although she was able to catch an occasional glimpse of the emerald blue waters of the Atlantic dotted by multitudes of white caps. She listened contentedly to the rushing white foam of the surf rolling into the shore.

The morning was still fairly young. But the beach goers were already out in numbers enjoying themselves and splashing about in the surf. She caught a glimpse of several quaint bicycles; the ones with the very large front wheel as compared to the tiny wheel in the rear which sat so high off of the ground. The muffled squawking coming from a flock of seagulls as they flew in off of the Atlantic also got her attention.

She began to feel wonderfully refreshed as she closed her eyes and wished that the present moment might somehow go on forever.

The cooling breeze suddenly grew much gustier and she was forced to hold onto the wide brim of her hat as the carriage passed beyond the large open gates and along the narrow road with open stretches of beautiful verdant green which were the grounds surrounding Warlock Inn. As the imposing outline of the large Queen Anne Victorian refurbished house came into view, Francis sensed right away a powerful area that radiated from the large dwelling with its lofty turrets. An enormous observation weather tower stood above the center of the building which was graced with spire gables.

The house cast an immediate spell on her as she studied carefully the carnation pink structure as the carriage moved up alongside the large steps leading up to the L-shaped veranda and came to a halt.

The old man escorted her over to the large front desk. A pleasant balding man in his early middle years smiled at her and wished her a good morning. "Neil Young madam. I'm the manager of this establishment." His introduction was polite and business-like as he adjusted his bifocal wire frame glasses when the slipped down the long, thin bridge of his nose.

"T.M. Beacham," she answered. "I believe a reservation has been made in my name." She matched his business-like deportment step for step.

He quickly glossed over the reservation cards, pulling one out of the file and smiled pleasantly. "Yes madam. Room 212 is booked in your name. If you will just sign the registry, I'll have one of our bellboys collect your suitcase and escort you to your room."

Francis felt the hairs on the back of her neck suddenly bristle. A low whispering voice spoke to her. The voice was coming from inside her head. It repeatedly ordered her to demand that she be given room 207. She had to have room 207. No other room in the inn would do.

"I'm sorry Mr. Young. That room will not do. Is room 207 occupied at the present time?" She smiled sweetly and batted her eyelashes. "I would very much like to have room 207 if it would not be too much trouble."

Mr. Young looked at her with an astonished and puzzled expression. After regaining his composure, he answered, obviously very curious about her request. "Well, I suppose so madam. That room is presently available. However, I must warn you about that room. It is, how shall I put it, a trifle unusual. Indeed. It is on the bizarre side and probably not the sort of room that a lady of your obvious refinement would be comfortable staying in if I may be so bald as to say."

"It shan't bother me, Mr. Young, I must insist on room 207," she demanded.

The manager was taken back somewhat by her rebuke and showed his displeasure in the tone of his voice. "Very well, madam. If you will just sign the registry."

The elderly colored carriage driver placed the suitcase on the soft velvet textured carpet next to her and graciously wished her a good day before departing.

As she signed the book under the alias of T.M. Beacham, Mr. Young vigorously rang the bell on the counter next to him. A pleasant appearing young man with curly, flaming red hair and the most freckles she had ever seen on a fellow human being soon appeared.

"Show this lady to room 207 Tim." There was a definite feeling of unease and even anger in his tone.

"Room 207?" the boy quipped in disbelief.

"That's what I said, Tim." Mr. Young was showing signs of increasing irritability.

"Yes sir," Tim replied in snapped attention and quickly picked up the small suitcase, asking her to follow him. They proceeded across the lobby to the stairs. The bellboy gingerly took two steps at a time as Francis followed close behind him.

Once they were at the top of the stairs, they proceeded halfway down the dimly lit corridor and stopped. Tim took the key to the door of room 207 and quickly unlocked it. "Room 207" he announced politely and stood aside, allowing her to enter the room. He followed her inside and went over to the large four-poster queen-size bed with a white lace fringed canopy and placed her bag on top of the elegant amber satin bedspread.

Francis began to carefully scrutinize her surroundings. She took particular note of the bizarre pattern of amber-colored wallpaper that contrasted sharply from the richly embroidered pattern of the scarlet oriental carpeting on the floor.

She paid particular attention to the various paintings and tintype photographs and placed strategically about the walls that depicted all manner of chaotic disasters of man and nature.

"This room is a real doozy, ain't it ma'am?" Tim commented with an elfish grin.

She smiled sweetly and reached into her purse and gave him some of the loose change in the bottom. "Yes, it certainly is unique," she replied.

Tim tipped his cap and wished her a pleasant stay before leaving.

She removed her wide brim hat and carefully placed it on the dresser across from the bed.

A particular painting caught her eye as she began removing the straight pins from her hair. She was mesmerized by the portrait of a man with a thing and foreboding face. The eyes were deep-set and penetrating. They seemed to burn right into her very soul. The eyes of that man took command of her. She felt as though her will was slipping away.

Chapter 8

A BANK OF low grey clouds moved swiftly out of the east across the late morning as Francis stepped outside the lobby onto the large veranda. The wind rose and fell in a rapid succession of gusts, which afforded considerable relief from the oppressive closeness of the early morning as she took a brief walk around the inn. Her walk was cut short by a band of showers that seemed to come out of nowhere.

It was typical of the weather pattern since her arrival at Warlock Inn. Fast moving clouds with gusty wind followed by oppressively still mugginess.

Vernon and Mimi Seawell, the pleasant middle-aged couple from Pittsburgh with whom she had several pleasant conversations and a nice walk along the beach the day before, sat in large rocking chairs enjoying the cooling effect of the sea breeze.

Mimi smiled at her, giving her a pleasant good morning greeting of her own. Mimi asked her to join them. At first, she was reluctant. She feared any familiarity with the other guests, especially that nosey travelling salesman, Ernest Thompson. He had a revoltingly thick southern brogue that along with an unpleasant nasal quality made her want to cringe. He had tried on several occasions to make overtures in her direction. She politely but firmly rejected his attention. Vernon and Mimi were nice and warm and seemed to take an interest in her without any of the customary prying she had encountered in the past.

Vernon Seawell had even tried his best to put a stop to Thompson's unwelcome intrusions, telling the salesman straight out on one occasion that she was not interested. Thompson had tried to get her off in a corner. She was afraid a scene might develop between the two men. But after a minute or so, the salesman smiled nervously. "Sure, can't blame a lonely unattached fella for wanting the company of an attractive lady," he said lamely. Francis felt some sympathy for the lanky drummer as he tipped the derby he wore and sauntered away dejectedly.

Francis went over to the whitewash wooden swing, which was close to the rockers in which Mimi and Vernon sat and seated herself in the middle of the swing, allowing it to move back and forth in a slight swaying motion. "Looks as though the weather may take a turn for the worse," she commented. Another bank of low, ominous-looking dark clouds came blowing in off of the Atlantic and the wind grew much stronger.

"Yeah, looks kind of nasty. Mr. Young was listening to his crystal set last night. He picked up a station between Savannah and here. According to what he could hear through all the static, a tropical storm is out there in the Atlantic not all that far away from this part of Florida. Pretty near to hurricane strength," he said. "I think they're calling this gal Carlotta." Vernon did not seem to be worried about the news that Mr. Young related to him. He sat back in the rocker lazily with his white shirt opened down the front, exposing the upper part of his chest and his straw panama pulled down slightly over his forehead.

"Oh dear. That sounds rather ominous," she said with a cautious note of weariness.

Mimi looked over to her husband as he proceeded to prop one leg over the other with as much concern as Francis had displayed. "Vernon, do you thing it is safe here with a possible hurricane out there?"

He pulled the brim of the Panama up slightly and smiled. "It's about as safe as you can get in these parts. Mr. Young said he is prepared to open up the big cellar if the storm reaches hurricane strength and comes this way."

"But is the inn strong enough to sustain a blow from the kind of winds a hurricane can produce?" Mimi demanded.

"Don't you worry, honey bun," Vernon said. "Mr. Young has offered the use of the inn's cellar to the locals living nearby. Fools are refusing the offer though if we were to take a direct hit from the storm, this place will be standing after a good many of those flimsy little frame cottages which the locals call home are knocked flat."

"Why are the local people refusing the shelter of the inn's cellar?" Francis asked pointedly, her curiosity intensely aroused by Vernon's remarks."

He shrugged his broad shoulders and looked just a little disgusted. "A lot of superstitious claptrap from what I gather. It goes back to the last century just after the civil war. Seems the fellow who built this place originally was into black magic and all sorts of mumbo jumbo. Even practiced human sacrifices or so I'm told. I gather that they believe the cellar is haunted by the evil spirit of the man. They say that there is supposed to be something down there. Just a lot of superstitious bull."

"Warlock Inn… Warlock. I remember having read something back in my school days. I believe warlock is the term used to denote a male witch," Mimi said with a hint of trepidation.

"Yeah. That's what Mr. Young said. This fella was a male witch," Vernon confirmed.

"Must be the origin of the inn's name," Francis said. The image of the thin-faced man with the penetrating eyes in that portrait up in the room seemed to loom right in front of her.

"That's right, Miss Beacham," Vernon confirmed.

Mimi Seawell began rocking vigorously. She grew quite nervous. "I don't know if I care to go down into that cellar if the storm should hit here after hearing a story like that."

Vernon looked over at his wife and smiled reassuringly. "Oh, come on honey bun. Don't you go fretting any. We're as safe as we can be. Another week from now and I'll be back in the sales office and you will be back attending to the house and the church socials and all the regular business."

The wind suddenly gusted with furious power. An ominous muffled roar accompanied the gust. The air suddenly became much cooler as the wind gained additional strength. Vernon had to hold tight to his Panama as vivid flashed of lightening began to streak across the dark sky followed by the low ominous rumble of thunder. A sudden torrential downpour came bursting out of the low clouds in sheets of cascading water.

Vernon bolted from his rocker as Mimi jumped up out of her own. He shouted for them to get inside. They were already drenched as the fierce winds whipped the heavy downpour in all directions.

Vernon threw open one of the large double doors at the front entrance and held it firmly, allowing Mimi and Francis to enter the lobby before him. Once they were inside, he slammed the door shut.

"My, but that was sudden," Francis smiled nervously.

Vernon smiled. "Sure was. If you'll excuse us, we'll get up to our room and change into some dry clothes. I suggest you do the same."

She smiled, saying that she would as Vernon and Mimi quickly ran across the lobby to the stairs and son disappeared at the top.

Francis stood in the lobby in her wet cotton print dress. A voice that seemed to come from the inner depths of her mind spoke to her. "Come to me. Come to me. You are one of us now. Come to me," it said.

Some instinctive compulsion guided her as she slowly walked in the direction toward the back of the inn past the front desk. She found herself in a narrow corridor where she topped and faced a large door, which was padlocked, located halfway between the back of the inn and the area around the front desk.

The voice inside her head spoke again, "I am here. Soon. You will come to me. You belong to me."

She pressed her wet body against the old brittle wood of the door and caressed it with the palms of her hands as the face of the thin man with the burning eyes floated in the air in front of her.

Chapter 9

THE WIND HOWLED with a deafening impact as the small fishing troller was tossed about in the turbulent waters of the Atlantic like some insignificant toy. Enormous waves billowed up over the bough, flooding the decks, cabin, and holes below with a steady stream of churning ocean water.

The lithe and lean muscular London cockney in command of the troller guided the wheel at the helm with all the precision in him as he did his damnedest to keep the boat afloat and as steady as possible under the circumstances.

He kept one eye on the compass direction, making sure the Lady Jane did not veer off of her course and the other shut tight as he prayed to whatever God that might be willing to listen to a world-weary bloke like Harry Dunke.

The whipping wind and waves continuously exulted unbearable degrees of force upon the small vessel as the cockney opened both steely blue eyes wide. It as an almost impossible situation. All he could make out was blinding rain and crashing waves pounding against the glass of the observation ports.

The but storm had been building out in the Atlantic even as they left the concealed lagoon in Nassau under the cover of darkness in the night before with a consignment of banana rum bound for a secluded rendezvous point just north of Fernandina, Florida. Harry Dunke knew that this run was a calculated risk at best. But he never figured on the storm reaching hurricane strength as fast as this mean lady.

His boys thought that the run was worth the risk just as he had when considering the payoff. Raymondo, the young colored buck from Bimini and the surly hard drinking Cuban from Santiago, Raphael, were more than ready for the handsome payoff which this load would fetch.

He had taken chances like this on many occasions in the past several years. Each run turned out just fine. He had always made it to the rendezvous points and back with the illegal hooch as the yanks liked to call it in this day and age of prohibition. He had always enjoyed the challenge and adventure of runs like this one, particularly with a prize of thousands of Yankee dollars at stake. It was good as gold since prohibition was enacted in the states thanks to the 18th Amendment to the US Constitution and the earlier Volstead Act passed by the American congress. But on this trip out, the percentages had caught up with him as this mean little mama developed faster and with greater intensity than any storm he had ever tangled with before in these waters.

The waves grew larger, pounding the small boat with even more unmerciful force. Harry knew full well that the troller couldn't take the beating much longer from the storm's fury. He had to get the Lady Jane into a safe harbor or she would break up eventually under this kind of a battering.

He ordered Raymondo, whose solid black features were awash in heavy perspiration from his ever increasing sense of terror, to take the helm and hold her on course as best he could just as the door to the bridge opened wide. Raphael came scurrying inside along with a sheet of ocean foam. He was decked out in his whale skin storm coat and cap. It took a tremendous amount of effort between Harry and himself to secure the door to the bridge. He had to catch his breath before speaking; "The cargo is all secured below, Harry. We gotta get out of these waters soon or we've had it."

"That's right man. This little boat, she cannot take this much longer." Raymondo shouted over the deafening turbulence of the wind and rain and pounding sea. His voice was tense with near panic.

"All right. All right. Don't you think old Harry knows about it." The cockney shouted back at his shipmates and partners in the smuggling trade. The wheels in his steep-trap brain were spinning like dynamos. They were right off the coast of north Florida somewhere between Daytona and St. Augustine. He had been through these parts some years ago when he worked for a brief time as a ticket agent for the Harrison Steamship Company out of Charleston.

There was a small grotto just below the little town of Seville, which was south of St. Augustine that he discovered when he and a business companion explored the region while staying at a nearby inn for a few days rest. If he could make it to that grotto and not land up on a sandbar or get trapped in shallow water, they just might have a chance to save themselves and the cargo of rum as well. He had nothing to lose at this point in making a run for the coastal grotto. According to the navigational compass, he figured that it must be somewhere close by.

All Harry Dunke had to go on was gut instinct. He had to maintain radio silence while approaching U.S. Territorial waters. The coast guard was beginning a nasty crackdown on smugglers in these parts. He wanted to avoid mixing it up with those boys and a coast guard cutter since the only weapons they had was a Thompson sub-machine gun and a Winchester rifle.

The cockney quickly formulated his plan and relayed it to his mates. They would make for the grotto. Once the Lady Jane was safely secured, they would head for the nearby inn that wasn't that far away from where the grotto lay.

He ordered Raymondo to relinquish she helm back to him. The black man quickly stepped aside while Raphael nervously made the sign of the cross and started praying in his native Cuban tongue for the protection of the sainted Holy Mother.

Harry Dunke turned the boat about in the direction of the coastline as the vessel tilted to the port side at such an extreme angle that he feared for a moment the little troller would capsize. He managed to steady her and breathed a deep sigh of relief once he had the boat headed toward the coast.

They were absolutely blind now and had to rely totally on the navigational compass and Harry Dunke's own inner reliance to guide them. Fifteen minutes later, Raphael cried out at the top of his lungs, "Land dead ahead!"

A slight let up in the pounding rain allowed Harry to just be able to make out the beach head which was the general area where the little grotto was located. "We made it lads. We made it," he shouted and began laughing heartily. Raymondo laughed and shouted with great relief as he slapped Harry affectionately across his lean muscular shoulder while Raphael yelled and rejoiced like someone at a New Year's Eve celebration in Times Square at the countdown to midnight.

Harry got his breath and barked his orders. "Raphael, get below and breakout the arms and ammo. Raymondo, check below for sings of damage and report back to me."

Raphael came topside a few minutes later with the Thompson sub-machine gun and the Winchester along with several belts filled with numerous rounds of ammunition. He was soon followed by Raymondo, reporting that the Lady Jane was secure.

Harry grinned proudly, "Right, lads. Once we've anchored the Lady Jane, we'll make for the inn. I'd say it's not more than half a mile from the grotto. We'll take it fast and hard. Let them know we mean business and hold up there till this mean little lady blows over. Then we'll march the able-bodied gents back here and make 'em help us get the old gal seaworthy again."

Raphael was hesitant. "But Harry, do you think that's wise? They will probably go straight to the law as soon as we're out of here."

Harry Dunke's deeply tanned and lined face twisted into a grin. He reached inside a cigar box on a little stand next to the helm and got out one of the fat, long Havana stogies. He ordered Raphael to break out a box of matches from the grey cast-iron cabinet anchored to the starboard bulkhead.

Raphael dutifully obliged and proceeded to light the cigar for Harry after biting off the tip and spitting it on the deck. Harry began to puff away on the stogie, filling the bridge with the pungent aroma of strong cigar smoke.

He took the stogie out of his mouth and grinned, holding on tight to the wheel with one hand. "We'll gag and tie everyone we leave at the inn. On the other hand, the lads we'll oblige in makin' this lady seaworthy won't be goin' back to the inn. Do you get my meanin' mates?" He began giggling and his two companions eyed each other knowingly as they grinned and joined in the laughter.

Chapter 10

THE WIND SPEED increased significantly in the advancing hours of the afternoon. Francis grew perceptibly more uneasy by the increasing force of the storm as it battered the large house with mounting strength. It was becoming apparent to everyone that hurricane Carlotta was now a major threat to this part of the Florida coastline.

Mr. Young once more did his best to reassure everyone that Warlock Inn was one of the safest and sturdiest structures in Seville. The old house had withstood some of the harshest weather Mother Nature could possibly dish out since it was built in the era following the civil war. In all that time, the structure had sustained only minimal damage. He also pointed out that the house had been substantially reinforced and strengthened several times in the past quarter of a century. Mr. Young, nevertheless, had a number of his most able male employees hurriedly boarding up windows during the morning in the upper turrets of the house as well as the main windows on the first floor.

In addition, he had inventories accessed of the food stock provisions on hand in both the pantries and the large meat locker to the rear of the kitchen, checking on the perishables such as the sides of beef and pork that were skewered there. He happily reported that there were enough large blocks of ice on hand to maintain the perishables for days. When the electricity finally failed, he told them that it could be off for days once the hurricane came inland.

Mr. Young assured everyone again that he would go open the large cellar. "It should be ample protection if we need to go down there."

The men who stayed on at the inn, when it became apparent that the hurricane might indeed hit the area, such as Vernon Seawell, Rufus Hagen, the tall, lanky, night man who did duty at the front desk with a thick and heavy southern cracker accent, Tim Rich, the young stocky bellboy, and the lecherous tacky drummer, Ernest Thompson agreed wholeheartedly with the manager's confidence as to the sturdiness of the building. The large downstairs cleaning lady, Juanita Leech, agreed with the men. But Mimi Seawell had worked herself up to an awful state of anxiety. Vernon had all he could do to keep her from going into a nervous fit.

Harriet Martin, the only other remaining female guest, wasn't nearly as tense as Mimi Seawell, although she too had voiced her reservations concerning the safety of the inn if the hurricane proved to be a truly bad blow. She had gotten hold of a bottle of sherry and was pretty well away after having imbibed on most of the decanter of liquor.

The other people which were staying there left the day before having anticipated the possible move in this direction of the storm as the gale force winds grew increasingly more ferocious with the passing of time.

Ernest Thompson expressed utter contempt for those who cleared out. "Craven cowards. The lot of them. If the storm does hit within a hundred miles of here in either direction, north or south, some of them won't make it out of the area in time. The railroad will most certainly shut down with a storm such as this on the way." He looked over at Francis. "On the other hand, we're in pretty fair shape I'd say. Snug as a bug in a rug. Ain't that right, Miss Beacham?"

The lout actually had the nerve to leer at her as he grinned foolishly and winked. "Who knows, we might even enjoy ourselves if we have to go down into that big, dark cellar." His stupid grin widened.

Francis turned away and promised herself that if the oathish lout so much as touched her she would kill him if it was the last thing she ever did.

The roar of the wind increased significantly with each rising gust and the force of the rain became almost overpowering. When Tim Rich forced one of the front doors open, he found it nearly impossible to see anything on the outside as he peeked out.

Mr. Young got his crystal radio out and placed it on top of the front desk and did his best to listen with his earphones. But it was impossible for him to pick up an intelligible signal. All he could hear was the constant drone of static.

Francis found herself growing more apprehensive. The house seemed to be creaking and buckling on its foundations. It was an odd and nerve-wracking noise. She was glad that she hadn't gotten into the state poor Mimi Seawell was in. But she was becoming more afraid with every passing minute.

After a short period of time, Mr. Young gave up on trying to listen for an intelligible signal on the crystal set. He had a sufficient number of oil lamps ready for use when the electricity went just behind the desk as well as a stock of them in the ballroom and dining room.

Francis did her best to show a good front for Mimi's sake, as did the men.

She hoped her example might help Mimi from going into a real fit. But even with the building fear of the storm without, the voice inside her head continued to speak with her. It did not converse all the time. It spoke in intervals, particularly during the evening hours last night. It spoke in a forceful whisper and demanded that she come down into the cellar as soon as she could. She belonged to whatever or whoever was down there. She must do as it told her. She must do its bidding no matter what it wanted of her.

When she first heard the voice, she did not try to resist it. But after a while, she grew fearful, sensing that it wanted something from her that could endanger the others in the inn. She tried her best to resist the voice. She did not want to hurt anybody… not even that oathish salesman unless he tried to force himself on her.

Vivid flashed of lightening illuminated between the seams of the boarded-up windows interrupted her train of thought as the roar of the nearly ear splitting thunder followed. Mimi Seawell began to cry in a hysterical manner. Vernon took her in his arms and did his best to reassure her.

A drunken Harriet Martin stumbled over to them and offered Vernon what was left of the decanter of sherry. He thanked her as Mr. Young came over with a small glass. Vernon quickly measured out a small amount of the sherry and ordered Mimi to drink it down.

She gulped it down and began coughing fitfully as the warmth of the liquor coursed down her throat. After a few seconds, her nerves quieted.

There was a sudden loud pounding at the front doors by the lobby. Voices from just outside demanded entry. Mr. Young scrambled from behind the front desk. Together with Tim, he ran across the lobby to the entrance. They managed to open the. They were nearly knocked off their feet as the doors were thrown all the way back against the walls.

Three armed men came bursting into the lobby. They were drenched to the skin. One had a Thompson sub-machine gun while another pointed a rifle nervously at everyone. They were obviously dangerous types. The deeply tanned, fair blond man among them yelled, "All right ladies and gents… you got some unexpected guests stayin' with you until the little lady out at sea blows over. Name's Harry and my mates here are Raymondo and Raphael. If everybody stays calm and collected and does as what we three blokes tells 'em… then we'll all get along just famously. But, if any of you has a mind not to follow orders… well, he or she might just wind up poppin' up flowers for eternity. So… I suggest to one and all that we all try to gets along real well. Then everything will be just fine."

The steely-eyed leader had a colourful English cockney accent. The black man and swarthy Latin stood on either side of him with the guns ready for use.

Francis cringed as the Latin looked at her and grinned with a lusty leer every bit as offensive as Ernest Thompson had been.

Chapter 11

WITH THE COMING nightfall, the hurricane-driven rain and wind pounded the house unmercifully with increasing force. The structure continued to buckle and sway under the unrelenting attack of the storm. The wind howled like a thousand shouting banshees. The hard driving rain sounded as though it would tear right through the sturdy solid timbers, mortar, and brick.

The gunmen forced everyone in the house to remain in the confines of the lobby. A table had been brought out form the dining room and placed near the front desk where they could keep a close eye on everyone.

The electricity went shortly after the three stormed the inn. Mr. Young, along with Tim and Vernon quickly broke out the oil lamps and lit them up on the barking orders of the cockney leader, moving as fast as they could in getting the lamps strategically placed around the periphery of the lobby. It was obvious that the cockney had a volatile temper and was a dangerous character as were his two companions; particularly the black Bahamian as he barked orders with a tense finger on the trigger of the tommy gun as though he would open fire at any moment.

Once the wicks of the lamps were adjusted so that there was enough light to see by adequately, the cockney leader told the men to return to their places. The flames from the numerous lamps produced an eerie soft flickering light.

Poor Vernon Seawell continued to have all he could do in keeping Mimi from going to pieces. The cockney exploded earlier, threatening to beat Mimi if she continued the crying jags and whimpering. Vernon vowed to himself that if the thug laid so much as one finger on her it would have to be over his corpse.

Fortunately, she was able to get control of herself enough to stop grating the cockney's nerves.

As the afternoon came to an end, it was becoming apparent to the seasoned veterans among them that the eye of the storm was coming in somewhere along the coastline the their vicinity at some point in the next few hours. Mr. Young, along with Rufus Magen and Juanita Leech, agreed on that. They had all been through more than one storm before. The signs were all there. Warlock Inn would not escape the brunt of this hurricane.

Harry Dunke ordered to get some grub pronto, telling Raymondo to accompany Juanita Leech to the kitchen to get out the food while he stayed in the hallway close to the corridor which led to the kitchen area and the food locker, keeping a nervous eye on everyone. He then barked at the dusky Cuban, ordering him to take a position by the doors at the front entrance. Raphael snapped to the orders and ran over to the entrance with the Tommy gun poised.

Francis shuddered as the Cuban once more lustfully eyed her. He wanted her. That was obvious. She resented it utterly at first, but the voice inside her head whispered to her again. It wanted her to come down to the cellar soon. It wanted her to bring someone down into the cellar with her. The chubby Cuban liked her and desired her and wanted her. She should encourage him. They should come down to the cellar together. The voice wanted to be nourished. It would have an offering after many years of going without.

When the voice ceased whispering to her, she looked over at the Cuban and smiled while fluttering her eyes. He grinned stupidly at her, displaying a set of disgustingly, ugly, yellow-stained teeth, some of which looked half-rotted.

Ernest Thompson sat languidly in a large chair off to the side of the lobby close to the entrance of the ballroom. When he saw the Cuban begin to make eyes at her, something inside him snapped. He sprang up out of the chair. "Leave Miss Beacham alone, you greasy Latin thug. Isn't it enough that you come in here with guns and frighten the death out of the women? Do you have to make insulting gestures at a refined lady? If you weren't armed, I'd give you a beating you wouldn't soon forget."

The Cuban's features went wild with rage as he spat and cursed at the salesman.

Harry Dunke sat back in the chair at the table and laughed mockingly at the salesman's outburst. "This Yank is full of spunk ain't he mate?"

Raphael spat again. "Let me clip his balls off Harry. This Yankee pig needs to be taught a lesson."

Harry looked up at Raphael and grinned. "No. No. We won't clip his balls. But I am going to let you have one of his ears, mate."

The cockney looked over to Mr. Young and Vernon, ordering the two men to get hold of Earnest Thompson by the arms in such a manner as to prevent him from being able to move or squirm about. Then he barked at Raphael, telling him to give the Tommy gun to him. Raphael could use his big knife to gain his trophy.

Mimi Seawell became almost hysterical again as Mr. Young protested loudly.

The steely blue eyes of the cockney flashed with anger. "Do what I tell you or I'll put a couple of slugs into that sobbin' bitch."

A feeling of emasculated helplessness took hold of Vernon as he and the dazed manager of Warlock Inn proceeded t obey their oppressor. There just did not seem to be any other avenue opened to them.

The two men reluctantly approached the salesman. He looked at them with an expression of utter disbelief and horror.

"I'm real sorry about this, believe me." There was a note of personal disgust in Vernon's shaky voice. "But if I don't do as he demands, he'll kill my wife. I'm certain of that."

They grabbed the horror-stricken salesman by the arms and held him fast. Thompson tried to resist as he shouted, "My God, you can't let them do this to me." He was wild with panic and terror.

Raphael handed the machine gun to the cockney and giggled with a wide toothy grin as he whipped out the large skewering knife from its sheaf that was attached to his wide belt. He laughed mockingly as he advanced menacingly in the direction of the salesman.

When he was upon Thompson, he proclaimed, "This is going to be a real pleasure." The Cuban grabbed hold of the terror-stricken man's lover left ear-lobe and stretched it as tight as he could. Thompson screamed in agony ad the Cuban took the razor-sharp blade of the skewering knife and cut straight down, slicing the earlobe clean off.

Thompson continued screaming even as he nearly passed out. The Cuban held the earlobe above his head triumphantly as the blood spurted and flowed from the ugly would where the earlobe used to be.

"My God, let me got some slave and bandages before this man bleeds to death," Mr. Young shouted as he desperately tried to keep from being sick.

"All right. Raphael will go with you. But you mind yourself of that poor bastard won't be the only one to suffer." The cockney spat his words out with an unmistakable brutality of will.

He threw the Tommy gun to the Cuban as he went along with Mr. Young to a storage room in the rear of the inn after the manager got an electric torch from behind the front desk. He then whipped out the Bowie knife he carried on his belt, telling them not to get any foolish ideas.

The viciousness of the act and the sight of all the blood proved too much for Mimi Seawell's sensitive nature and she mercifully fainted. Vernon quickly caught her in his arms as she started to fall.

Francis and Tim guided the half conscious salesman over to the large sofa in the lobby and had him lay down while Tim pressed one of the large table napkins he had gotten from the dining room against the stump of Thompson's left ear and did his best to prevent as much bleeding as was possible under the circumstances.

Juanita Leech and the black Bahamian returned from the kitchen with several trays of cold raost chicken, pork and a large pitcher of cold tea along with a plate filled with rolls and slices of bread. Raymondo had the rifle tucked between his large muscular left arm and side as he carried the second tray with the plates and cups. They sat the trays on the table by Harry.

Raymondo looked over at the wounded salesman. "What happened, Harry?" His voice was filled with mirthful curiosity.

The cockney smiled, telling him that Mr. Thompson had been a naughty boy. Raphael punished him and now he had one less ear.

Mrs. Leech nearly dropped some of the plates she was preparing when she heard that. The cockney barked at the frightened woman. "Watch it, old lady. I ain't above punishin' bad little girls either." He began to laugh mockingly as Juanita Leech cringed and backed away from him.

Mr. Young returned with Raphael just behind him. He carried a small tray which held packages of gauze and surgical bandages along with a tin container of medicated salve.

"Poor Mr. Thompson has lost a lot of blood," Tim shouted excitedly. The manager began to immediately treat the salesman. Thompson began to slip into a state of shock.

"I suggest we all be good lads and ladies and enjoy the nice meal which this good lady and my mate got up for us. Let's try behavin' ourselves. I don't want to do nasty things. But I will have my orders obeyed. I won't have anybody talkin' back to me or my mates. Is that understood?" he barked.

The area around the lobby remained silent save for the howling wind and rain. "I want to hear a yes from you people," he shouted as he waved the rifle above his head with menacing gestures.

It provoked an immediate "yes" from everyone.

The cockney grinned, "Good. That's what I wants to hear." He looked over at Raphael and ordered the Cuban along with Francis to dispense the food.

The voice inside Francis' head whispered again. It told her to do as she was ordered and to play up to the plump and juicy Cuban. Before the night was over, it would enjoy a savoury meal.

She went to the table. Raphael handed her a large carving knife and told her to carve the meat and serve it. He grinned at her. She returned it with one of her own.

Chapter 12

AN ORNATE GRANDFATHER clock, which stood just inside the entrance of the ballroom, began chiming the hour of midnight. The wind continued to roar with a deafening intensity. The large old house seemed like it would shake right off the foundations. But the inn held its ground despite the murderous beating Mother Nature was giving it. Several windows in the upper turrets of the house along with a number of windows on the second floor were shattered under the tremendous pressure of the wind and rain.

Most of the oil lamps had been turned down with the exception of two large ones near the front desk and another on a small pedestal in the lobby close to the doors at the front entrance.

Most everyone was trying to get some rest in the various chairs that were scattered about and the benches that were brought out of storage. Ernest Thompson lay sprawled upon the sofa in a bad state of shock.

Francis sat limply in a large upholstered chair that Mr. Young brought in from his office. She was able to doze on and off for the past few hours.

The chubby Cuban sat in a large straight back teak wood chair of oriental design close to the doors at the front entrance. He cradled the Tommy gun in his large lap. The cockney leader lay sprawled across the table fiercely snoring while the Cuban stood first watch.

The Cuban was in the midst of smoking on of the strong, smelly Havana stogies such as the cockney smoked before assigning the Cuban first watch. The Cuban continued to eye her. His desire and lust was obvious. He acted like a young school boy hoping to make his first sexual conquest.

The voice inside her head hadn't spoken to her since the Cuban and she served the cold meal and drinks earlier. But she did as the voice demanded and occasionally looked over at him and smiled encouragingly.

The voice began to whisper again and instructed her to look over at the Cuban again and tease him. She obeyed and smiled at him, running the tip of her tongue over her upper and lower lips suggestively and then proceeded to apply a fresh coat of scarlet red lipstick to her full lips. She continued to eye him in her most provocative manner.

Beads of sweat formed along the deep lines of the Cuban's broad brow as she got up from her chair and sauntered sensually over to him. She put an extra umph into the swaying motion of her hips.

She smiled at him with a glint in her eye. "What some company, big fella?" There was a earthy sauciness in her voice.

The Cuban grunted slightly as he cleared his throat. "Si," he replied.

Her smile broadened as she applied the tip of her fingers along the rough stubble of his beard along the lower cheeks. "I like big guys like you. I like you. I'd like to get to know you much better… if you know what I mean." Her vice was filled with a seething, seductive charm.

His large head bobbled up and down eagerly. He reminded her now of a large mongrel dog hot to hums some bitch in heat in a back alley. "Si! My little conchitta. I think I know exactly what you mean." He placed the Tommy gun up against the side of the chair and grabbed her as he got up from the chair. He began pawing at her roughly as he awkwardly began to smother her cheeks and lips with sloppy, disgusting wet kisses. His breath stank of cigar smoke. For a moment, she thought that she might become sick from his breath and the rough way he handled her, but she had to obey the voice no matter what.

She suddenly pushed him away. His swarthy features became flushed with anger. "What's wrong?" His demand for an explanation was given in a harsh whisper. He did not want to arouse Harry or the others.

Francis smiled pleasantly as she caught her breath. "Not here. Not like this. Not in front of all these people."

He looked at her for a second and nodded in agreement. Then he looked all about the lobby, taking particular note of Harry as he slumped across the table snoring away. Raymondo was slumped against the chair and snoring almost as loudly as Harry was.

He looked at her as his anger returned along with a desperate feeling of frustration. "But where? I got to say here on guard duty until two."

"Oh, nonsense. Everyone is well away. I know a perfect place; the cellar. We can go down there and not be disturbed by a soul and be back up here before anyone misses us," she said.

He remembered what Harry told them about this place. He liked her idea. The bulge in his pants began to grow hard and became quite noticeable.

She grinned, "Oh, yes. There's a big cellar. It's the perfect place. Just to the back of the inn. And it's close enough so that if you hear anything… you can get right back."

The Cuban began rubbing the stubble on his chin as he pondered her proposition. He wanted her badly. But he knows what Harry was capable of if he got sore. And he know that Raymondo would do anything Harry told him even though they were close amigos.

But he wanted this Yankee woman more than any woman he had seen in many a year. His burning need was tremendous. He had to quench the fires of desire that she had stirred up in his groin.

Raphael decided it was worth the risk.

"Okay, conchitta. Let's go." He grinned at her with lustful intent as he picked up the Tommy gun. She smiled teasingly as they tiptoed down the hallway and into the connecting narrow corridor, which led to the back of the inn. He carried one of the oil lamps with his free hand so they could see their way along the narrow passage.

Francis stopped in front of the large, brittle, cypress wood door which opened onto the stairs leading down into the cellar. She took the oil lamp and turned the light on the large padlock.

"Damn," the Cuban growled under his breath when he saw it.

"Can't you get it off?" she asked teasingly. "A big strapping man like you shouldn't have any trouble," she goaded him with a mocking tone.

Raphael was filled with anger as he told her to stand back. He took the butt end of the Tommy gun and struck as hard as he could at the padlock. It took four powerful blows before it gave way and the wood splintered where the metal collar was screwed into the wooden frame. He easily tore it loose. The long, rusted screws came popping out of the wood.

"No trouble, my little conchitta." He grinned at her again and it nauseated her.

He grabbed hold of the doorknob and found that he could hardly turn it. He had to apply a considerable amount of force before the door would open. There was a nerve-grating squeak and squeal that almost drove her up the wall as the Cuban forced the door wide open. The large hinges had almost frozen in place from years of corrosive oxidation acting upon the metal.

Raphael then eyed her curiously. "How did you know about the cellar in this joint? It's been years since anyone has been down here."

The voice in her head told her how to answer and she obeyed dutifully. "Why… I had a chat with the manager a few days ago. He fold me something of the history of the inn. That's when I learned about the cellar. This place is one of the few around these parts with a cellar."

Raphael nodded as he took the oil lamp from her and preceded her down the stairs. A pungent and highly foul odor permeated the large cellar of the inn. The place was damp and mildewy with greenish grey fungus and mold staining the ceiling and walls with a sickening scent. "It stinks down here," he complained. He played the light from the lamp all about the parameters of the stairs, observing the huge silken strands of gossamer-like spider webbing which hung from the ceiling and large sturdy oak crossbeam supports and columns. The pitted and porous coquina stone walls were stained black from years of increasing discoloration in addition to the greenish mold and mildew stains.

Large roaches, beetles, and other vermin scurried and pranced about the cellar. The pronounced squeal of rats hidden in their lairs within the walls of the cellar did not escape their attention.

Raphael turned on her and growled, "I don't like this fucking hole."

She grinned as she proceeded to raise the hem of her dress, revealing the black mesh silk stockings caressing her shapely legs. "We haven't got much time, big boy." There was a throaty quality in her sultry tone.

The bulge in his pants grew heard as a rock. He felt the sticky wetness begin to ooze from the opening of his shaft. "To hell with the damn rats and bugs. Come here baby." He placed the Tommy gun down on the damp stone floor along with the oil lamp and started to grab her when his attention was arrested by the sight of the large half-ruined Satanic altar in the rear of the cellar. He shuddered and made the sign of the cross. The Cuban knew instinctively that he was in a place of great evil.

A low, guttural growl reverberated through the cellar. It sounded as though it was coming from a large cistern well which was off in a corner close to the unholy altar. He asked himself repeatedly why he had not noticed these evil things the minute he came down into this pesthole.

"What was that?" he shouted as he experienced a penetrating chill. His voice quivered slightly as he spoke.

Raphael looked at her and swallowed hard. She already had her dress off, revealing the large cupped brassiere and corset she wore so alluringly. He wondered why he could not make out the fullness of her breasts. Her arms and shoulders seemed too large for a woman her size.

She smiled and spoke seductively as she told him she was his for now.

"So, she's a little large in places," he mused. She was here and he was here and they both wanted each other and time was wasting away.

He grabbed her and crushed her to him. His eager trembling hand sought inside her garment, seeking the warm, moist opening between her thighs. When his fingers came to rest on a large bulge similar to his, his hand jerked spasmodically away as he went cold inside. "Goddamn. What is this?" he swore under his breath.

Her smile became teasingly seductive. "Why, whatever is the matter?" she said.

A rage of uncontrollable fury took hold of the Cuban. He grabbed her by the hair and yanked hard. He yelled when her hair came off in his hand.

"You fucking Yankee pervert," he screamed as he spat at her and whipped out his large skewering knife from the sheaf attached to his belt.

He rushed her and a great struggle developed. The noise caused the rats to go into a frenzy of squealing and squeaking which echoed throughout every part of the cellar. After a few minutes of struggle, she gained the upper hand due to an enormous surge of adrenaline coursing through every part of her body. She was soon able to get the Cuban in a vise like headlock. A strength which she had never known before allowed her to rest control of the large razor-sharp knife. She managed to get the blade up against the fat soft flesh of his throat. She proceeded to slice straight across the flabby, soft folds.

Frothy blood squirted and poured from the gaping wound. He made a low gurgling noise as frothy blood began to pour from his mouth and nose as well.

She held him in the bear like grip as she continued to slice back and forth as though she was carving a piece of meat at the dinner table. She sliced through flesh, muscle, and bone. The head was soon free of the body. The decapitated body fell to the cold stone floor of the cellar with a sickening plop.

The voice inside her head instructed her to bring the head over to the well. She dutifully obeyed, approaching it with a reverence and respect like a parishioner taking part in a solemn religious act.

Francis held the head up high above her. The voice told her to give the offering to it. She dropped it down into the dark confines at the bottom. There was a soft thud followed by what seemed like powerful animal teeth biting and tearing through flesh and bone.

Chapter 13

A DEAFENING CRASH resounded through the lobby as one of the large royal palms facing the front of the inn was uprooted and sent smashing into the veranda at the south end. Harry Dunke jumped up like a bullet being fired with the Winchester ready for use. Everyone else was jolted wide awake by the crash as well.

It took Raymondo and Harry a few seconds before they realized that Raphael was no longer at his station by the front entrance. "Raphael! Where the hell are you?" Harry shouted above the deafening roar of the elements outside.

There was no reply. The cockney ordered Raymondo to turn up the wicks on several of the lamps on the countertop of the front desk as he proceeded to take a head count of the hostages. One of the women was missing. He remembered how Raphael kept making eyes at the rather tall attractive woman earlier. She appeared to have encouraged him.

Harry Dunke shook with rage. He was filled with disgust as he yelled for Raymondo to find Raphael and the woman. He glared at Rufus Hagan as he sat in a straight back chair next to one of the large potted plants close to the entrance of the dining room. He took aim at the tall, lanky man and shouted, "Get off your bottom, mate. Take a look outside and see what the big noise was all about."

The lanky man gulped hard as he bolted out of the chair. "Yes sir. Right away." His voice quivered as he ran over to the large double doors and with a considerable effort managed to force one of them to open. He braced himself against the door as he peeked out. He was immediately drenched in rain. He was nearly blinded by the fury of the storm. But flashes of vivid lightening clearly illuminated the immediate surroundings. He could just barely make out the uprooted palm and the smashed in portion of the veranda on the south end.

Rufus forced the door to close as Harry Dunke shouted, demanding to know what had happened as he cocked the rifle.

Rufus wiped the water out of his eyes and off of his brow as he answered, "One of the palms fell against the porch." He screeched as he spoke, betraying the terrible anxiety he felt.

The cockney grinned. "fine, that's what I like. A bloke that knows how to take orders without talkin' back."

Rufus' slim, drenched form slumped back down on the straight back chair. He shook badly from the chilled rain and wind and nerves.

Raymondo ran back into the lobby and reported that there was no sigh of Raphael or the woman. But there was an open door halfway down the hall that opened into a cellar. The Bahamian reported that it looked to bed a very large cellar although he was only able to see the area around the stairs clearly.

The cockney spit. "Damned fat Cuban. He gets the hots for the lady and just has to get a piece. And now the sonafabitch is too scared to come and face ole Harry. Well — the dumb bastard has got good cause to be afraid."

He looked around him at the apprehensive faces that stared back at him. "All right ladies and gents… everybody on their feet. We're all goin' to take a little walk down into the cellar. Ole Harry is goin' to give you a demonstration of what it means to cross a bloke like me. Jump to and I mean now," he barked.

The cockney looked over to the wounded salesman as he lay sprawled on the sofa. He would not be any help to them when this storm ended and he marched the men back to the Lady Jane to get her seaworthy.

Mimi Seawell saw the way he looked at the salesman. "You can't mean poor Mr. Thompson as well. He's lost so much blood and is still in shock," she pleaded.

He looked at Mimi tellingly. "Yeah, you're right lady. He ain't much use to me." A grim expression developed in his deeply lined and tanned features. He took aim at the salesman with the Winchester and fired. The bullet smashed into the temple of Ernest Thompson's head. His body jerked from the impact of the bullet as the blood poured profusely from the fatal head wound.

Mimi Seawell, Juanita Leech, and Harriet Thompson screamed. Mimi buried her head in her husband's shoulder and sobbed uncontrollably.

"You filthy, murdering bastard," Vernon shouted in outrage and anger.

The cockney grinned. "Careful what you say, mate. I still got a number of rounds in this piece. Everybody move," he shouted.

Raymondo kept an eye on the hostages as the cockney used the rifle to point the way. They slowly began moving in the direction of the narrow corridor that led to the back end of the inn in single file except for Mimi, as she had to cling to Vernon's arm for support.

Raymondo and the cockney brought up the rear. Raymondo held an oil lamp while Harry kept the rifle trained on their frightened captives.

The cockney ordered them to stop by the door leading down into the cellar and form a cluster around it. He kept one eye on them as he opened the door wide.

There was a deathly silence augmented by the dim and ghostly flickering light coming from the oil lamp. "You down there, Raphael, ole mate?" the cockney shouted. "Just couldn't wait to get into the panties of the pretty miss. Well mate… you're goin' to be awful sorry for leavin' your post like that. You hear me?"

There was no answer.

Harry smiled wickedly at Raymondo as he told the black Bahamian to take the rifle.

"Lover boy knows his arse is goin' to get flayed for this one. I bet the poor bastard is shittin' his pants right now," the cockney screamed and then laughed heartily. "We're comin' down Raphael. You better not try anything."

Harry Dunke motioned to the frightened group to proceed down the stairs. They showed a reluctance to follow his orders.

"Go or me and my mate will finish the lot of you right here and now." The sound of his voice seemed like venomous snakes coiled and ready to strike.

Each of them slowly made the descent down into the dark underbelly of the house. It seemed at that moment more like a tomb rather than a cellar.

As the cockney and his Bahamian mate started down the stairs just behind the others, piercing screams and shouts of horror and shock erupted from both the men and women. They literally bounded down the stairs.

When they saw what the others were looking at, their eyes popped in disbelief. The large, bulky body of their comrade lay on the floor. The head was no where to be seen. Large rats had been at the fat meat on the arms of the corpse, chewing away bloody strips of meat. They had also been feasting on the stump of the neck.

The area around the decapitated body was awash in crimson red gore.

The rats went into a frenzy as they scurried away from the body back into their invisible lairs.

"Maan, whaat happened to him Harry?" Raymondo shouted. He was crazed with fear.

"I don't know. I don't know," was the cockney's stuttering answer.

Something moved out of the shadows at the rear of the cellar. Harry and Raymondo turned about like steel spring traps that had suddenly snapped tight.

"What the hell," Harry yelled as he looked on incredulously at Francis. She wore only her black corset, panties, brassiere, and black mesh stockings. There was no longer the full head of hair. The face seemed more like that of a pale, delicate, thin, young man.

Francis had the Tommy gun and proceeded to take aim at the cockney and the Bahamian. She smiled sweetly at them.

The voice in her head told her it wanted all of the people. It had fed on the brain of the Cuban and wanted more food… much more food.

Raymondo snapped out of his initial shock and fired at her. But it was too late as she began firing wildly. The bright, rapid flash of machine gun bursts momentarily illuminated the near darkness. Bodies jerked in spasms of bullet-ridden violence. When the clip was empty, the cellar resembled a slaughterhouse full of blood drenched corpses.

The thick stone reverberated with the high-pitched squealing and squeaking rats. They went wild as a result of the explosive machine gun fire followed by the warm smell of much spilled blood in the close, stinking air.

Francis went about the business of dragging the bodies over by the well. With the large knife in hand, she busily went about the task of removing the heads so that it could feed on the many brains.

Chapter 14

SHE SAT PERFECTLY still as traces of new morning sunlight filtered through the seams of the boarded-up windows in the double doors at the front entrance. A quiet lull hung heavy in the air making her feel as though she was entombed. It had been like that for more than an hour when the fury of the hurricane moved out of the surrounding area.

Warlock Inn stood its ground firmly, sustaining only minimal damage from the force of the storm.

She sat perfectly still in the straight back chair Rufus Hagen occupied before he and the others became food for the thing down in that well within the dark, rancid confines of the cellar. It all seemed like an eternity had gone by since then. She felt a wariness since the carnage down in that small piece of hell. She also felt utter disgust. She could still smell blood, urine, and feces from several of the victims that came from their clothing at the point of death when their bladders and bowels erupted.

The sickening aroma had been even worse in the gateway fro hell due to the stink which already permeated the cellar. The odor now issued from the corridor into the main hallway and lobby and was made even worse by the close summer heat that was rapidly returning.

Loathsome, filthily bloated flies seemed to come out of nowhere and buzzed all about the body of Earnest Thompson as it lay stiffened in rigor mortis on the sofa. They made a hideous droning noise as the body began to add to the already horrible odor.

She wondered why the voice in her head hadn't told her to take his body down into that slaughter room so that it could feed again. Perhaps it was full now and required nothing more from her. It hadn't spoken since the massacre.

She began to experience great remorse as the tears began to run down her cheeks, streaking what was left of her makeup which she had applied just before that gang of brutes forced themselves into the inn.

She wondered how in the world she was going to live with herself with the blood of so many innocent people on her stained hands. She told herself that her will was not her own when she did the bidding of the voice. But it was her hand that fired the terrible machine gun and blasted all those innocent people into eternity and then afterward hacked their heads off so that it could feast upon their brains.

She kept telling herself over and over again. It was the killer. She had no choice but to obey.

Her thoughts turned to cousin Thaddeus then. She grieved intensely as she began to dwell on his untimely end. After all those years in incarceration at Lakeshore and the humiliation she had endured as they tried to make her believe that she was her dead brother, it was cousin Thaddeus who liberated her. He just should not have changed his mind like he did. But, on the other hand, these people were completely innocent with the exception of those disgusting thugs. She was glad that they were dead.

She would somehow have to convince the authorities when they came that she was not responsible for this carnage. They simply had to understand what really happened in this place.

Francis got up and went upstairs to the large guest bathroom at the end of the hall. Once she was inside, she drew herself a soapy bath in the large ivory colored porcelain tub.

After removing the blood splattered undergarments, she immersed herself in the cool, cleansing water. Numerous goose bumps formed on her smooth white skin as she got a large bar of perfume scented soap and a long stemmed soap brush and proceeded to vigorously lather her body in an effort to quickly rid herself of the dried blood, gore, and gritty dirt which clung to her in a most offensive manner.

When she was finished bathing, she got out of the tub and dried herself with a large, soft, pink towel. She unstopped the drain, allowing the soapy, pinkish water to go down with slurping and gurgling noises.

Her body was now free from the sickening, unclean feeling. But inside her mind and soul, it still remained as she went to her room and put on a fresh petticoat and large cupped halter and finally the extra light print cotton dress which cousin Thaddeus had ready for her.

She retrieved the wig from the cellar and brought it back up to the room, after all that horror, and placed it on the bed. She proceeded to put it back on. The womanly head of hair made her feel ever so much better. Her real hair hadn't yet grown back sufficiently. The brutes at Lakeshore had cut it short. It would take a great deal more time for it to grow back the way she wanted it to be.

She applied a fresh coat of lipstick to her full lips and then put on her tiny ring-shaped earrings that she purchased in the little s hop back in the Jacksonville depot.

When someone did finally come, she wanted to look as presentable and normal as she possibly could She didn't want anyone thinking of her as being any way but normal under these circumstances.

After putting on her sky blue high heels, she went back downstairs to the doors at the front entrance. It took some effort to open the doors. The wind and rain had damaged the locks to some extent. But after several minutes, the doors opened wide and she walked out onto the large veranda, taking note of the uprooted tree that had caved in the roof of the veranda at the south end.

Palm prongs, snapped boughs, leaves, and pine needles were scattered all about the grounds surrounding the house. The big house itself appeared to be in good condition.

She heard the hoof beats of a horse then looked up at the drive that led up to the front of the house. A man wearing a wide-brimmed straw Panama, loose white cotton slacks, and a striped cotton shirt riding a spotted grey more came trotting up to the front of the inn.

When she saw who it was, she almost fainted. It was cousin Thaddeus. She could hardly believe that he was alive and here as he reigned in the horse by the steps and dismounted.

He did not say a thing. He just looked up at her shocked features and proceeded up the steps and finally stood confronting her.

When the initial shock wore off, she spoke, her voice shaking, "Oh, Thad. I thought I killed you. You don't know how glad I am to see you. Everything has been so horrible."

His features showed no emotions. "As you can see… I survived, Frank."

"Don't call me Frank!" she screamed.

Thaddeus closed his eyes momentarily and breathed deeply. "All right Francis. I survived. I regained consciousness shortly after you put that knife in me and was able to summon help despite a considerable loss of blood."

"Dr. Gilmore came. He got the police and I was later arrested and charged with aiding in your escape. Nurse Higginbotham apparently had a guilty conscience and confessed her role in the plan. I posted a hefty bond and was released. I managed to allude the police after escaping from the hospital I was in and hopped a train out of Trenton," he solemnly concluded.

"Oh, my poor Thad. I'm so sorry about all this," she said as she put her arms around his neck and gently placed her head against his chest and began to weep.

"That's all right," he replied as he continued to show no visible signs of emotion. But there was a determined weariness about him as he gently disengaged himself from her.

It was then that she noticed for the first time the gun and holster which was strapped around his waist. His right hand reached down and undid the guard on the holster. He pulled out the sleek, cold, grey, steely 44 revolver which he purchased in St. Augustine at the same time he rented the horse to ride over when the fury of the hurricane subsided.

It took most of the morning for him to get from St. Augustine over to Seville due to the badly impaired roads and the thick mud he had to forge as he moved through woods and swampy marshes. But he made it. There wasn't anything going to stop him from doing what he knew he must do.

He pointed the revolver dead center at her.

She looked at him incredulously, "Why, whatever is this Thad?" Her voice trembled with anxiety.

He showed the first real sign of emotion then as he smiled. "I realized what a terrible mistake I made by doing what I did. I robbed you of any real chance you may have had in ever facing the truth about yourself and ruined my life as well."

A tear came streaking down his cheek. "I'm truly sorry Frank." There was great sadness in his voice as he pulled the trigger.

She hardly believed what was happening as the slug from the 44 tore into the pit of her stomach. The force of the slug sent her falling back, crashing against the hard floorboards of the veranda.

The bullet lodged in her spine. She felt nothing nor could she move.

As she began to slip into a deep shock, she heard the voice once more inside her head. But this time it spoke to Thaddeus. It was in his head as well.

It told him to take her down in the cellar. It was once again hungry and wanted fresh food.

Thaddeus' hands slipped underneath her armpits. She lost consciousness as he began dragging her limp body back into the house.

Trance Two
Their Perilous Mademoiselle
June, 1943

Chapter 15

HORACE TATE SWATTED at the air about his large, sunburned nose. A pesky deer fly was trying its damnedest to get at him. He hated the damn critters. They could bite almost as bad as a bee could sting. The hot air was filled with too many of the mean little stingers this time of the year.

He had been patiently waiting by the little train depot for the arrival of the Silver Eagle, which was due in from Miami on a run to New York at 9:42. His wait was made double uncomfortable not only because of the deer flies, but also from he close morning air which was as still as death. The lack of any sea breeze just added to his misery.

Horace removed the ponderous black coat and tie which was part of his uniform and placed them neatly in the passenger seat next to him. It was just too damn hot to wait inside the sleek, black Pierce Arrow touring car circa 1937. He began sweating profusely. His shirt was soaked with sour-smelling sweat.

But even with the coat and tie off, it wasn't enough to give him the relief he sought as he proceeded to unbutton the top button of the white cotton shirt and remove the stiff collar. He just was not going to suffer any more while being forced to wait for that damn train to arrive on a hot summer morning like this one.

That damn Elwood Spencer could take a flying leap into the ocean if he didn't like it upon returning to the inn with the newly arrived guest. Spencer had dressed him down in recent weeks for doing what he just did. But he wasn't worried. Spencer would have a tough time finding a driver and mechanic for the guest's limousine as he liked to refer to the '37 Pierce Arrow, particularly one as good as him what with the war on and everything.

Horace picked up the morning edition of the Times Union out of Jacksonville and tried to read the latest war news from the European and Pacific theatres. It was useless. The heat made him feel just too damn miserable. He threw the paper down in disgust and got out of the car. He grabbed hold of his suspenders and began strolling up and down the length of the platform by the front entrance of the little depot.

If Spencer so much as made one remark when he returned to the inn, he was going to quit that little shit of a manager as he still couldn't get any relief from the sweltering heat.

After all, he was fifty-one years old now. He had his veteran's pension which he drew due to a back injury and other wounds he sustained in the First World War while taking part in some of the fiercest fighting along the Maginoal Line. He could get by on that if he had to.

Horace got out his pocket watch and checked the time. It was now 10:05. "Damn. Late again," he swore under his breath.

There was to be only one passenger for the inn this morning. But then, one passenger was better than none. Warlock Inn along with the other accommodations between St. Augustine and Daytona weren't doing the kind of business they had begun to enjoy in the several years before America entered the war when the damn Japs bombed Pearl Harbor.

He had to hand it to the owners of the inn though. They hit upon a clever innovation in maintaining a certain level of GI business along with a moderate amount of civilian patronage by converting the old ballroom and the dining room into dance floors along with a small stage large enough for a moderate size dance band to perform on.

The bands they were able to book were pretty decent too. That was probably one of the big reasons why so many of the sailors, coast guard boys, and Army Reserve GI's came down from St. Augustine and nearly packed the place on the weekends.

He would drop in himself occasionally just to hear those real fine renditions of Glenn Miller, Artie Shaw, Harry James, and the Dorsey Brothers. And the inn had that real nice jukebox to play the best recordings of the genuine real McCoys. The guys could really do some juken. The local gals really turned out a Saturday night in droves didn't hurt either in maintaining such good weekend business.

Horace figured that the weekends were the best time in this chicken liver job. He really enjoyed coming down here and picking the guys up and talking about the war and learning what there was to learn along with reminiscing about his own experiences in the last big one.

There wasn't anything too good for those boys. They were the nation's pride. The fellas that were going to stop Hitler's Nazis, Mussolini's fascists, and Tojo's

Japs from getting their hands on the great nation.

He wanted to help make this GI's a little bit happier. Some of them would be going overseas and would not be coming back. This was the one aspect of his job that made him feel like he was contributing something to the country's war effort.

He thought about it all and decided that he would hold onto the damn job after all as he stepped down from the platform and leaned against the Pierce Arrow and cursed the damn late train under his breath.

His disposition sweetened considerably as he heard the faint whistle of a train off in the distance. The sleek lines of the Silver Eagle pulled up to the train depot and came to a swooshing halt seconds later.

"About time," he huffed as he reached inside the car and retrieved his jacket, quickly putting it on. But he still refused to put on the damn collar and tie.

Horace went around the side of the little wooden frame building and gingerly hopped up onto the platform as the Pullman conductor stepped out of the nearest coach with a large brown suitcase in hand.

When Horace saw the only passenger for Seville get off the train, his mouth nearly fell open. The young woman was one of the most stunningly attractive gals he had ever laid eyes on in his entire life.

The lean black features of the conductor, Henry Gates, smiled at him. Horace gave the colored conductor a hardy smile and greeting just as he did on each encounter. They had become pretty good friends over the years. "This is your passenger Horace, Miss Bridget Bollier."

Horace smiled broadly as he gave the stunning girl the once over. She had silky, long, blond hair that cascaded perfectly over the straight shoulder pads of her blouse and jacket. One large bang of blond hair fell sensually over her left eye. Her complexion was pale and creamy in texture. Her eyes were like pale blue sapphires. They seemed to have a shimmering quality. And she was one of the most regally tall dames he had ever seen. In short, she was a grade-A knockout.

With her black purse tucked under one arm, she had the bearing of real continental charm and sophistication.

Henry cleared his throat and excused himself as he went back inside the coast after handing the suitcase to Horace and wishing the gorgeous blond babe a pleasant stay.

She looked at Horace amusingly. He realized how he was just standing there gawking at her and turned three shades of red with embarrassment. "Welcome to Seville miss. Hope you have a pleasant stay," he quipped.

She smiled teasingly as she replied with a heavy French accent, "Thank you."

Horace asked her to follow him as he led her through the tiny depot out the front entrance and other to the Pierce Arrow. He held the door to the back passenger seat on the right side open for her as she climbed inside and then went around to the back, depositing the suitcase in the trunk.

Horace hurried around to the driver's side and quickly hopped inside and sped away from the little train depot grateful to be once again out on the main road and able to generate a slight breeze from the sheer motion of the car.

His gaze drifted up at the rear view mirror as much as he could while maintaining a margin of safety as he drove. He just could not keep his eyes off of her. He asked if she would be staying at the inn long.

"I'm not sure," she answered. "Maybe a few weeks… perhaps longer. I am a political refugee you see. My father is one of the key leaders in the Gaullist resistance in my native France. He was very fearful that the Nazis might retaliate against my mother, younger brother, and myself. So, we were smuggled out of France. My mother and brother wanted to stay in England. But I wanted to come here to the States. It has been a dream of mine for some time."

Horace found himself captivated by that alluring throaty French accent. It put him in mind of his time in France during the last war.

"Have any relatives here in Seville miss?" Horace asked. His curiosity roused. He thought he knew most everyone in the little coastal community. He hadn't noticed any foreigners moving into the area for quite a few years now.

"No," she replied. "My uncle is a businessman in Bayonne, New Jersey. You see… he used to vacation down here in this state of Florida at Warlock Inn often before the war. He will be coming down in perhaps in a few weeks or so. I will go back with him to this Bayonne in New Jersey. He thought it best to do it this way since I arrived in the states through Miami by way of Argentina. It was all done very quietly in the hope that Nazi agents would not learn about me being over here."

Horace nodded understandingly, "I see."

"Is it always this hot?" she asked while getting a lace hanky from her purse and daintily wiping the perspiration from her brow.

"I'm afraid it is miss, around this time of the year," Horace answered.

"I should be used to it by now, having spent the past few weeks in Miami," she replied.

He just couldn't keep his eyes away from the view of her in the rear view mirror. She was a real knockout for certain. He wondered if he should warn her about the weekends when the bays came down from St. Augustine. But then, she was an adult continental gal. She could probably take care of herself after all she had been through, living in an occupied country with the damn Krauts all around. He decided that it really wasn't his place to say anything.

It seemed like only seconds had gone by to Horace as he brought the Pierce Arrow to a stop in front of the large house. He gingerly stepped out of the car and went around to the trunk to collect her brown suitcase and then proceeded to open the passenger door for her. As she got out, one of the bellboys standing by the front steps of the veranda got a look at her. Horace chuckled under his breath as the boy's eyes went as round as saucers. There certainly weren't any women like her in Seville.

The bellboy rushed down the stops and over to the Pierce Arrow with a mixture of ogling shyness. He was relatively new. A local boy who had lived all his young life in Seville.

"This is Miss Bridget Bollier's suitcase Danny. Now you show her to the front desk and assist her in getting properly signed in." Horace gave the young man a firm look.

The bellboy blushed slightly as he realized he had been eyeing her much like Horace when he first saw her back at the depot.

"Yes, Mr. Tate. Right away," the bellboy replied nervously.

Horace smiled pleasantly, tipping his hat again and wishing her a pleasant say.

"Thank you," she replied with a wink.

Horace lingered for a minute as he watched her go up the steps and across the veranda to the double doors at the front entrance with Danny. If only I was twenty years younger," he sighed before getting back into the car to drive it around to the garage.

Chapter 16

SHE LOOKED AROUND the room and was again miffed by the manager's insistence that it was the only one presently available for occupancy. He explained that the staff was presently in the process of renovating and redecorating most of the other rooms in the inn. The bizarre wallpaper scheme and those curious paintings and tintype photographs were odd, to say the least.

She had been told that the Americans were such a happy-go-lucky people. She smiled, amused by what the silly young bellboy told her about the history of the inn as she removed her dress suit jacket and undid the top buttons of her blouse.

She opened the large window, allowing fresh air inside. A slightly stale, musty odor clung cloyingly to the air in the room. There were two small table fans in the room. One stood on an open secretariat and the other was on the little table by the large four-poster bed. She switched on both fans, welcoming the slight movement of the heavy air which the fans afforded.

A particular picture got her attention then. It seemed to hold her fast for a few seconds. It was of a grim, thin face with a large moustache. He had flaring widow's peak sideburns. His eyes were very lifelike. They seemed to be almost observing her.

This inn and the uniquely American Gothic quality of the house itself along with the portrait of the man who, according to the silly bellboy, was a male witch and was said to have sacrificed small children and young virginal girls to the devil, made her realize that the Americans may not be all that far removed from their predominantly European ancestry after all.

She shook herself out of the odd feeling as she quickly disrobed, taking her under things and placing them neatly in the lower drawer of the chest of drawers. She then took some of her better dresses and skirts and neatly place them across the coat hangers in the closet.

For the time being, she wanted only to draw herself a nice, cool bath and soak in it. She went into the adjoining bathroom and turned on the taps, making sure of the desired temperature. She then placed the stopper over he drain and went back into the room to get some of the fine bath powders she acquired during her time in Miami and then went back into the bathroom, measuring out just enough and pouring it into the fast filling tub of invitingly cool water. The surface of the water soon had a consistent coat of glittering bubbles.

She turned off the taps when the tub was filled to the desired level and got into the water, immersing her soft, creamy contours in the bubbly bath.

"This is much better," she sighed, wondering if she would ever get used to the hot Florida sun while staying here. But she was willing to do anything to help the fatherland achieve ultimate victory against the inferior allied forces.

Her slender, perfectly shaped body breathed again as little goose bumps formed around her midsection, thighs, and flanks. If she had to stay very long in this hot climate, she would sleep in the nude as she did in Miami and Havana. This was so different from Germany, France or Scotland.

She took the soft, velvet-textured washcloth from the towel rack next to the tub and began to softly soap her face, shoulders, and perfectly rounded breasts with it before she lay back in the cool bubble bath.

She smiled with a feeling of deep satisfaction as she though about how well her cover had worked for thus far since laving France on this assignment, following that last passionate night of lovemaking with Manfred Wilhelm. That was the height of ecstasy compared to the sexual encounters she endured with that ugly little Scottish professor in Edinburgh. How she hated having to submit to those indignities. But she was giving her body in the cause of the fatherland. She though about Manfred as the little man reached his climax, which made it easier to endure.

When she finally extracted the information she had been sent to get on the latest developments in British radar defences, she took tremendous pleasure on that last night with the detestable little man when she took her Luger and demolished his testicles, sending him into eternity while he slept.

She posed as a British citizen on that occasion. This time around was much easier, assuming the fictitious identity of Bridget Bollier. She was able to totally submerge her own real identity, Marisa Stohler. It was fairly simple. She already spoke fluent French. Her mother originally came from the little village of Louen near the Swiss-French border.

Her mother had met and married her father shortly after the First World War and moved to Munich where her father had his printing business. When the fuher came to power following the fall of the miserable weak Weimer Republic, she left her father when he swore his allegiance to the Nationalist Socialist Party and returned to France.

How she despised her weak, inferior mother. She ardently hoped that she was now dead. And she hoped it was at the hands of the superior soldiers of the fatherland. Her mother was so insipid and weak like the Jews and gypsies.

Her lover, Manfred, had already achieved a high position within the SS. She had become very curious about the camps where the Jews and other inferiors were taken and wanted to see one. Manfred managed to obtain permission for her to visit Auschwitz.

That was one of the most glorious days of her life as she witnessed a number of the hated Jews being hung from the numerous gibbets. She was thrilled as she was given a tour of the gas chambers. She almost achieved an orgasm as she looked upon the blackened, charred bones of numerous Jews following their extermination.

She looked forward to the day when all the Jews and every inferior on the face of the earth were finally exterminated and the iron boot of the master race ruled the whole of the earth.

She was more than willing to do her part, including the surrender of her body to any inferior male who could give her critical information useful to the intelligence network of the fatherland.

The toughest part of this assignment so far was crossing over from France on the small submarine to Argentina. Those waters were full of allied destroyers and frigates. The submarine was on silent running nearly all the way across. It was almost suffocatingly hot and the air was horrible.

She made her first contact on this assignment in Buenos Aires. He had all the necessary documentation ready, such as her passport and visas, as well as a fake birth certificate and other necessary papers. They went through a gruelling three days of non-stop briefings and debriefings.

After her orientation in Buenos Aires, she boarded a small tramp steamer destined for Havana. She met her second contact there after first getting settled into a little hotel close to the section which contained most of Havana's nightlife and received her final set of instructions, targeting her prime objective in great detail.

She took a seaplane from Havana to Miami. After successfully passing through customs and immigration, she laid low in Miami for several weeks, staying in a small hotel on Miami Beach.

She looked back on that period with a bitter taste in her mouth. That part of Miami Beach was crawling with other inferior American Jews. Some were very old. It made her skin crawl when she had to be polite and sweet to those inferior Jewish swine.

When it got too much for her, she would go back to her dark little room and lie down on that small, lumpy bed. She would dream of the fatherland and once again being in the strong, virile arms of Manfred.

She was certain that the fatherland would triumph in the end. Perhaps she would have the pleasure of personally executing some of the inferior, stupid Americans. It would be very special if they were Jews. When she though about those stupid Jews in Miami, she wanted to vomit.

She closed her eyes. A smile came to her lips as she thought only of the day in the future then the Jews would only be a bad memory on the face of the earth.

Chapter 17

THE LILTING AND melodious sounds of "Moonlight Serenade" echoed through the semi-darkness of the ballroom. Tom Sanchez started working on his second glass of beer. It was his turn to pick up the tab for the booze and food tonight.

The last time the guys and Marion came down for a weekend pass from the Coastguard Naval station in St. Augustine, Charlie Shears had to foot the tab for the food and rounds of drinks,

This weekend break from the murderous grind of practicing and memorizing for the big mission later this year around Matanzas Bay close to the Castilla de San Marco, the historical old fortress in St. Augustine, was particularly welcomed. He was completely wiped out and in real need of some R&R.

His unit was under a great deal of pressure. This was to be one of the biggest assignments yet; to quietly infiltrate the harbor housing the Nazi naval base at Toulon, France and plant enough charges and mines to effectively knock that key installation out and hopefully destroy some of the most effective warships in the Nazi arsenal.

There were certain topographical configurations in the geological makeup of Matanzas Bay, which made it ideal for the training ground of this mission. That was the prime reason why the Chief of Naval Operations at the war department picked St. Augustine for the gruelling exercises which would lead up to their deployment overseas.

As far as the citizens of St. Augustine were concerned, his group was just regular coastguard swobbies stationed at the base there, working in conjunction with the National Guard and Army Reserve boys.

Tom was thankful for these occasional weekend passes which allowed them to get out of the confines of St. Augustine and commute down here on the Florida East Coast Special that ran from Jacksonville down to Daytona and back on a twice-a-day basis.

St. Augustine wasn't as much of a sweat for him as it was for the rest of the guys, having been born and bred in this community. The Sanchez family want way back in the history of the town. The family was among the original Majorcan settlers, going back as far as the early Spanish period. Even so, most of his friends he grew up with were gone now, either fighting in the European theatre or in the Pacific.

Their unit was not allowed to go beyond a 25 mile radius from the St. Augustine area because of the top-secret hush-hush status of their mission. That meant the nearest big city to them, Jacksonville, was off-limits.

Seville was the next closest town. Thankfully, it was within that 25 mile limit. It was smaller than even St. Augustine in size. But thanks to the management of Warlock Inn and the policy they had of giving service men special discount rates and preferential treatment, the inn was a favorite meeting and watering hole for the boys in weekends. This was particularly true when some of the regional big bands showed up to play, like the Charlie Leonetti Orchestra out of Ocala, performing this evening.

The guys and gals really appreciated bands like the Leonetti band; the ones that could really belt out great musical renditions of Artie Shaw, Harry James, The Dorsey Brothers, and the one which really meant so much, the Glenn Miller Band.

The local gals were eager to date the fellas whenever they got into Seville on a weekend such as this. Most of the younger men from Seville were off fighting in the war just like his pals from St. Augustine and most every other place in this swell country. The single gals were really hurting for a lonely young man's company along with some of the married ones as well.

Archie Bronski, the tall stocky fella from the steel mills of Pittsburgh cracked a joke then which set their little group around the table rolling with belly laughs, including Tom's sister Marion.

His big sister's eyes sparkled as she looked over at his buddy Oliver Roberts. Marion was an attractive 22-year old sandy-haired brunette and as nice a sister as any guy could want.

When the war broke out, Marion went to work as an assistant secretary in the dispersing office back at the small coastguard-naval base in St. Augustine. She also did some nurse's aid work at the hospital in St. Augustine which was handling quite a few of the local guys, who came home from the war so badly mangled that for them the war was already over.

Tom and Marion had been very close ever since their parents were killed at the beginning of the war when the ocean liner they were on crossing over from

England, was hit by numerous torpedoes form a German U-boat and sunk. All passengers on board were lost in the attack.

Marion and he took an oath to do their part in helping to defeat the Nazi monsters after the memorial service for their folks was held. He had been a shrimper most of his working life and elected to join the Navy. He found his niche as a diver and eventually wound up as a frogman.

Tom observed carefully the way Marion kept looking at Ollie in that special way. It worried him some, realizing that things were getting serious between them. The status of their unit as some of the crack frogmen in the service made t hem particularly vulnerable as likely candidates for some of the most perilous assignments the service could throw their way. There was always the strong possibility that some day they might go on a mission and not return.

Marion already had suffered greatly from the loss of Mom and Pop, as he continued to think of them. He wondered what it might do to her if she also lost not only a brother, but the man she loved as well.

He tried to switch off his thoughts as the Leonetti Orchestra shifted gears and began performing a lively arrangement of a Harry James swing favorite. He got out his pack of Camels and lit up as Ollie asked Marion if she would like to dance.

Marion readily accepted. They were on the small dance floor in a flash with half of the guys and gals present and really juking to the jiving sounds.

Tom took a deep dreg on the cigarette and slowly expelled a haze of pale blue smoke. He began sipping his beer once again when Frank Frazetta leaned over and judged him with his right elbow. "Get a load of the babe what's giving you the eye, old buddy… over the table in the right corner of the room."

Tom looked quizzically at Frankie's strong square-jawed features as he rolled his eyes in a half disbelieving expression, knowing the way Frankie liked to put him on from time to time.

Tom turned about slightly and looked in that direction. He nearly fell out of his chair when he saw her. Despite the darkness in the converted ballroom, he was able to make her out pretty well as she sat at a table just under a pair of dim yellow lights shaped like candles.

She was drinking what appeared to be a martini and she quite simply was one of the most gorgeous dames he had ever seen. She raised her glass and smiled seductively at him. He, in turn, raised his glass of beer and toasted her.

"Well buddy, if I was you, I would make my move very soon. Most of the boys without dates tonight have been over to her table. She's been fighting them off. And once more, those gorgeous sparklers of hers have been trained on you pal since she came in here, you lucky stiff." Frankie winked and toasted him with what was left of his nearly empty glass of beer.

Tom quickly put his cigarette out in the little ashtray next to him and winked at Frankie as he got up. "Guess it's just my sheer animal magnetism," he quipped jokingly.

"Get outta here," Frankie retorted with a laugh as Tom slowly sauntered across the room, carefully making his way around the proximity of the dance floor over toward the beautiful lady's table.

He wondered just what sort of an approach he should use. This one definitely wasn't the typical girl next door here for the weekend shindigs. Her silken slacks fitted a tad too tight and were as black as night. They contrasted sharply with the billowy white lace gossamer-looking blouse she wore. Her clothes helped to accentuate her slender well-rounded figure.

There was no doubt about it; this babe was a real prize package. There was absolutely no doubt about that whatsoever.

Tom smiled nervously as he introduced himself. "Hello, name is Tom Sanchez. I noticed that you were all alone and looking like you might enjoy some company." He swore at himself under his breath. It was an old, corny line. But it was the best he could think of at the moment.

She looked up and smiled invitingly. "Thank you, oui monsieur. I could very much use some company." Her accent was French and very sexy.

"Beautiful and French, this must be my lucky night," Tom said to himself as he sat down in the chair next to her.

He asked if she would care for a cigarette. She smiled teasingly and replied that she would very much enjoy one. Tom quickly got out his pack of Camels, allowing her to extract one from the pack. He got out his brass-plated lighter and lit her up. She drew on the cylinder and expelled a thin, blue line of smoke in his direction. Her full, red lips formed a saucy smile.

"From overseas?" he asked. He listened enraptured as she told him about herself She was the daughter of a key leader in the Gaullist resistance movement back in France. She fled her occupied country along with her mother and brother and was waiting her for her uncle to arrive from New Jersey. She entered the country in Miami from Havana.

Tom told her about himself, beaming with enthusiasm whenever he mentioned Marion and proceeded to point her out to Bridget. Marion was really cutting it good on the dance floor with Ollie. They were really moving to the music.

"Your sister looks very nice," she commented.

Tom's pulse quickened as this seductively sensual French coquette eyed him hungrily. It almost seemed like she was devouring his lean and trim six-foot, one hundred and seventy-five pounds of manhood with her eyes and mind.

"Thanks. She's a swell gal," he replied and proceeded to tell her his cover.

He was a second class petty officer on a coastguard cutter stationed in St. Augustine and was down here with his shipmates on a weekend pass. She smiled and seemed to buy the cover.

"Tom, it's very close in here. Let's go outside. Maybe take a stroll on the beach.

Would you like that?" Her voice was filled with a sultry French throatiness that almost made him hard.

"Sounds like a fine idea to me. I'll let my buddies know and then we'll be off."

She smiled saucily again as she took several deep drags on the cigarette.

He quickly went back over to the table where the guys had been sitting and told Frankie that he made a solid score with the French chick.

"Ou la la," Frankie replied with a jealous laugh.

Tom left enough money behind for the food and drinks and left with is beautiful French mademoiselle.

Marion saw them out of the corner of her eye from the dance floor as Tom left the room with the attractive girl at the corner table… the one that had been eyeing him for so long.

Chapter 18

HE HAD NEVER before met a girl quite like Bridget. She was warm and cordial. At the same time, Bridget had an air of continental charm and worldliness he couldn't resist. Even so, she was so honest and sweet.

Tom was oblivious to everything but her as they strolled hand in hand under a full waxing moon that night. The shimmering gleam of moonlight reflecting off the calm ocean water made it an ideal setting. The lulling sound of the ocean surf as the tide rolled in close to the shore added just the right romantic touch. They stopped and took off their shoes, allowing the cool surf to rush over their bare feet. That evening proved to be one of the most pleasant moonlight walks he had ever been on with a girl in his life.

Bridget was so different from the local gals. She did something to him that no other woman had before that first night they met.

Since then, he called her from the barracks in St. Augustine every chance he could just to hear her compelling voice. It was long distance. Marion chided him about it when she found out, telling him it was very costly.

He had to agree. But it sure was worth it just to hear Bridget on those lonely nights.

He could hardly wait for the weekend passes to be issued. As soon as his buddies and he, along with Marion most of the time, arrived in Seville, he would meet with Bridget. They would first have a small brunch. Then they would change into their swim wear and head straight for the beach where they would frolic in the surf and sunbathe for hours on end. They spent the nights together on the dance floor along with Marion and Ollie a goodly part of the time, making it a foursome.

The other guys were really envious. He could tell by just looking at some of their sour grape expressions. He didn't blame them. He had the best looking babe there in his arms during those quiet, slow numbers with the lights low and the music of either Glenn Miller, Artie Shaw or Russ Columbo and numbers by some of the other big names in the music world contributing to the perfect mood.

When the dancing and the music was all over for the Saturday evenings, they headed upstairs and pretended to go to their separate rooms. As soon as everything was quiet for the rest of the evening, they would engage in the most passionate and intimate love he had ever known. Neither of them seemed to get enough of each other until the dawn arrived. Then they would lay panting and sweating in each other's arms for hours.

He was no virgin. He had known the intimacies of more than a few women in his life, particularly after entering the service. But never had he known a woman with such passion and staying power before. He wanted her more and more. He wondered what it was about her. Was it the scent of her arresting exotic perfume or the sweet, natural scent of her body that was so electrifying?

He wanted to tell her the truth about himself and be completely honest with her. Things were really getting serious between them. There was no telling how much longer they would have together here in Seville. Her uncle and his family could be coming down from Bayonne most any time, according to Bridget.

He found himself torn between duty and love. After the murderous night time drills in Matanzas Bay, he should have dropped off dead away in sleep from the backbreaking and nerve-wrenching time spent in handling delicate explosives and super sensitive mines. But all he could think about was Bridget and the short precious moments they may have left perhaps for keeps since there was a very strong possibility that his unit might not make it back from this mission. Toulon was very heavily fortified. They would have to get past numerous minefields and numerous other highly sophisticated defences in order to carry out this assignment.

If he asked Bridget to marry him and she said yes, she could become an overnight war widow very fast. He loved her and wanted to spend the rest of his life with her. But would it be right, asking her to marry him now? That was the question he asked himself over and over again.

He finally decided that the best thing for now was to get an engagement ring and ask her to wait until the war was over and hope that she would accept his proposal.

He began to dwell then on Marion's curious reaction to Bridget. For some reason that he could not comprehend, Marion was plainly cool when it came to his relationship with Bridget. She was friendly and polite whenever they were together, usually with Ollie along with maybe one of the other guys like Frankie. He would have one of the local girls as his date on the weekends. But he could sense that it was just a façade on Marion's part such as the last weekend when

Bridget came up to St. Augustine and they all went sight-seeing in the historical downtown district on one of the horse carriage rides followed by the best seafood dinner he had ever eaten at Captain Jack's Seafood Shanti, feasting on lobster and crab legs and finishing it all off with a fine, dry, white wine.

Marion's overtures of friendliness were all too obviously forced. It bothered him as much as his inner turmoil. Should he wait until this war was over or follow the commands of the heart and flesh and marry her now in spite of the not-so-great odds?

He finally told Marion a fortnight ago that he was in love with Bridget and intended to ask her to marry him. Marion was shocked although she must have known that he was getting serious about Bridget. Marion's obvious dislike for Bridget had gotten to him more than he realized after he told her of his intentions of making a proposal of marriage when he got the next weekend pass.

Marion seemed all too greatly relieved when he told her that he was thinking of asking Bridget to wait for him until the war was over. She seemed just a little too cheerful when she told him that the thought that was the wisest thing to do.

His anger built to the boiling point. He erupted, accusing her of not really being for this prospective marriage, demanding to know why she felt the way she so obviously did about the girl he loved.

Marion froze for a moment, shocked by his sudden outburst. He never before had gotten so angry with her. Tears came to her eyes. She lowered her head, trying to conceal them. "I don't know, Tom. It's just a feeling I have about her. I don't think it would work," her voice quivered.

"That's ridiculous," he shouted. "Sure, se's French and kind of on the worldly side. But if two people really love each other… I figure that nothing is impossible.

Marion frowned as she replied, "It's not that, Tom. I don't really know how to say it. I jus think she's all wrong for you."

He turned livid with an inner rage. He had never before that moment felt like striking Marion as he did then. "Well, Marion Sanchez, it's not gonna stop me. You got that, Sis? I'm going to ask Bridget to wait for me. If I survive this damn war, we are going to get married. I hope by that time you will have a change of heart for all our sakes."

Marion did not say anything as he stormed out of that little café on Aviles Street, deeply hurt and angry with her.

His inner conflict festered into something akin to real torment since then, as he found himself torn more and more between Marion's unreasonable doubts and his own gut need for Bridget.

He loved Bridget and not anything was going to stand in the way of that love. The only thing that was going to stop him now was death if it should come to him in this bloody war.

Chapter 19

SHE CAREFULLY CHECKED her appearance in the large mirror of the vanity while applying the finishing touches of makeup with the mascara and a fresh application of scarlet red lipstick to her full sensual lips. She wanted to be at her most alluring and provocative self. Her white shorts and low-cut cotton blouse trimmed in lace enhanced her curvy and petite form.

Tom particularly loved her Veronica Lake hairstyle she had done in the little beauty parlor on Miami Beach shortly before she left for Seville. She had that big dumb oaf right where she wanted him. Her intuitive instincts had once again served her well.

She sensed that Tom was her man right from the first night in the dimly lit converted ballroom of the inn. She had him eating out of the palm of her hands. This stupid American mongrel was convinced that she loved him and wanted him always.

So many of the stupid American men took things readily at face value and assumed a conceited machoism if a woman showed them any favourable response.

There was one thing about Tom that made the sexual side of her assignment pleasurably tolerable. His penis, when fully erect, was approximately the same size and fit as Manfred's beautiful instrument. When they were in bed together and she was close to an true climax, as she had been on the last three occasions, she closed her eyes and imagined that is was Manfred inside of her, bringing her to an ecstatic completion. Her fantasy made it all the more tolerable in submitting her body to someone like Tom in the manner of a common whore.

In that respect, this mission was certainly more pleasurable than when she had to bed down with that ugly Scotsman for the sake of the fatherland and the fuhrer. The Scot was short and stocky. He was covered with coarse, disgusting hair. When he was fully aroused, he had a hard time maintaining an erection. When she finally had the pleasure of putting a bullet into him, she did so with a profound sense of ecstasy before returning to Germany with the vital blueprints on the latest improvements the British had made in their radar defences.

Things were rapidly coming to a head in the current assignment. Tom had some very important things to say to her today. He sounded as though he was very serious the last time he called her form the base in St. Augustine. She was expecting that he might make a proposal of marriage. She felt sure that he had it on his mind.

She would make her big move today and get him out here this evening, pretending to want one additional night of passion more than anything. When she had him just the way she wanted him, she would strike.

She went over to the bed, sat down on the side and slowly pulled out the drawer in the intricately carved bedroom pulling out the 9mm Luger that she had acquired from another contact in Miami. She carefully checked the clip, making sure the gun was fully loaded and ready for use.

A long, narrow, velvet-lined case lay in the drawer next to where the Luger lay. She put the gun down on the bed next to her and got the case out of the drawer. After opening it, she removed one small vial in a row on nine vials, which contained sodium pentathol along with a hypodermic syringe. She proceeded to insert the tip of the needle into the bottle and extract the exact amount of serum needed with the plunger… just enough to put someone away fast.

She gazed lovingly at the tip of the needle. "You'll tell me everything I want to know tonight, Tom dearest, and then goodbye forever. I can return to the fatherland and Manfred and receive my reward from the fuhrer personally.

She closed her eyes and experienced a near orgasm as she thought about the wonderful future when the whole world would dance to the tune of the fatherland and what might be ahead for Manfred and herself in that perfect order.

Chapter 20

IT WAS NEARLY 10 a.m. when Tom pulled up to a stop in the parking lot of the inn. It had taken him quite a lot of time and effort to secure the little '39 Chevy coupe for this weekend. Lieutenant Holland had to pull a few strings for him to get the car along with a full tank of ethyl with what was left of the stamps in the gas rationing coupon book he was issued. He didn't have to be back at the base with the coupe until 6 a.m. Monday morning.

He spent the better part of the morning rehearsing in his mind what he wanted to say to Bridget as well as making himself look as spiffy as possible. He figured that he must have used most of the rest of the bottle of cologne that Bridget liked so much on him before packing his overnight bag and changing into his civvies at the little gas station on the outskirts of St. Augustine beach.

He wore his best striped cotton short-sleeve shirt and white cotton trousers. He wanted everything to be just right as he pulled out the tiny blue patent leather box from the right front pocket of his trousers and opened it.

He looked down at the small ring that was less that half a carat. It was all his. He was proud of the fact that he had been able to pay all cash from the money he'd been able to save in the past few years.

At the same time, he was nervous… very nervous. He hoped that everything would go smoothly. Most of all, he ardently wished that Marion felt differently. He was sure that in time Marion would come around and accept his decision when she finally could see for herself that Bridget was an all right girl. Things would work out. He just knew they would.

Tom gazed up at the clear blue morning sky and smiled as he bounced out of the Chevy coupe, humming the tune to "Blue Skies" as he got the overnight bag from the back seat. He closed the door and licked the car up, then headed around to the front of the inn. Once inside, he briskly walked up to the front desk.

He gave Fred, the man on duty, a friendly smile and asked for a room close to 207. Fred smiled and offered him the key to number 204 as Tom signed the registry.

Tom quickly paid the military discount rate for the weekend stay and asked Fred if Miss Bollier was in. Fred answered that as far as he knew she was still in the inn. Her key wasn't in the box for room 207.

Tom smiled and thanked him, telling Fred that he wanted to surprise Miss Bollier. He didn't want her to know he had arrived. Tom proceeded across the floor over to the stairs and took the steps two at a time up to the second floor landing and headed down the corridor to his room.

Once inside, he tossed the overnight bag down on the bed and then left the room, going straight down to number 207. He knocked vigorously on the door.

Bridget's sultry French accent came from behind the door, "Who is it?" He smiled teasingly. "Give you three guesses Mademoiselle and the first tow don't count."

The door opened wide and she greeted him with a warm smile. "Tom, I thought you said that the commuter special wouldn't arrive until the noon hour."

He grinned, "Well, is that the best my little French mademoiselle can do for a poor lonely sailor?"

She giggled as she fell into his arms and gave him a long, deep, wet kiss. "Is that better?" she asked teasingly.

"Oui, much better, my little coquette," he quipped, smothering her with kisses.

She told him to come in. She was just about ready. He took the chair close to the bed as she went over to the dressing table and proceeded to put on two tiny bell-shaped earrings.

He got out a Camel, lit up and asked her if she wanted one. She replied that she didn't care for a cigarette just then and asked him why he was early as she inspected her appearance one more time.

After expelling several puffy rings of wispy smoke, he told her about Lieutenant Holland helping him get the loan of the Chevy coupe for the entire weekend. She glanced back at him and smiled broadly, saying that the use of a car sounded wonderful.

He took another deep drag on the cigarette while observing the more bizarre aspects of room 207 once again, as was his custom every time he had been in the room with her, shaking his head in disgust. Surely the management could have seen fit to change Bridget over to another room. It seemed like such a goofy place for a generally class act such as Warlock Inn.

"Damn shame you still have to be in here. If this wasn't the best place to say in Seville, I would find you something else but fast."

She smiled, replying that the room wasn't all that bad. She had gotten used to it while patting a few drops of the heady scented perfume to the soft contours of her face and slender neck. The fragrance of that perfume drove him crazy with desire whenever they made love.

Tom glanced up at the portrait of Jonas Van Gilder. Looking at that man's mug always gave him the creeps. He shrugged his broad shoulders as he took another drag on the cigarette. "Boy, he sure was an ugly little SOB."

"What?" she asked, somewhat taken aback by his off-the-cuff remark.

"The fella that built this house just after the Civil War. As I understand it, he was supposed to be a male witch. Said that he used to slice up kids and young girls as human sacrifices to the devil; that kind of garbage. Looking at the picture of the old boy, it's not hard to believe all those local tales."

She looked at the picture again and it had the same effect on her as that first day she'd seen it. She had to agree with the American mongrel. This Jonas Van Gilder looked as though he might make a perfect SS officer if he was living today, or perhaps a fine guard at one of the camps busily eliminating the Jewish swine.

Chapter 21

THE DAY WENT by gloriously Everything had gone as he had planned it. The inn's kitchen prepared a picnic basket which consisted of fried chicken, homemade potato chips, sweet pickles and topped of with a large container of iced coffee. It was Bridget's favorite beverage for chasing away the close sultriness of the hot Florida summer heat.

They drove down by the beach and spread out a large, striped beach towel close to where the tide was just going out. The muffled churning of the ocean surf augmented by the occasional chirping of a seagull along with the visual treat of watching a group of pelicans in flight, all helped to crate the perfect mood as he prepared to pop the question to Bridget.

He lay on the soft, damp sand, content with the world. She sat next to him, looking down with a saucy smile that made him wish he could have her right there.

Finally, he got up the nerve to ask. She immediately said yes. He had the ring in the pocket of his swim trunks and quickly got it out. She beamed as he gave it to her, saying that she loved it. She placed it lovingly on her ring finger with ease. It fit perfectly.

Tom felt like he was on top of he world. Nothing else mattered in this crazy-mad world but Bridget. He took her into his arms and crushed her yielding body to his. They fell onto the sand and rolled around in it, kissing and caressing passionately.

He made a promise to her that he was going to be the best damn husband humanly possible. She smiled saucily again and darted her tongue between his lips and French kissed deeply. Afterward, she promised to always be his one and only.

After the picnic, they shook off the fine beach sand as best they could and spent the rest of the afternoon cruising along the coastlines in the Chevy coupe. Bridget couldn't keep her hands off of him. She teased him and played with him.

At first, he was a little shaken by her horny forward actions. He thought that maybe they should hold off on bedding down until after the knot was tied when the damn war was over. But that might be a very long time from now. Bridget was very French. She needed the physical side of love as much as he did. He needed her love and passion and decided that conventions be damned. And there was that constant awful thought he tried to keep in the back of his mind: there was the very real possibility that he might not make it back.

They didn't even attend the Saturday night dance that evening. They headed straight upstairs to her room and proceeded to make the most intense physical love he had ever known in his life. By the fourth time he came, he was totally drained and lay back panting on the large, inviting bed as she huddled close to him and softly stroked his chest, kissing him lightly on the chest and neck.

After she finished with her petting, she laid her head against his chest. "I'm so glad my darling," she said with a saucy bite. "So am I," he replied sleepily.

Her voice was soft and warm as she told him to think of beautiful and wonderful things like a picturesque waterfall and beautiful verdant green valleys such as she had so often visited in the old country in the more pleasant days of her childhood. She then told him to think of a quiet and wonderful time from his past and to count slowly from one to twenty to further relax him.

He became really loose as he yielded to her suggestions. He began to feel really at peace with himself. He was soon at a point of almost dropping off into a restful sleep.

She had him just the way she wanted him as she quietly slipped out of bed and opened the drawer of the little table. She got out the already filled hypo and checked it once again, making doubly sure she had the correct dosage. She bent over him like a bird of prey ready to swoop down on its unsuspecting victim and plunged the sharp needle into his neck in the area of the carotid artery and injected him with the serum.

The searing sting of the needle caused his eyes to fly open with a spasmodic jerk. His last thoughts were "What has she done to me? What kind of a joke is this?"

Tom tried to get up and immediately fell back against the soft mattress. The effects of the potent serum was almost immediate. Everything before him became wobbly and out of kilter. He rapidly lost consciousness.

She told him to count backward from twenty. He would the open his eyes.

He began to slowly count s she went over to the large bureau and got out a small tape recorder and quickly went back to the bed with it. A spool of tape was already in position as she put the recorder on the table next to the bed and plugged it into the wall outlet close to the bed. She then took the microphone and placed it near his lips.

At the end of the count, his eyes opened automatically. He seemed to stare off into empty space. She immediately went to work, pumping him for all the vital information related to the allied plan to destroy the fatherland naval installation at Toulon: she had him name the date of executions, key details of the plan of attack and the exact procedures to be followed. How they intended to get past the Nazi defences, the names of all the key people involved in the operations, and any other incidental pertinent details he might know. She finished by demanding the names of any French operatives who might be involved.

When she had everything she needed, she ordered him to get up and get dressed. They were going on a night time drive in his car.

She put the tape recorder back in the bureau drawer and closed it before hastily getting dressed, putting on her light cotton blouse and silken light beige slacks. She hastily applied her makeup and got her large, black purse. Then she got out the Luger and placed it inside the purse.

"All right, lover boy, let's go." Her tone was filled with venomous hate.

Tome walked slowly over to the door and opened it. "After you… you American swine," she spit.

They proceeded down the hall to the stairs.

Chapter 22

A LIGHT SEA fog settled in along the shoreline and the immediate surrounding inland areas. She slowly drove the Chevy coupe south along the major road which ran parallel to the coast. Across the rising dunes and flat beaches, she listened attentively to the gentle sound of the waves rolling into the shoreline.

A low bank of clouds obliterated the moon. She was forced to turn on the headlights of the coupe as she looked over at Tom. He was glassy-eyed and completely unaware of his surroundings.

She decided to drive a short distance from Seville to a lonely stretch of road that veered off the main beach road into an area that was totally wooded and relatively isolated. When she found a good, secluded spot, she would liquidate Tom and return to the inn, leaving an order at the desk to prepare her bill. She would leave at the break of dawn.

Tom's getting hold of the car was exactly the kind of opportunity she had hoped for since she zeroed in on him that first night. She would abscond with the car and drive to Daytona and board the Silver Star destined for Miami. She would then rendezvous with her contact there and under the cover of darkness, be taken out to sea and put on board a submarine, which would take her back to France.

The one part of the plan that she did not like was having to stay for a time in the Miami area even though she would switch to another identity. During the train ride, she would put her hair up and put on a wig of full, red hair. Her alternate false ID would identify her as Margo Devareux. Once Tom turned up missing and his body found the authorities would be hot on her trail.

She breathed deeply as she reached inside the purse and pulled out one of the American cigarettes which Tom smoked. She stopped the coupe long enough to get the cigarette lighter and quickly lit up. She took a deep drag and expelled a heavy trail of smoke from her sensual mouth and nasal passages before continuing on.

It wasn't long before she reached the lonely stretch of winding road that seemed to lead to nowhere. She drove approximately three miles inland along the rough pavement and stopped the coupe close to a large drainage ditch next to the road. It was the same stretch that Tom drove along after he made his proposal of marriage.

She reached down inside the large, black purse again and got out the 9mm Luger and looked over at him. A thin smile formed on her lips as she ordered him to get out of the car and stand next to the ditch.

He responded automatically to her command and opened the door, stepping out close to the edge of the ditch. He stood there and faced her with that music, blank expression etched into his features.

Her smile widened as she got out of the car and faced him. She took dead aim at his right kneecap and pulled the trigger. He screamed in agony as the bullet tore through the kneecap, completely shattering it. He polexed backward into the deep, vicious mud, sharp bull grass, and painfully thorny creepers in the deep ridges of the ditch.

"This is for the humiliation of having to endure the pawing and the penetration of an inferior," she hissed under her breath like a serpent spewing its venom. She took aim at his disabled form once again and pulled the trigger. The second bullet tore into the region of his scrotum, destroying his testicles as blood poured from the destruction of his crotch.

She chuckled with a smug satisfaction arising from bloodlust and vengeance as she again took aim. This time, the bullet entered the head just above the right temple. Great gouts of blood poured freely from the wound.

The sounds of the night surrounding her increased tenfold as a result of the three explosive shots from the Luger. The cacophony lasted only a matter of seconds and then the unseen squeaks, squeals, chirps and growls of the nocturnal inhabitants of the woods and marshy swamps nearby died back down into their natural pattern.

She stared down at Tom's broken and bloody body for a short time with a sense of deep satisfaction. She finally shook herself out of that momentary state of contemplation and got back inside the coupe.

A thrill of fear came over her as a sudden shrill-low wailing oscillation shattered the wooded tranquility around her. She gasped as she spotted a pulsing icy-blue light coming from an area not too far away from the car.

Her heart was in her throat as she realized that she wasn't alone. Whoever was out there must have heard the gunfire and would probably be around shortly to investigate. What if this was from a night time military manoeuvre? After all, the relative isolation of this area was perfect for a military exercise under the cover of night.

She took a deep breath and scampered down and across the recesses of the ditch after bolting away from the car. Her low-heeled shoes sank deep into the soft, slimy mud. Sharp blades of bull grass and prickly creepers bit into the soft flesh around her ankles. The air was thick with mosquitoes as they busily feasted on the exposed portions of her body as she made her way through the heavy growth of woods.

She came upon a clearing a short distance away from the narrow road. Her eyes nearly popped out of their sockets. A large, oval-shaped, shiny, metallic object stood in the clearing. The ground surrounding the other worldly appearing mechanism was singed and scorched as though by some very intense heat.

The object appeared to be more than twenty feet across in diameter. A strange icy-blue glow pulsated off of the glistening, metallic surface of the object. A weird rasping and whirring sound issued from it.

She jumped as something that was both cold and hot at the same time grabbed her by her left shoulder and forced her around.

She screamed. Something which looked human but wasn't in the normal sense of the word stood next to her. Its features were pale and thin. It had no earlobes. The pupils of the eyes were metallic black. Those eyes were large and saucer-shaped. The nose was long and thin with flaring nostrils. It had no hair and the dimensions of the cranium were extremely disproportionately large. It stood no more than five feet in height and probably weighed less than a hundred pounds. The suit it wore glowed with the same icy-blue light as the mechanism in the clearing radiated.

She fired two rounds from the Luger into the thing's chest. It made an indescribably shrill of a scream as it stumbled and fell to the damp earth.

She ran through those dark woods faster then she had ever ran before in her life back to the hoped-for safety of the Chevy coupe. Once inside, she gunned the engine hard. She managed to turn the car around and tore down the fog-shrouded road at better than fifty miles an hour until she was back on the main road, hugging the coastline.

It took her less than fifteen minutes to get back to the inn. After parking the car, she hurriedly ran around to the front of the house, charging up the steps onto the veranda and over to the e double doors at the front entrance. She threw one door open and immediately calmed down. She casually walked over to the front desk.

When the night man on duty saw her dishevelled appearance, he asked if there was anything the matter.

She took a deep breath and composed herself as best she could, saying that she as all right. She planned on leaving first thing at dawn and to please have her bill ready for her at that time.

He was taken aback slightly by the sudden turn of events, saying that he understood she would by staying for a while longer. She lost her cool at that point and shouted, demanding that her bill be prepared for her departure.

"Yes miss," he replied coolly, watching her suspiciously as she ran over to the stairs. She practically flew up them.

She had been in such a hurry that she did not notice Marion sitting on the upholstered sofa off to the side of the lobby near the entrance of the little bar and grill located next to the converted ballroom.

Marion became desperate with worry when she saw Bridget's dishevelled appearance and overheard what she had told the clerk at the desk. Tom was to have proposed to her tonight. Perhaps Bridget turned him down and they had had a big fight as a result. That might explain why she planned on leaving. At least, that was Marion's ardent hope and that there wasn't anything more to it. But in the back of her mind, she knew something was very wrong here.

She walked up to the desk and cleared her throat. The night man smiled pleasantly at her. She asked him how long he had been on duty. He replied that he came on duty just before midnight.

She asked him if he might have seen Miss Bollier leave one of the coastguard boys who came down frequently on the weekends. He replied, saying that he hadn't and then motioned for the bellboy on duty to come over to the desk.

"That pretty French lady in room 207, you see her leave with one of the sailors that comes her on the weekends?" The boy replied with a smile that he saw Miss Bollier and Mr. Sanchez leave between eleven and midnight.

Mar iron swallowed hard as a cold, tight sensation developed in the pit of her stomach. She smiled nervously as she thanked them before starting for the stairs.

The night man called out, "Hold on there, miss. It's almost the middle of the night."

She looked back at him before starting up the stairs. She forced herself to smile. "It's all right. Miss Bollier is expecting me. I want to say goodbye before she leaves."

Marion turned away and wiped the smile from her lips. Her soft features took on a fearful and grim expression.

Chapter 23

MARISA STOHLER THREW the suitcase down on the dishevelled bed. The sheets and pillows still bore the imprints of the passionate interlude of lovemaking. The miniature tape recorder and the case containing the hypodermic and vials of sodium pentathol were on the bed next to the small table.

She ran over to the closest and hastily threw her clothes on the bed when a loud pounding at the door caused her to momentarily freeze.

She stood very still as a familiar voice cried out, "I know you're in there, Bridget. Open the door, and I mean right now."

She quickly composed herself and walked casually over to the door and asked who was there. "Marion Sanchez," came the crisp response from the hallway.

She already knew that it was it sister. She wondered why in the world she wanted at this hour of the night. She unlocked the door and slowly opened it.

Marisa forced herself to smile pleasantly at the angry and frightened sister of the man she had killed. "Why Marion, what can I do for you?"

"Where is my brother?" Marion demanded. Her tone was filled with a desperate frustration.

She smiled, raising her hands in a puzzled gesture, "I don't understand, Marion. He isn't here. I haven't seen Tom all day."

Marion exploded after hearing her obvious lie. Marion almost screamed as she exclaimed that Tom and she had been seen leaving the inn earlier. "You tell me where my brother is or perhaps you might like to tell some of his shipmates where he is… or maybe even the police."

Marisa Stohler's demeanor turned positively icy. She told Marion that she would explain everything, gesturing to her to come into the room.

Marion quickly stepped inside. Marisa slammed the door shut and slowly walked over to the bed. When Marion saw the suitcase and other things sprawled across the bed, she demanded to know if the woman she knew as Bridget Bollier was planning to leave.

"Yes, Marion, I'm going," she said as she reached down and picked up her large handbag which lay at the foot of the bed. She reached inside and slowly pulled the Luger out, taking aim at Marion.

"You're going to leave with me a daybreak, dear, and you are not going to say anything to anyone if you want to go on living."

Tears streaked Marion's cheeks. She instinctively knew that Tom was dead. "Who are you and what are you really here for?" Marion demanded as she fought to hold back the tears.

Marisa smiled. She started to answer Marion when the room was suddenly filled with a low, oscillating, weird, restless noise that was like the sound in the woods just after she had disposed of Tom. The noise was so intense that is seemed to cut straight into her brain like hot needles.

Both women began screaming as the door to the room melted and vaporized seemingly into thin air. One of the strange, little humanoid creatures stood at the entrance of the room. It held a thin, shimmering, metallic, wand-like instrument in its right hand. A thin spider's thread of glowing, blue light came from the tip of the wand straight at Marion, rendering her totally inert. She was alive and aware but totally disabled as a numbing paralysis spread through her body.

Before Marisa could pull herself together and fire at the creature, another thread of glowing, blue light pulsed from the weapon, hitting Marisa squarely between the eyes. Everything melted away as a curtain of darkness came over her.

Chapter 24

SHE SLOWLY REGAINED consciousness. At first, her vision was badly blurred. Everything appeared to be out of focus. Several minutes went by before she could clearly see again.

Marisa Stohler screamed once only, as she realized that she was bound by some invisible force to an enormous table. She looked all around her, turning her head rapidly from side to side. Her eyes rolled up into her sockets and from side to side as she took in everything she could within her limited range of vision.

She had never before seen anything like the chamber she now found herself imprisoned within. It was totally alien to anything she had ever known before, including her privileged visits to the scenic centers of Nazi experimentation which used the Jewish swine as guinea pigs or at the concentration camps, for that matter.

The chamber was large, with a glistening, metallic quality quite unlike anything in her experience. It had a rotunda shape and a sloping curve to the overhead.

Unfamiliar machinery and instrumentation abounded within the chamber.

There appeared to be no external source of lighting, but a soft, bluish-white light pervaded the whole of her prison and bathed everything in a soft sheen of light. It was as though the very bulkheads themselves served as the conductor of the light.

There was a crystalline sheen to the various instruments that she would see.

"The Americans must be far more advanced than anyone in the top command of the Reich realized,"she reasoned to herself, given this totally alien machinery. "This little wand-like weapon which the humanlike creature used to render Marion inert and herself unconscious was a very formidable weapon. If the fatherland was to win the war, the Reich must have the weapon and improve upon it," was her immediate thought.

It all seemed like something out of an American Flash Gordon movie serial or the fatherland's own Baron Munchausen tales. It suddenly dawned upon her then that she might not be a prisoner of the Americans after all. This strange chamber might indeed be within the alien craft she saw in the woods near Seville.

That shattering, oscillating sound began, driving her nearly insane as the decibel level was so intense that it caused a slight haemorrhaging from both her ears and nose.

She then experienced a tremendous force that pressed unbearably against her body. The agony and pain was so great that she nearly passed out. She thought for a second that the force of pressure might crush her like an ant being crushed under the heel of a shoe. The threshold of pain lasted almost a minute and then the killing force instantaneously went away.

A new terror began almost immediately. She could not breathe. There was a strong rush of swishing air pressure that instantly filled the chamber. Color returned to her feature as she gulped in the life-giving air into her lungs, relieving the aching pain which was created by the temporary vacuum of oxygen from the short seconds the crushing force ended and the air swooshed in.

She gradually became more accustomed to the changed taking place in her bodily chemistry. She instinctively knew that this was some kind of ship which had come to earth from the other planet, probably from outside this solar system. She also realized at that moment that she was no longer on earth but now out in space rapidly leaving her world behind.

Marisa sobbed, fully realizing that she might never again see her world. She would not know that future time when the fatherland would rule the whole of the world. She would not be there to share in the fuhrer's triumph, which was the purpose of her life since the rise of the National Socialist.

An aperture in the bulkhead of the chamber slid open then and two of the humanlike creatures entered and walked over to the table. They spoke in voices that had an odd, high pitch and strange electronic quality.

They did not speak in any language or dialect that she was familiar with as they proceeded to examine her thoroughly, pointing at various portions of her anatomy from head to foot. The way they looked at her with those strange eyes made her feel like they could see right through her.

She screamed hysterically at them in her native German as well as French and English. She demanded to know where she was and who they were. Neither one of the creatures replied. Instead, they immediately disappeared through the same aperture they had entered the chamber.

An opening appeared in the center of the overhead then. A huge version of the wand-like weapon that the little humanlike creatures carried emerged through that portal. It took direct aim at her disabled form.

Marisa's heart began pounding furiously as she anticipated what was to come. She began to scream hysterically. But her screams were instantly cut short as a thin beam of blue light lit her dead center at the top of her skullcap. It moved slowly down along the center of her body, dividing it in half.

Organs and other viscera spilled out onto the table and fell down into the deck of the chamber along with all the blood and other bodily fluids that had not yet vaporized from the intense heat that was generated.

Trance Three
The Quest of Bobby Sailor
June, 1955

Chapter 25

BOBBY LOOKED ALL about the room again, experiencing a sense of wonder. He was also just a little bit scared. He felt very cold despite the summer heat of the day. When he was playing outside, the strong Florida sun had beat down on him unmercifully.

The cold, scary sensation was similar to the one he experienced when he first entered the room several days ago. He and his parents had just arrived at Warlock Inn and checked into their room.

Almost immediately, Daddy and Mama got into a fight after Daddy went into Seville and came back with a large bottle of whiskey. Mama broke down and cried. She begged him not to start drinking now that they were so close to getting their lives back into shape.

Charlene Sailor had left Burt about a year ago. He had been drinking too much beer and whiskey and had lost another job. Money problems were getting to be too much for her to handle. She took Bobby and went to Grandma Belcher.

Life hadn't been too bad for him at Grandma Belcher's home. Bobby did miss his old friends and neighborhood where he had lived most of his young life. He really missed Cypress Grove Elementary most of all. He liked all the teachers he had since he began school. He made so many friends while going there.

He was glad when Daddy went to the place Mama called Alcoholics Anonymous and especially when he sopped drinking the beer and whiskey about six months ago.

Burt Sailor had gotten another job as a car salesman at Jim Tillar's Car City back home in Birmingham. He started getting good money again and asked Charlene to give him another chance.

Bobby knew that Mama thought a lot about the bad times when Daddy would come home drunk after being all right for such long stretches of time. When he was drinking, he would stay drunk for what seemed like eternity to Bobby and just lay in bed. Sometimes, he wouldn't eat for over a day or more and he would puke all over himself and get to stink real bad. He lost his job almost every time he got drunk like that. When he dried out, as Mama called it, he always had to look for another job for a long time before he finally got one.

It happened like that too many times in the past few years. Mama would get so sick and scared. That's when she decided to go back to live at Grandma Belcher's house. The last time it happened was the most awful.

Charlene had a lot of misgivings, but she agreed to go home with Burt. Bobby knew that she really did love Daddy despite his drinking problem. She would give him another chance like he wanted so badly.

Bobby was feeling real good about things in the last few weeks. It was so good being in his own home and getting reacquainted with his pals like Jimmy Clay, Roy Apple, and Cheryl Schwamgure. He liked Cheryl more than most girls. She was more like one of the guys. She liked to play stickball with the guys and trade baseball cards during the season. She also did so many other neat things that the guys liked.

Daddy had some time off coming soon and asked Big Jim if he could take it now. He wanted to take them to Seville and stay in this big house called Warlock Inn.

Burt told Bobby that he would love the sandy beaches and ocean surf. This trip would be a second honeymoon for Mama and him. When he and Mama got married, they stayed at Warlock Inn. He wanted everything to be like it was for them that first time and Bobby would be part of it this time around.

It sounded great to Bobby, but things started going wrong the day they arrived at the inn. Daddy showed signs of getting real edgy and nervous like during the bad times. He fussed at Mama about things that didn't even make sense. Mama struck back by chewing him out for picking on her. It all seemed to get real big just the way it did before Daddy would go get the whiskey and start drinking heavy.

It ended with Daddy storming out of the room. He went into Seville and came back with that large bottle of whiskey.

Mama broke down and began to cry and locked herself inside the bathroom. Bobby felt all cold and empty inside and had to get out of the room. He put on his gun and holster set and pretended to be his favorite cowboy star, Hopalong Cassidy. He wandered around the halls and corridors of the inn on the trail of cattle rustlers.

When he went back upstairs and started back in the direction of the room, he noticed that the door to the inn's spooky room was open. Several cleaning women told him that it was called the spooky room when he came past it earlier and peeked inside the door. There wasn't anyone staying in the room at the present time. He felt a strong compulsion come over him. He had to go into the room.

When he stepped inside, his mouth fell open. His green eyes went wide as that feeling of being wowed came over him much more so his time. He couldn't get over the neat room. The little elf and impish demons and fairy tale creature design of the wallpaper was something to behold — not to mention all the yellow-looking photographic pictures and paintings on the walls, depicting things like bad storms at sea, the sinking of a big ship and other bad things that happen such as that.

Finally, his attention became fixed on one particular portrait, that of a man. He had a long, thin face and a large, hook like nose and a bushy moustache and long, wide sideburns that were real old-fashion.

The man's eyes were large and dark. As Bobby stared at that face in the painting, he got goose bumps all over his body. A chill went up and down his spine. It seemed like that man's eyes were looking right into his very soul.

It suddenly got so cold that he felt as though he was going to freeze. The light from the hallway filtering through the half-open door began to suddenly dim.

Bobby became frightened when a large, glowing light appeared out of nowhere in a corner of the room and took on a definite form that became a woman. The light faded and a pretty woman dressed in a real old-fashioned gown stood before him. The ghostly lady spoke to him in a low, sad voice.

Hackles formed on the back of his neck. He fled from that spooky room and ran back into his own.

When he told Daddy and Mama what he had seen in the room, Daddy became furious with him. He shouted at Bobby. He was doing it again, living in a make believe world. He yelled at Bobby, telling him he should not make stories up like that. There wasn't room in the real world for make believe and pretend. Life was too hard in the real world. Someday, he would have to face that fact. There would be no room for that kind of nonsense.

Charlene sided with her son. She rebuked Burt sharply, saying that pretend and make believe was normal in a growing boy. It was all part of being a kid and having a childhood.

They began to argue and shout and made so much noise that it brought the stern-looking man with grey hair who was the manager of the inn. He said that other guests had complained to the management about the loud fighting coming from the room. They would have to stop having loud words or he would be forced to ask them to leave.

Daddy's face became real red. Bobby had never seen him that embarrassed before. Mama broke down and cried like she did a lot when they had fights.

Bobby felt even more scared and lonely. It was just too soon after everything seemed to be getting better between them for it all to be falling apart once again.

Mama and Daddy continued to squabble. Daddy went into town the next morning and didn't return until late that afternoon. He had the bottle of whiskey with him.

He had been drinking before he came back to the inn. It was strong on his breath. Daddy laid down on the bed. Mama ran into the bathroom and cried.

Bobby felt so bad. He had to do something. He immediately became Hopalong Cassidy again still after those rustlers and the stolen cattle from the Bar 20.

He began to play in the hallway like before. He suddenly stopped dead in his tracks. The door to that spooky old room 207 was open just like before.

Bobby was even more frightened this time, but he had to go into the room.

Everything about it was the same, including that funny sensation he felt of being too cold like the other day. He again looked carefully at the neat wallpaper and old pictures and paintings and especially the picture of that evil man with the dark, penetrating eyes. He shuddered as he gazed up at the face in that portrait. He decided to call the man in the picture the bogeyman of Warlock Inn.

He felt a shock of fear run through his young body like a surge of static electricity had gone right through him and jerked him around. He looked on wide-eyed in the direction of the large four-poster bed with the frilly lace canopy top.

Bobby shuddered as goose bumps formed all over his arms and legs just like before. It seemed as though the room was so cold that he was freezing. The large glowing light formed by the bed and shortly assumed the shape of that woman. The light faded and the ghostly woman stood smiling before him. She had long locks of flaming red hair. Her skin seemed as white as new fallen snow. Her eyes were wide and green like his own. She was real pretty in an old-fashion way. She wore an old-fashion green dress with a high lace collar and a large bustle in the back.

At first, Bobby was as scared as he was the first time she appeared. He wanted to run from the room. When she smiled at him in that same gentle and sweet way, he rapidly lost his fear. It was replaced with a strong feeling of curiosity and even sadness.

She spoke to him in a soft and gentle tone in a cultured southern accent. She told him not to be afraid of her. She had been waiting for a brave young lad such as himself for a very long time. She needed his help desperately and begged him to hear her out.

Bobby got his courage back and asked the ghostly lady who she was. He knew that she wanted something real important from him.

She told him that her name was Jeanine Van Gilder. During the final years of her brief life upon this earth, she had been the wife of that evil man in the portrait that Bobby had been looking upon.

She had lived at the time of the great war between the north and the south back in the last century. Her family was a fine high station southern people. They had a large cotton plantation near Savannah, Georgia. Her father also owned a large steamship company with headquarters in Savannah and Charleston, South Carolina. He was an important gentleman. His name was Nathan O'Rourke. Her mother was a genteel Georgia aristocrat, Abigail O'Rourke.

With the defeat of the south at the conclusion of the war, the family plantation was in a state of near ruin due to a number of battles, which took place there in the last year of the war as the union forces penetrated deeper and deeper into southern strongholds. The steamship company had incurred tremendous debt running union blockades in order to get much needed goods and war supplies from English and French ship well out to sea.

The family assets and holdings were in near ruin and the family holdings were to have been sold off by union sympathizers during the occupation in the years immediately following the war.

About a year after the end of the war, she met the man in the portrait, Jonas Van Gilder, at a fund-raising ball in Savannah. He was a Yankee from somewhere up in New York state and had recently come to north Florida to plunder the area south of St. Augustine for all the wealth it could yield. He was on a business trip to Savannah at the time.

He took an immediate fancy to her that night. He stayed on in Savannah for a period of time, ingratiating himself into the confidence of her father and mother. He spent all his time courting her. He made frequent trips back to Savannah.

When her father's creditors demanded payment of the huge debt which Mr. O'Rourke owed (as she referred to her father), Jonas said that he would pay those debts and rehabilitate both the family plantation and the steamship company in exchange for her hand in marriage.

Father had taken greatly to Jonas and her mother told Jeanine that he was a fine prospective husband. She felt a tremendous obligation to the family. If the pressing financial obligations were not met, they would be turned out on the streets and would be destitute until such time as Mr. O'Rourke was able to secure proper employment.

She did not want to marry Jonas, but she really felt that she had no choice but to do so. Despite the fact that there was something about him which left her cold and even somewhat repulsed, she did agree to marry him.

As soon as they were wed, Jonas fulfilled all the financial promises he had made to Mr. O'Rourke and made arrangements for them to have an extensive honeymoon in Paris, France. It was while they were on the continent that the house which is now known as Warlock Inn was built.

Jonas had already had the plans drawn up with one of the best architectural firms in the country at that time. No expense was spared in the building and furnishing of the house.

Shortly after they returned from the continent, they took up residence in the newly-completed house.

The ghostly lady paused for a moment. Bobby felt sad for her. He had never seen such a look of sadness in another person before in his young life; not even his mother, like now that Daddy was drinking again which made her so upset.

When the ghostly lady spoke to him again, he felt a seething anger issue from her spectral form. She swore to him that she had no idea at all of what a wicked person Mr. Van Gilder had been in life. She would never have consented to marry him if she had known about his evil and vile ways and the murderous assignations that he had been a party to.

Jonas was, in life, a tyrannical monster. He treated people beneath contempt and made many enemies. Almost everyday, he would throw up to her all that he had accomplished for her fine southern family, reminding her that if it had not been for his personal intervention, she might be a beldame in the streets or something even more wretched.

Jonas would frequently disappear for several days at a time. She felt great relief during those times. Life with him had proven to be a living hell. Although she did not know it at the time for a certainty, there was talk among the household staff that Jonas was a practitioner of the black arts. The talk was that he was accomplished in evil sorcery. People perceived by Jonas as his rivals and competitors would suddenly die for no apparent reason. Several farmers around the Seville area died. Their farms were on land that he wanted desperately in his unquenchable lust for power and vast amounts of land holdings. It was whispered that they died as a result of death curse conjured up by Jonas and tow women witches that came to Seville from time to time to take part in ritual witch' sabbats and the obscene Black Mass. They were his confederates in the art of satanic magic.

During their stays in the area, it was rumoured that children and young girls were snatched and made human sacrifices to the devil's dominion at these unholy ceremonies.

Life within the walls of the house became unbearable except for a few sympathetic servant women. She was a virtual outcast from the rest of the society in and around Seville.

An outbreak of yellow fever took place in the region and she came down with the dreaded illness shortly after it began to spread through the community. While she lay dying on her deathbed, that monster became enraged. He had always looked upon her as a prize and a coveted possession. His enormous ego could not accept loosing her in such a manner while he still wanted her for his won personal needs and to display to the few business associated he could get to come to the house.

Before she died, he placed a curse on her. Her soul would forever remain within the walls of this house. After the house was gone, she would remain to wander the grounds which encompass the house until such a time as she could enlist the aid of a male child approaching the age of accountability to assist her in the necessary steps needed to release her soul to the peace of death and the next stage beyond in the hereafter.

Her eyes firmly met Bobby's wide-eyed stare. She told him that she was sure that he was the young man she had been waiting for all these years to help her gain her freedom and release from that monster's terrible spell.

Bobby swallowed hard when she finished and simply replied, "Gosh."

She asked him how old he was. "Ten, ma'am. I'll be eleven in November," he replied. She smiled, saying that she was absolutely certain that he was the boy she had waited for. She begged and pleaded with him to hear her out.

He swallowed hard again. "Yes, ma'am. I'll listen."

She gave a sigh of great relief. Bobby had never seen anyone look so relieved in his young life.

There was a sense of urgency about the ghostly lady as she continued. "When that monster was executed for his crimes against man and God, he was buried somewhere around the general area of Seville not too far from where this house is located in unconsecrated ground. The earthly symbol of his allegiance to the fallen angel was consigned to his unmarked grave with him. It is a pendant which is fashioned from pure gold. He always carried it with him wherever he went. It symbolized the power of Lucifer granted to him in his studies and adeptness at practicing the black arts. This golden pendant is called the Broken Cross of Belberith. It is named for the demon that inspired men to lust and murder. You must find the ground where the remains of Jonas Van Gilder lay and unearth those remains. You must first obtain a small container and fill it with holy water blessed by a priest from the baptismal font if a Roman Catholic Church. You must pour the holy water directly on the pendant. This act will destroy the power that holds my spirit imprisoned within the walls of this place. I will at last be free and know the peace of death and whatever lies for me ahead in eternity.

Bobby nervously swallowed hard again. His young mind was trying to fully grasp the awesome responsibility that the spirit of Jeanine O'Rourke wanted to place upon his shoulders.

"I know that I am asking a great deal of you, Bobby Sailor. But I know that you are the one I have waited for and this is part of your destiny also."

Bobby screwed up his courage again. "I won't fail you ma'am."

She smiled sweetly. "I know you won't, Bobby Sailor."

She continued, "Now watch the space in front of me. You will shortly see what the Broken Cross of Belberith looks like."

Bobby's eyes went wide again as a stream of light began to form in mid-air. It took on a definite shape and pattern. There was a circle with what looked like a Nazi emblem from the World War Two days. Daddy told him that it was called a swastika. They had been looking at a picture book together which depicted the big war and he had seen several photos with swastikas in them and asked what they were. In the center of the swastika was an animal skull. The skull figure had two hooked horns coming out of the top. It looked like the skull of a goat.

"Gee, that looks like a Nazi swastika," Bobby exclaimed.

The ghostly lady (as Bobby continued to think of her) explained that the symbol of the German nation during that turbulent time was a very old one dating back in history to ancient India. Its origin could be traced to the beginning of the Hindu faith. In olden days, its likeness was found in ancient Greece and Rome as well as many other areas of Europe.

Bobby was fascinated by the history lesson she gave him. His reply was another awestruck "Gosh."

He wondered how the ghostly lady knew his full name and asked her. His curiosity was greatly aroused.

Her eyes seemed to look deep into his own much as the eyes of the wicked man seemed to cut right through him as he looked at the portrait. "My spirit knows of all who enter this room. When you came into this room the first time — it was no accident, Bobby. When you and your parents entered this house, I knew immediately that you were the boy I have waited for through the years. This is part of your destiny."

She told him to study the design in the air before him and notice the animal skull in the central axis point of the swastika. It is the skull of a ram.

The ghostly lad instructed him most carefully to be sure that the holy water completely immersed the portion of that golden pendant with the skull of the ram more so than any other part of that blasphemous symbol of deviltry.

"I know that I am asking a great deal from a young lad such as yourself. You must be very brave and strong." The ghostly lady spoke very sternly and yet there remained that genuine tenderness in her tone.

Bobby felt a stirring of manhood within his breast. He felt that somehow by helping this trapped soul be free from her imprisonment within the wall of the inn that he could prove himself worthy of his Mama and Daddy. He could not explain why he felt the way he did, but he knew that this great task before him would help to pull his parents together the way they should be. He just knew it would although he could not reason out in him mind why that should be so.

"You have my word, ma'am," Bobby swore with commitment and pride.

"Thank you, lad. God will bless you for what you are going to do on my behalf. I will be forever eternally in your debt." Although she was just a spirit appearing before him as she looked in life, Bobby thought he saw tears fall from her pretty green eyes. He became misty-eyed himself.

Her form became immersed in the glowing light then as the ghostly pattern of the Broken Cross of Belberith faded from sight. Moments later, the light was gone and he was again alone in the room.

Chapter 26

BOBBY WIPED THE seat from his brow, using the blue bandana he liked to wear whenever he was playing like he was Hopalong Cassidy. He put the damp, large handkerchief back in the pocket of his dungarees as the family's '52 Nash Rambler convertible came to a stop in front of Dan's Clip and Cut Salon, which was at the south end of Seville's main street.

As the noon hour approached, the heat of the day had turned angrily hot and still. Burt Sailor leaned over the seat and looked sternly at Bobby. Burt warned his son in no uncertain terms not to go talking about the ghost in the inn to anybody. He had had enough of that foolishness, particularly since the manger of the inn came to him earlier in the morning and complained that Bobby had been pestering the staff, asking all kinds of questions about something that really shouldn't concern a small boy. Mr. Freeman told Burt that Bobby was not to ask anybody else about the man who originally built the house and definitely not anything more about where his remains might be buried. Bobby was not to talk about this thing he called the Broken Cross of Belberith. It was crazy nonsense anyway.

Bobby cowered before Burt's angry outburst. He was so angry that he was visibly shaking as he reproached Bobby.

Bobby felt real bad inside. Daddy was nervous again and acting like he was needing another drink of whiskey real bad. He had seen Daddy like this too often in the past during those long spells when the whiskey and beer was running low. He would demand that Mama go to the liquor store and get some more so that he could get over his drinking… at least that was always what he would say to her.

Charlene nudged Burt, demanding that he not be so rough on the boy. "Perhaps if you did not find so many excuses for getting a bottle, Bobby might not have such a need to escape into a fantasy world." Her remarks carried a stinging rebuke.

Burt's face was red with rage as he struck back, "Perhaps, if that son of yours faced up to the real world a little more instead of always pretending — maybe I wouldn't feel the need to drink so damn much." He nearly shouted it out, drawing attention to himself from several pedestrians passing by.

"All right, Burt. Keep your voice down. People are looking at us." Charlene's voice quivered. She did her best to contain her own seething emotional hurt.

Bobby felt all empty and sick again. Mama and Daddy had been fighting too much since Daddy came back to the inn with that bottle and began drinking. Mama threatened to leave him again and go back home to Grandma Belcher if he did not come into Seville today and see the marriage counsellor she found in the phone book. She called this Mr. Baker and made an appointment for them to go see him. Daddy wanted to wait until they got back to Birmingham, but Mama was so sick that she said something had to be done right now. She just could not take it anymore.

Daddy knew she meant what she told him. It was just like before when she left him.

Despite their problems, Bobby felt in his heart that Daddy loved him and Mama. He was all edgy and nervous and didn't like having to do this in a strange town, but Bobby was thankful that he did agree to see Mr. Baker.

Their appointment was at 12:45. Bobby needed to get his hair cut. Dan's Clip and Cut Salon was the only barber shop in Seville.

As he climbed out of the backseat of the Nash Rambler sped down the street and turned the corner, disappearing from view.

Bobby quickly glanced up at the white-hot noonday sun and again wiped the perspiration from his forehead with the back of his left hand. He walked toward the front door of the wrap-around glass storefront barber shop, passing by the tall striped barber pole that he thought was real neat looking. He opened the glass front door and stepped inside. A large fan blew the cool air coming from the large air conditioner above the door evenly about the shop which had originally had been a shoe store. Bobby welcomed the immediate cooling effect that the drier, colder air gave him. The angry heat of the day had added greatly to his already troubled spirits. At least, for a little while, he wouldn't have to suffer in the torrid summer heat. He hoped that another strong breeze from the ocean would come along like earlier in the morning.

Bobby looked across the checkered tile floor at the large heavy-set man in the white jacket as he busily attended to his customer. He was giving the man a shave with a straight-edge razor. It was the kind of old-fashion razor he had seen his granddad use when he came visiting from time to time from up in Nashville.

Dan Marchotti smiled pleasantly at Bobby, telling him to take a seat. He would be finished with his current customer shortly.

"Yes, sir," Bobby replied and walked over to a chair close to where the air conditioner was located at the front and sat down.

He was greatly taken with the large mirror on the wall in back of the barber chair. It seemed as though the image of the barber and the man he was shaving and everything else was reflected in the highly polished surface of the mirror went on and on with Dan and the other man being repeated over and over again until there wasn't any more room in the mirror for their images to go on. There were at least eight of the barber and eight of the other man reflected in that neat mirror.

"Gee, that's some neat mirror you got there, mister," Bobby said with tremendous enthusiasm.

Dan Marchotti smiled at the boy and chuckled. "Thanks, kid. That's what they say. I like it cause it reminds me of the barber shops in Brooklyn. That's where I come from, kid."

The man in the chair smiled and with a heavy cracker accent quipped, "Yeah, and the way you go on about Brooklyn and the Dodgers and Marciano's last fight, I sometimes think you still want to be up there in good Ole New York town."

Dan Marchotti observed the smirk on his customer's face as he quickly scraped away the remainder of the shave cream from around his firm jaw line. "Hey, Brooklyn will always be in my heart, Hank. You know what I mean. But I can live without the hustle and bustle of the big town. That's why I came here," he responded with wit, humor and a slight frown.

Dan looked curiously at Bobby. "Haven't seen you before kid. Just come into town?" he asked as he carefully wiped the slender man's freshly shaven face and applied some fine, manly-scented cologne around his cheeks and neck.

"My folks are here on vacation. We're staying over at Warlock Inn. They had to come into town on some business. They wanted me to get a haircut."

"Well kid, you'll get the best haircut in town. Of course, Dan is the only barber in town," the lanky man called Hank said with a wide grin.

"Very funny, Hank," Dan said while removing the towel and the thin paper from around his slender, long neck.

Hank got up out of the chair and pulled out a light beige cowhide wallet from the back pocket of his khaki slacks and whipped out a dollar bill while observing with approval the flat top and shave which Dan had given him in t he large multi-image mirror. "Perfect Dan, perfect as usual."

"Of course. Nothing but the best is guaranteed when Dan Marchotti cuts your hair," the portly barber quipped mirthfully.

The two men chuckled. "See you next time," Hank called out as he walked to the door which opened suddenly as he started to reach for the door handle. This next man to come into the barber shop immediately put Bobby off as he walked past Hank and sat down in a chair near Bobby just as he got up and went over to the barber chair and hopped up in it.

For some reason, Bobby could not take his eyes off the man despite his drab and disagreeable appearance while Dan tied the apron around his neck and tucked a clean sheet of waxy, thin paper around the collar of his striped T-shirt.

"How do you want your hair cut, kid?" Dan asked as he looked over at the man and frowned.

The drab-looking man wore clothes that seemed entirely too warm for a hot day. He had a decidedly offensive body odor to boot.

Bobby glanced away from the man long enough to look up into Dan's smiling features. "I'll have a regular haircut, sir."

"Sir, is it? I like that kid. Not too many kids are all that polite to their elders these days. Okay, kid, a regular it will be," Dan exclaimed as he got his shears and clippers and went to work.

Bobby continued to stare at the man as much as he could while Dan adjusted the position of his head before starting the cut.

The old man wore a dirty grey old sports coat and loose, baggy trousers that were grimy with deep, soiled stains. His shirt was opened down to his chest. He wore a small, weather-beaten narrow-rim walking hat. His features were deeply lined and craggy. His skin was sunburnt brownish-red. There was a hardness bred of deprivation about his demeanor. There was a sort of vacant stir in his brown eyes. He looked back at Bobby as attentively as Bobby looked at him.

Dan frowned at the town tramp he called Ole Man Ritchie. "I don't know why you come in here, Ritchie. You never get one of my famous haircuts. But then, I'll bet you don't have any money for it."

The old man rebuked Dan, "I got money. Can't a man come in here out of the heat and sit for a spell and maybe get a cold Coke out of yur drinkin' machine?"

The old tramp wiped the corner of his mouth with a stained, old, yellowing handkerchief as he got up and went over to the Coca-Cola vending machine and placed a dime in the coin slot. He pushed the dispensing button. There was the familiar cranking sound as the six ounce green bottle fell down into the dispensing slot.

He quickly reached down and got the familiar green bottle and placed the top of the bottle under the metal rim of the opener and pulled the cap free from the head of the bottle. He took a large swallow of the cold pop and sighed. "Man, that sure hits the spot on a hot day. Ain't that right, boy?"

Bobby smiled nervously while Dan began to work at the back of his head.

The old tramp sat back down in his chair. He began to rub the greyish white stubble on his chin as though it was itching real bad. He began to gulp down the cola until the bottle was more than half empty. His eyes stayed on Bobby the whole time.

Dan and Bobby became more and more aware of the disagreeable odor coming from Ole Man Ritchie. Finally, Dan went, "Pew-w-w, I sure wish you would take a bath every once in awhile, Ritchie. I'm getting fed up with you coming in here smelling like a pole cat most of the time."

The old man put down the bottle of Coke. He pulled the handkerchief back out of his pocket and blew his nose hard before answering; "You mind your own business, Dan. I wash up when I need it."

Dan rolled his brown eyes in disgust. "Mama Mia. Christ. I bet he's crawling with fleas and lice," he swore under his breath.

Bobby smiled in agreement with the portly barber.

Bobby was put off even more by the old tramp. Whenever he opened his mouth wide enough, Bobby could plainly se that many of the tramp's upper and lower teeth were gone. What teeth he still had were terribly stained with dirty yellowish-brown discoloration. Whenever Ole Man Ritchie spoke, it was with a deep southern drawl that was somewhat slurred due to so many missing teeth.

Bobby was overtaken suddenly with a strong inner feeling as he watched the old tramp. Something instinctively told him that now was the time to bring up the subject of Jonas Van Gilder. "Dan, you know anything about the man who built Warlock Inn around the end of the Civil War?" Bobby asked with a sense of apprehension, remembering his Daddy's stern warning.

Dan looked down at Bobby curiously while he worked on the sides with his clippers and shears. "That's a funny question, kid."

"What ayah want to know, kid?" the old tramp asked eagerly. His interest had suddenly been aroused.

Bobby knew immediately that Ole Man Ritchie could tell him a lot. "I heard some people talking about that man while they were working in that weird room upstairs in the inn."

"That must be the famous number 207. That was the crazy loon's bedroom according to local history," Dan commented rather matter-of-factly.

"Yeah, that's right, Dan," the old tramp verified before taking another sip from the nearly empty Coke bottle."

Bobby's strong instincts were intensified. "Does anyone around here know where that man was buried?" Bobby asked straight out.

The portly barber did a double take and stepped back from the chair. "Wow, kid, that's some question. Why would a kid like you who isn't even from around here want to know something like that?"

Bobby's focal point stayed squarely on Ole Man Ritchie. The tramp's eyes got real bit and intense.

"I've picked up a little smattering of the local history in my nearly seven years here in Seville. Wasn't that dirty, killing scumbag cremated by the federal troops after he was hung for his crimes?" Dan exclaimed with a strong sense of contempt.

Ole Man Ritchie leaned forward. He took out his stained handkerchief again and wiped his thin, cracked lips with it and then spoke. "Ain't true. They tried to burn old Jonas up after they stretched his neck, but every time they tried to put a torch to the dry pine box they put him in, the flames always went out before it would start to burn. The Yankee soldiers got real spooked after a number of tries. They took his body and buried it in a secret place somewhere around here."

Dan looked at Bobby sternly, asking pointedly; "I would still like to know why a nice kid like you would want to knew about something like that. I mean… that was a long time ago, kid. It ain't exactly the sort of thing a kid like you should be interested in."

Bobby was becoming nervous. He did not want to come on too forcefully. He cleared his throat. "I heard these two cleaning ladies back at the inn talking while they were doing that room. The door was open and I listened to what they were talking about. I heard one of them say that a magic gold necklace was buried with him. They said that it was real valuable. I think they called it the Broken Cross of Bel-Bel-e-rith or something like that."

The old tramp's eyes seemed to light up as he grinned at Bobby. "Yeah, kid. I know all about that. It's a pendant. That's what they call that kind of a necklace. It was buried with him just like you said. It was supposed to be what gave old Jonas his black powers. He was a male witch, a warlock. His powers were granted to him by old scratch himself and the Broken Cross of Belberith represented his mastery of the dark forces."

Dan's eyes flashed with a spark of anger as Ole Man Ritchie finished. "That's enough, Ritchie. You're getting a little too familiar with this boy. I want you out of here, now. Go on. Get out."

The old tramp sprang up out of the chair and scowled back at Dan. "All right. Don't get your feathers all ruffled, Marchotti. I'll leave."

The old tramp started for the front door and then looked back at Bobby. There was a gleeful glint in his eyes.

Dan took a deep breath, trying to control his temper as the old tramp left. "Dirty old man. Don't know why I let him come in here. He always stinks the place up. I don't thing I will let him come in here anymore," he said in a huff.

Dan soon finished with the basic trim cut on Bobby's curly, brown hair and finished by giving him a thorough brushing off around the neck and cheeks before removing the apron and thin, waxy paper from around his neck.

Bobby hopped up out of the chair and reached into the back pocked of his jeans for the half dollar piece Mama had given him to pay for the haircut just before they left the inn to come into Seville. He quickly put it in Dan's outstretched large right hand.

"Okay, kid, you're all set. Will your parents be back soon?" Dan inquired.

Bobby smiled, nodded yes before starting for the front door.

Dan called out to him. "Kid! That old tramp seemed much too interested in what you were talking about. He's sort of the town wino. We tolerate him. He seems harmless enough. A word of friendly advice, though. If you see him around, I wouldn't have anything to do with him."

Bobby could tell that the portly barber was entirely serious. It was firmly etched in his swarthy generally pleasant features. Bobby gulped hard. "Yes, sir," he said and quickly went outside.

Clouds were beginning to come in from the east partially blocking the strong summer sun. With the clouds came a cooling breeze, which helped in lessening the stifling noonday heat.

There was a small Rexall Drug Store about a half block down the street. Bobby decided to go in there and get a nice cool chocolate soda with two big scoops of vanilla ice cream while he waited for Daddy and Mama to come back and get him. He figured that he might have just enough time.

As he started down the sidewalk, a shrill whistle got his attention. The old tramp stood in an alley three store fronts down from the barber shop, holding onto the handle bars of a large, black bicycle.

Bobby felt a slight sense of trepidation as he slowly approached the old man. He looked up attentively at the tanned, deeply-lined features of his weather-beaten face. "Whatta you want, mister?" he asked guardedly.

There was a growing intensity coming from the old man. "You want to know where the secret grave is, kid? Where old Jonas is buried along with that big gold necklace?"

Bobby tensed up and swallowed hard. "Yeah, mister. Do you know where the grave is?" Bobby asked warily.

Ole Man Ritchie grinned; displaying what was left of his yellow, rotting teeth. "Yeah, I'll take you there. I can help you. We'll get that pendant and we'll split the money we get from selling it two ways right down the middle. You and me kid. I've been waiting for someone like you for a long time kid, cause nobody else would believe Ole Ritchie when I told 'em where old Jonas' bones are buried. You see — I'm gonna need some help in diggin' him up."

Bobby was scared, but he had made a commitment to the ghostly lady. If he did not free her soul, he would feel guilty about it for the rest of his life.

"You really know where he's buried," Bobby demanded.

"Didn't I just say so?" the tramp replied with a slight scowl.

Bobby steeled himself. "Okay mister. But before I go with you, I got to get a bottle and go to a Catholic church."

The old tramp was taken back as he shouted testily, "Catholic church! Why the hell do you have to go to a Catholic church?"

Bobby stood his ground. "Never mind that, mister. If you want me to help you — you gotta take me to a Catholic church."

The old tramp rubbed the stubble beard around his chin like he did in the barber shop and agreed to Bobby's demand. "All right, kid. I gotta small canteen here in the basket of my bike." He pointed to the rusty, wire basked attached to the handlebars of the bike. A small canvas-covered canteen lay tucked in the bottom of the basket.

"I'll take you over to St. Mark's Then let's be on our way." Ole Man Ritchie said anxiously as he looked all about the street.

Bobby was more afraid than he had ever been, but he knew that this was something he h had to do. Nothing else seemed to matter.

Chapter 27

BOBBY HELD ONTO the handlebars of the bicycle tightly, balancing himself on the front end. His uncertainty and fear continued to mount as the narrow trail through the woods skirting the edge of swampy marshland opened into a clearing where an old wooden cabin stood which the tramp called home. On one edge of the clearing, there was an old, neglected, small cemetery, which was all grown over by shrubs, vines, tall grass, and creepers. It was in a shambles and clearly showed signs of long neglect. The cemetery was a faded memory of the forgotten dead that lay moldering there.

The tramp had vividly described the place to him after they left the little Catholic church on the outskirts of the small town. It was located a block west of the beach. According to Ritchie, the bogeyman of Warlock Inn was just outside the grounds of the cemetery in a secret place that he discovered one day after a terrific thunderstorm. An old swamp oak fell over crashing into the ground. It smashed through the soft ground, exposing the rotted casket with a name plate clearly visible atop the broken lid. It read, "That accursed monster, Jonas Van Gilder, one of the devil's very own."

Bobby was glad that they were nearing the end of the bike ride from town. Every minute he had to be close to the old tramp became more and more menacing, not to mention the repulsive body odor coming from him. It got even worse while heading down the coast highway and finally off onto the side road leading to the narrow trail through the woods. The deadly, still heat became unbearable, particularly when the breeze blew toward them. It was all he could do to keep from gagging and retching. That was how foul his odor was.

As they came out onto the clearing, a bank of low, grey clouds moved swiftly overhead. That, along with an increase in the easterly breeze, made him feel some better as the tramp brought the bike to a stop and ordered him to hop off.

Ole Man Ritchie leaned the bike up against the dry, brittle, old, hickory wood logs the cabin was made from and grinned wickedly at Bobby. "Sure was hot coming back here from town. Gotta have some cool water to drink before we go dig old Jonas' bones up and get that gold pendant. How about it, kid? Could you use some cool water?"

Bobby gulped. His throat was dry and felt parched. "Yeah, mister," was his simple reply.

The old tramp threw open the door and yelled, "Com on inside, kid. Water is in here. I got a shovel and a pick axe inside. We'll need 'em."

Bobby's misgivings grew to a nearly intolerable level. He held back.

The old tramp looked at him with a scowl. "What's wrong with you?"

Bobby gazed with morbid fascination at the skull of the child to the right of the chest. Somehow the eyes had remained in a nearly perfect of preservation. They seemed to stare at him accusingly in the pitiful silence of death.

Bobby was overcome with sobs. He screamed, "You lied to me, mister. You dug up those bones a long time ago. You got the pendant already. Whatta you want with me?"

The old tramp grinned and laughed. There was an evil mockery about it. "Yeah, kid, I've had Jonas with me for many years now. You see kid — a voice spoke to me one night in my sleep back then. It told me where to find the old warlock. It told me all about the Broken Cross of Belberith. It told me that if I brought it young, innocent sacrifices like old Jonas made in his day, except mine had to be males, that it would reveal where a large treasure chest is buried somewhere around here with gold and silver from old Mexico and other parts of Central America."

"Hundreds of years ago, this was part of an inland route used by the Spanish to bring gold and silver up from south Florida to St. Augustine for shipment to Spain when the waters became too dangerous in the Florida straits with British buccaneers and other pirates.

A far away look came to the old tramp's eyes. He continued, "A platoon of Spanish soldiers got pretty close to where we are now with that treasure trove. They were ambushed by a war party of Seminole Indians. They were killed and buried in a mass grave along with the treasure."

He stopped again and rubbed the stubble on his chin as though it was itching real bad and then continued. "The voice told me to get some young kids. I needed three young boys and I was to offer them as sacrifices to it. The third sacrifice had to be made after some period of time had gone by from the point when the first two were offered."

"Little Bennie Edwards and Jeff Shuttleworth. That was a long time ago." He raised a shaking outstretched right hand and pointed to the mummified skeletal remains on the floor. "Yeah, that was several years ago. I followed its instructions to the letter. They looked high and low for those little shits, but I was real careful like the voice said to be. They never suspected me for a minute.

"I waited patiently for the sign as to the next offering. It's been a long time since the voice last spoke to me. This morning when I woke up, it told me to go into town to Dan's place. When I saw you there kid… I knew that you are that third boy I have waited for all this time to come along."

Bobby struggled to control his ever-increasing fear. He screamed, "You won't get away with it mister. The barber saw the way you looked at me and the way you talked about the Broken Cross of Belberith and Jonas and everything." He clutched tightly to the canteen as though he was holding on for dear life.

Bobby swallowed hard, trying to work up a little spit and saliva in his dry mouth. "When are you going to show me the secret place?" he demanded.

Ole Man Ritchie became flustered by the boy's flinching manner. "Don't you worry yourself none, boy. I'm gonna show you where the spot is in just a minute. Now, do you want some goddamn water or don't you?" the tramp barked testily.

Bobby swallowed hard. "Yeah, I'm pretty thirsty."

"Then come inside and get it. I ain't as young as I used to be. Gotta rest a minute. Then we'll be about our business."

Bobby grabbed the old, beat-up canteen, which contained the holy water he had secured from the baptismal font at St. Mark's and slung the strap around his neck and left shoulder. He wearily followed the old man inside.

The one room cabin was a foul smelling pest hole. An old fashion hut with a dirt floor from days of old. There was a fairly large fireplace built into the area where the small chimney protruded from the top of the north corner of the log roof of the cabin. A large, cast iron cooking pot was suspended just above the open grate of the fireplace where the tramp cooked stews and other concoctions when he got hungry enough to eat a meal.

A sturdy, long, pine wood table stood in the center of the cabin. There were several mildew-stained and corroded metal cabinets as well as several wooden chests placed around the room. A small cot was up against one corner of the room across from the fireplace, which was where the tramp slept. But what caught Bobby's undivided attention sent the hackles rising on the back of his neck. His fear and uncertainty was not fully justified.

His eyes went wide in shock as he gazed at the weird altar at the opposite end of the room. A human skull sat atop a human rib cage with a number of large bones placed strategically about the area of the skull and rib cage. This mockery of death lay on top of a solid cedar wood chest. Draped over the skeletal rib cage around the bottom jaw hinge of the skull was a pendant necklace. It was fashioned out of solid gold in the form of a swastika with a ram's skull molded into the exact center.

Bobby experienced a sickening panic when he realized what the objects were which lay grotesquely on the floor on either side of the elongated chest. His young heart raced even faster as he stared at the mummified skeletal remains of two very small children. Judging by the size of each one, they must have been much younger then he was when they died.

Only dried tattered bits of skin that had long since turned to a form of leather covered the heads and certain areas around the upper portion of the rib cage and lower region where their abdomens had been in life.

The old tramp grinned sardonically. "You're right, kid. As soon as I have done with you, it's gonna tell me where that treasure is buried. I'm going to dig it up and put it on an old pickup truck I got stashed away back in these woods. Then I'm gonna haul ass out of these parts. They ain't never gonna see Ole Man Ritchie around here again. I got a connection lined up ready to fence the loot. I've been planning this for a long time kid."

The old tramp bent down under the table and pulled a large razor-edge sabre, which had been worn by a confederate officer in the Civil War, out from under it. There was a gleam in his eyes which hinted at madness and possession. "Found this beauty a few years ago back in these woods. I just strangled those two over there. That's all I had to do to them. But this time, it has told me to remove the head. It wants your head. It's gonna materialize and eat your brains."

Bobby's heart pounded harder and harder. The tramp began to slowly move threateningly toward him. Bobby began to move away as Ole Man Ritchie raised the sabre high above his head in a striking posture.

"My Mom and Dad are probably looking for me right now. They'll find you. My Dad will kill you for this," Bobby screamed in a near fit of hysteria.

The tramp giggled mirthfully as he came closer to the boy. Bobby's mind was swimming around and around as he tried to think of some way to save himself. His attention was caught by the fireplace while keeping one wary eye on Ritchie. There were quite a few solid pieces of half-burnt pine logs in the bottom of the fireplace. An idea flashed into his tortured mind as he manoeuvred as close to the fireplace as he could, realizing that the tramp could lash out with the sabre at any moment.

A hard blowing wind came up just at that instant which was followed by the booming and crackling roar of thunder.

When Bobby was right up beside the fireplace, he quickly reached down and grabbed one of the more solid charred pieces of wood just as the tramp again raised the sabre high in a striking posture and sent it through the air a second time. Bobby jumped out of the way barely in time. The sword would have most certainly split his skull open if he had not been as nimble and as fast as he was on his feet

A heavy rain began to pelt against the wooden timbers of the cabin as Bobby sent the half-burnt, charred log hard into the tramp's midsection. The force of the impact sent the tramp reeling backward. He cried out in agony due to the hard blow.

Bobby made a dash for the door and threw it open, running out into the nearly blinding downpour as fast as he could just as several powerful strokes of lightening connected with the ground near him followed by ear splitting, crackling thunder.

The water cascaded so torrentially from out of the clouds — Bobby found himself running blindly through tall bull grass and dodging around palmetto thickets and huge looming scrub oak and live oak which proliferated in those woods. Sharp and prickly thorns and stickers stabbed at the exposed parts his ankles from just below the cuff of his jeans to the top of his loafers. The sharp thorns and stickers along with a number of soldier ants that were on him and spreading fast up his legs itched and stung like stabbing bits of fire.

His feet suddenly hit against a solid undergrowth, causing him to lose his balance. He went forward through the rain-drenched air into the wet ground. He was covered from head to foot with thick clots of mud. The thorny stickers bit through his drenched T-shirt into his flesh. A sharp, stabbing sense of nausea and pain coursed its way up from his left ankle o settle in the pit of his stomach as blinding sheets of water continued to pound hard against his inert body. Strong, powerful bolts of lightening continued to lick the land all around him.

Not very far away from where he lay, Ole Man Ritchie began to cry out in a fierce, resounding voice, screaming that he would find Bobby. There was no place for him to hide. He had waited a long time for this and nothing was going to stand in his way. The Spanish treasure was his.

Bobby watched in horror from out of one corner of his eye as a large, sinewy, diamond-back rattler slithered past him within inches of where he lay. His terror became almost too much as his heart beat faster and still faster.

He put his left hand in his mouth, doing the best he could to keep from crying out, lying as dead still as he could until the slithering poisonous serpent was completely out of range.

He breathed a deep sigh of relief as he managed to painfully get to his feet. He nearly fell as sharp, stabbing jolts of pain shot up through his leg. He realized that when he took the spill, he had turned his ankle rather badly. He looked down at his left ankle. It was beginning to swell up fast.

Bobby knew that he had to have a crutch of some kind to lean on before he could start of walk as the blinding sheets of water gave way to a moderate downpour.

He frantically looked all about him and spotted a fairly long, straight branch which had fallen from one of the tall live oaks. His body shivered from the cold, drenching rain he had endured while taking three hobbling steps in the direction of the branch. He went crashing forward into the earth again. The pain was excruciating due to the impact against he sharp, tufted grass, causing more of the stickers to bite through the T-shirt into his chest and belly.

The old tramp continued to bellow thunderously, demanding that Bobby stop this foolishness. He was only prolonging it this way.

Bobby started crawling feverishly through the muck until he was beside the branch. Despite the pain and mind-shattering itch that covered much of his body due to his coming into contact with a large growth of poison oak while manoeuvring toward his goal, he continued to stifle the overwhelming desire to cry out.

He grasped the wood firmly and slowly pulled himself to a standing position, which was excruciating, and looked all about. He had a good idea as to which direction the cabin was. He wanted to get back there as fast as possible. If this was the end for him, he wanted more than anything to fulfill his promise to the ghostly lady and pour the hold water on that accursed pendant, destroying the monstrous hold old Jonas left behind when he imprisoned that poor soul in this world, denying her the peace in the hereafter that she deserved. If this was it, at least he would have done this good deed so that his life would have meant something to someone.

He kept low and as quiet as he could while hobbling back to the cabin. His eyes continuously searched for any sign of the tramp. He was a formidable enemy. He was also half-mad and half-possessed and truly believed that by taking off his head, a valuable treasure would be revealed to him.

Bobby jumped aside as a bolt of lightening hit the ground just inches from him. He couldn't help but cry out from his sudden brush with near electrocution. He looked ahead of him. The cabin was in sight. He was just on the edge of the clearing.

He hurriedly looked all around. When he was sure that the tramp was nowhere within range, he hobbled as fast as he could under the circumstances, in the direction of the cabin and threw the door wide open. He nearly fell as he hobbled over to the obscene altar to the dark powers.

He placed his makeshift crutch against the large chest and quickly got the shoulder strap, tethering the canteen, from around his neck and shoulders. He rapidly recited the Lord's Prayer while nervously removing the cap from the mouth of the canteen and proceeded to douse the unholy pendant with the holy water, making sure that the most of the liquid fell into the image of the ram's skull in the center of the swastika.

The close, damp air of the cabin was suddenly filled with a cacophony of tormented screams and wailing that sounded like tortured soul in the very bowels of Hell itself to the frightened boy.

Bobby looked on in wide-eyed amazement as the accursed object began to pulsate with a brilliant, pulsating reddish glow. Within moments of that phenomena, the Broken Cross of Belberith began to melt down into a boiling puddle of golden liquid. Finally, there was a puff of blue smoke followed by a strong acrid odor. The thing had completely vanished.

Bobby felt a serenity and inner peace at that moment as the skeletal remains of Jonas Van Gilder crumbled into a fine, calcified ash. A feeling of pride swept through Bobby. He had been successful in freeing the soul of the nice ghostly lady.

Bobby's heart jumped suddenly back into this throat. Mama and Daddy were shouting frantically for him. Judging by the sound of their voices, they were not far away.

All this fear and horror rapidly returned. Ole Man Ritchie was still out there. He was a big threat not only to himself, but to his folks as well.

Bobby grabbed the branch and painfully hobbled over to the door and carefully peeked out. He watched with bated breath as Mama and Daddy emerged from the woods into the clearing toward the cabin.

He started outside when he caught sight of the old tramp approaching Mama and Daddy from behind with that long, razor-sharp sabre raised high and ready to strike. He stopped dead and cried for them to look behind.

Charlene screamed in relief when she saw Bobby and ran as fast as she could to him. Burt harkened to Bobby's warning and turned just the sabre went cutting through the heavy, damp air toward him.

He jumped out of the way. The blade just missed him by less than an inch. The tramp bellowed like a madman as he tried again to lash out at Burt. Burt jumped Ritchie before he had a change to deliver the flow.

Ritchie lurched backward just as Burt lost his footing when he stepped into a gopher's hold and went sprawling backward into the muddy ground.

Charlene and Bobby screamed in helpless shock as the tramp stood looming over Burt with the sabre raised high and ready to strike the fatal blow. Just then, a blinding bolt of lightening jumped out of the sky and connected to the tip end of the sabre blade. For one riveting moment, the sword and the man were lit up with the powerful charge.

Seconds later, the twisted, melted, blackened steel that was the sabre lay in the ground fused into the remnants of Ole Man Ritchie's right hand. His scorched and charred body lay plastered in the mud and much as wispy curls of white and greyish smoke rose up from the charred remains. The awful scent of burnt, wet human flesh was heavy in the air as the rain came to an end in a slow drizzle.

Burt got to his feet. He was shaking badly as Bobby and Charlene ran over to his side. He grabbed his wife and son and clung to them for dear life. He swore to himself that he would not do anything to ever again cause him to lose that which meant the most to him… far more than the bottle ever could.

Chapter 28

BOBBY STARED AT the door to room 207. He had no fear t his time. Instead, he felt a strong sense of inner peace and fulfillment. Daddy and Mama were truly together now. The most important thing of all, Daddy swore off the beer and whiskey for good.

Daddy actually believed his explanation of why he had to do what he did. Daddy really seemed to understand why he played make-believe so much and liked to live in a make-believe world.

Daddy told him that when he was a boy, he played make-believe games a lot, pretending to be all kinds of great heroes doing battle with evil villains and saving the world from nasty monsters. Apparently, Granddaddy drank a lot when Daddy was a boy. He scolded him a lot about his pretending. Granddaddy had many problems during those bad years Daddy grew up in that was known as the Depression. It was a time when there wasn't much work and it was hard to earn money.

Bobby just could not get over Daddy's acceptance of what had happened. It was like he knew how it was for him after not understanding for such a long time.

Daddy now believed everything he told him about his room. He truly believed in the ghostly lady, the Broken Cross of Belberith, and why it was so important for him to keep his promise to the ghostly lady.

Daddy said that things were going to be a lot different in the future. They were going to talk more often, play ball, and do more things together.

He was glad that Dan from the barbershop told Daddy and Mama about Ole

Man Ritchie and the way he was so interested in the Broken Cross of Belberith and Jonas Van Gilder when they came back to the barbershop and couldn't find him. He thanked God that they didn't stop looking until they located Ole Man Ritchie's cabin in those woods. Somehow, he knew that Daddy and Mama would find him and protect him from that crazy old tramp.

Bobby was glad that he found the courage to face death. A sad, earthbound soul was now free. The family was now bonded together like they had never before been in his young life.

He was glad that Daddy gave him permission to come to room 207 for the last time while Mama and he packed the suitcases and took them down to the car before checking out of the inn. He was glad that they stayed over the several extra days that the police required of them in order to get their statement and his statement. The police were able to positively identify the skeletons of the two missing boys. Their families now knew what had become of them and they would at last have the proper burial they deserved. Bobby felt sad for the boys' parents, but they did at least know what had happened to them. The old tramp would face eternal damnation in the hereafter for what he did and would have done to him if he had succeeded.

The door was unlocked. He slowly opened it and stepped inside. It was very dark. He immediately felt that freezing cold sensation as a light appeared in the center of the room. The light took on a soft phosphorescent globular shape. The room was filled with the pleasant scent of a woman's perfume. It was like jasmine.

The soft, warm voice of Jeanine spoke to him. There was a distant echoing ring to her voice like it was coming from some place along the way off. It reminded him of when he had spoken long distance on the telephone to Grandma Belcher and the connection was real bad. "Thank you for what you have done for me, Bobby Sailor. I will forever be in your debt, young man. I shall always be with you in spirit. You have given me the peace and love I have yearned for since that time when I died so long ago. I love you, Bobby Sailor. Have a good life. One day in the future, we shall meet in the afterlife. Until then, be happy."

Tears come to his wide eyes as the light faded away and the perfume scent, which was so heavy in the air, was no more. The ghostly lady was now truly at peace and would not be bound to this room ever again.

He left room 207 and flew down the hall to the stairs. He was joyful and happy. He knew that whatever would happen to him in the years to come, he would always have a very special guardian angel to comfort him.

Nate and Sally
Summer, 1968

Chapter 29

"MAN! WHAT A far out pad. Looks like something out of a friggin' bad trip." Nate Holden drank in every inch of the room with his wide, popping eyes. He just couldn't picture a straight place like this having such a far out room like number 207. The amber hue of the wallpaper with patterns depicting elves, fairies, trolls and demons was just too much.

Sally Wood looked all around her again, transfixed by the designs on the wallpaper, the old paintings, and tintype photographs, rubbing her long, tapered fingers as she squealed "o-o-o-w!"

Sally sauntered over to the large brass bed where the bellboy had thrown the carpet bag and the military-style seabag. She opened the seabag and got out a clear plastic bag filled with a generous amount of grade-A hashish along with sever smaller bags of sugar cubes impregnated with LSD. They had used the drugs to finance their way from California across the country to Florida.

Nate plopped down in the large, upholstered chair close to the door to the bathroom. He watched Sally attentively as she got some of the things out and placed them in the large chest of drawers facing the bed. A few days had passed by since he last banged her. It was the night before they left southwest Texas. They nearly were nabbed as he attempted to exchange some of the hash for a tank of regular at a Sunoco station. They were fortunate that the grease monkey at the pump wanted no more trouble with that overweight pig of a state cop that showed up just before the buy went down. The cop had busted the gas jock earlier in the year during a local war protest.

Nate became aroused as Sally bent over the bed. Her delightfully curvy bottom began to jiggle; the cheeks moving up and down so sensually. He was getting a tad bit horny what with those tight cut-away jean short prominently displaying the lower curve of her beautiful cheeks. Sally had a fine tale on her and great long legs to boot.

He got turned on the most when she wore her long, dark brunette hair in braided pigtails and had on a tank top halter. When she wasn't wearing a bra, he really got hot watching her large taut nipples jutting against the fabric of the halter.

Sally was a real fine old woman to him ever since they got together at that anti-war rally in San Francisco about a year ago. Whenever things were tight and there wasn't enough bread, Sally would find one of her ready contacts who would let them have enough pot, acid, or speed to hustle up some ready cash with until things got better.

He would sometimes take some straight jobs to get by, such as a dishwasher in a truck stop, day laborer when the call went out for unskilled labor, and short order cool stints in the little greasy spoons which proliferated in and around the small towns out on the coast.

They always had enough to get by but it was getting tougher. In short, it was becoming a bad scene. He was 22 now and without any solid prospects. The California scene had been a gas up to a point. When he reached that point, it became a very bad scene.

He was no big musician on the rise like he hoped to become after the blow up with Uncle Daniel when he told dear old uncle he wasn't going to the University of Florida like he wanted him to. He was headed for the coast instead to become a rock musician.

Dear old uncle gave him an ultimatum, which still rang in his ears and gave him a lasting bad taste in his mouth. He could still hear it now. "You leave here like this, Nate Holden… and I'll disown you and see to it that you never see any of the company money. I can promise you that, my boy."

That was almost four years ago. That whole scene grated on his manhood since that time. The old bastard raved and ranted. He was nothing more than a fourth rate musician at best. It was a fool's dream and nothing more.

Nate got up and walked over to the large, ornate dressing table then and took a hard look at himself in the highly reflective, polished surface of the mirror. He was still lean and trim with a deep California tan contrasting sharply with his bleach blond mane of long and stringy hair. His pale blue eyes, which Sally liked to call his Paul Newman eyes, could still get the attention of a good looking chick. Yes, he was still a pretty good looking dude. But the cheap love beads and light yellow T-shirt was the psychedelic pattern across the front depicting Jimmy Hendrix on a wild trip just did not seem to cut it anymore.

His thoughts returned to the present and their arrival at the inn. The tall old fart at the front desk had looked them over like they were yesterday's garbage as he signed them in and got the key to the room, demanding a day's room rent in advance. He nearly did a double take when Nate pulled out a big was of bills from the back pocket of his tattered jeans and paid the man. Nate gave him a toothy grin. The old fart was really pissed off. Nate was glad.

The jerk of a bellboy was just as much as an establishment square as the old fart at the desk. The young dude's mouth nearly fell open as he looked them up and down like he couldn't believe that a pair like them had the nerve to lay over at Warlock Inn.

Once they were upstairs and the kid handed them the key to the room after unlocking the door, Nate cornered him, asking if he would like some fine hash to groove on. He would give the kid a good price.

The damn jerk began sweating like a pig and told him that he didn't use the stuff. Nate grabbed him by the collar and slammed him up against the wall, telling him that he better not fink on them to the fuzz or anyone else or he would stick him or maybe worse.

The kid gulped hard, "Don't worry mister. I don't want any trouble."

Nate slapped him lightly on one cheek and smiled. "That's cool. As long as we understand one another… everything is cool." The jerk off bellboy practically ran down the hall. The sight of the kid nearly pissing in his pants as he took off was good for a short belly laugh.

Nate chuckled as he thought about it while continuing to stare at his reflection in the dresser mirror.

His thoughts wandered back to the reason for his return to Seville. The chuckles ended and his features became hard and grim. Uncle Daniel and his father had been partners in a very profitable trucking firm. When Daddy and Mama died in that car crash while on a trip to New York, Nate came to live with Uncle Daniel, moving in from the family ranch house over in Ocala. He was the only child of Steve and Mary Holden.

Uncle Daniel, as he was told to call the old coot, never married. The old boy was something of an eccentric and oddball, having lived in the small Spanish hacienda-style house out on the outskirts of Seville by himself ever since he could remember.

Nate wondered if that skinny, wrinkled prune, Mrs. Freed, still came over to the house twice a week and cleaned the place for him. She was a face full of wrinkles even then and always had a cigarette dangling out of the corner of her mouth.

He focused in on good old Uncle Daniel again. They had never gotten along even when he first came to live with the old boy. He knew that his presence had put a heavy crimp in the old boy's lifestyle. The old bastard really made life shitty for him.

When he refused the old boy's ultimatum about attending the university and then establishing himself in a respectable career, Uncle Daniel told him to get out of his sight. Go to California. See where it would get him. "You won't get any goddamn money. I promise you that, Nate Holden," was the dear old bastard's parting remark.

Nate almost cursed the memory of his parents. Dear old dad never made a proper will and the courts gave Uncle Daniel full control of their estate.

It hurt in the gut to think about it, but the old coot was right about California and his dreams of becoming a big time rocker. He couldn't get anyone really worked up about his music. One promoter in Fresno frowned after he finished an audition and called him a two-bit bum with nowhere music… told him to get out of the club before he personally kicked his butt out the door.

Yes. He was 22 now and he wanted better things than to just crash some hippie pad and get stoned for a night or two. He wanted better things for Sally. She deserved it the was she stuck with him and not complained.

He was going over to the old coot's house tomorrow and have it out with him. Good old Uncle Daniel was going to give him a fair share of the company or come across with the money from his share if he had his part of the business put up for sale.

He needed a solid stake to get a fresh start in the straight lane of life. Uncle Daniel was going to belly it up or else.

His thoughts were interrupted again as Sally told him she was going back to the Volkswagen Bus and get her other two small bags which contained some cosmetics and Hopi Indian jewellery and other trinkets she acquired when they visited a reservation while passing through New Mexico and the large expanse of mesa country.

"Man, I'm glad this pad has a good air conditioning system. The damn humidity and heat here just about knocks me out," she quipped before leaving the room.

She stopped dead in her tracks just as she started out the door when the portrait of a thin-faced man with a large, bushy moustache stared down at her from the wall. The dark eyes of the man in the portrait seemed to reach out and burn straight into her very soul. Sally shuddered slightly as Nate walked over to her and put his arms around her slender waist.

"What is it, baby?" he asked as he looked up at the portrait of the compelling, thin-faced man.

"The eyes of that dude, They seem to hold you in a spell. It's like too creepy." She said with a shudder.

Nate nodded in agreement. "Yeah, I think that's a picture of Jonas Van Gilder. He's the cat who built this place just after the Civil War. If I remember some of the local history, he was into black magic, Satanism… that kind of scene. I think they were supposed to have hung the old boy or burned him after they found out he had some young chicks and kids wasted in ritual sacrifices to the devil. I think that's how this joint got the name kids wasted in ritual sacrifices to the devil. I think that's how this joint got the name Warlock Inn. Old Jonas was a male witch and really far out in a friggin' kind of way."

"A real loony tune," was Sally's comment before leaving the room.

Nate walked over to the bed and took out a long, thin case from the carpet bag. He carefully opened it and removed the paper-thin titanium needle that lay inside the case. The needle was more than ten inches long and as sharp as a razor-edge sword. He had to look directly at it in order to see it clearly. It was that thin.

He had acquired the needle while working for a gas company one winter in Sausalito, primarily cleaning open space gas heaters.

"Yeah, uncle. One way or another… you're gonna give me what's rightfully mine." He smiled broadly as he placed the needle carefully in the groove of the inner lining of the case and closed it.

Nate walked over to the antique nightstand next to the bed and placed the case in the top drawer next to a Giddeon bible before going into the adjoining bathroom to relieve his bladder.

Chapter 30

DANIEL HOLDEN WAS a precise and punctual man both in business and the way he fastidiously led his Spartan lifestyle He had a rough but distinguished aura. Despite his age and greying hair, he was a trim and fit six feet of manhood. The iron grey moustache he sported was meticulously groomed and trimmed.

His daily routine adhered to a fixed schedule: he was of to the central offices of the Holden Trucking Company at 5:30 a.m. every morning. He worked straight through to five in the afternoon. He came straight back home just long enough to fix his usual meal that consisted of either fish, such as deep sea trout or Spanish mackerel, along with a Caesar salad. Sometimes he would substitute broiled chicken with his salad. Pork or beef in any form was taboo.

He would then return to the office or attend some local civic or business function either in Seville or up in St. Augustine. He would sometimes remain at home for the evening and consult his various astrological charts and books when he was in the process of making a major business decision.

He promptly retired every evening around 10:30 unless some demanding social function or business activity kept him from doing so.

He took three twenty minute breaks each work week for an intensive physical workout in order to maintain his peak vim and vigor.

Daniel Holden had been an intensive workaholic during most of his 59 years of life. He never married nor had he indulged in any affairs, although he did have an occasional session with several very discreet and trustworthy call girls from the Daytona area. A permanent and intimate relationship was not a part of his lexicon. He never saw a favourable percentage in such a relationship.

He diverted from the pattern of his usual evening meal this evening with a serving of pheasant along with the usual Caesar salad. In addition, he enjoyed a glass of dry white wine.

The doorbell began to chime from the small alcove vestibule at the front door just as he was finishing the last morsel of pheasant. He tried to ignore it. The chiming continued. He swore under his breath as he threw his table napkin down after neatly wiping his lips.

Absolutely no one at work was ever to disturb him at this time. If it was any of his numbskull employees, he or she would be very sorry as he intended to fire whoever it was right there on the spot.

Daniel Holden got up in a huff and stormed out of the dining room through the living room past the small arch of the vestibule and threw the large oak door wide open. He was astonished for a moment, gawking at the dirty hippie young man and girl. They stood there smiling at him with stupid smirks all over their asinine features.

He waited for a moment for one of them to speak. They remained silent. "Well, who are you people?" What do you want here?" he snapped. His pompous outrage amused Sally. She began to giggle while Nate continued to sheepishly grin, fully revealing his yellow stained teeth.

"Look here. You better explain yourselves or I'm calling the police." Daniel Holden's anger slowly changed to unease by the actions of this dirty hippie pair. He had read more and more in the papers about hipped, vagrant types getting high on whatever it was they used and killing people for no apparent reason such as what happened recently to that actress out in Hollywood, Sharon Tate, who was killed by a crazy bunch of hippie cultists.

"Oh man! Come on, Uncle Daniel. You don't remember your own nephew, man?" Nate was incredulous with disbelief.

Daniel Holden looked hard at the young hippie. "Good Lord, it's really you, Nate."

Nate giggled in a silly fashion. Sally joined in with a similar silly smirk that instantly irritated the older man.

Both Nate and Sally were feeling real loose, having just smoked a couple of joints before coming to the front door of the house.

"Yeah man, it's me. I've come home Uncle," Nate proclaimed.

Daniel Holden's features went rapidly through three shades of red as he looked perturbed at Sally and asked who the silly girl was with him. Nate's grin faded instantly by the cutting way his uncle talked. "She's my old lady. Her name is Sally Brent. Sally and me met up in San Francisco. We've been together for some time now."

Sally continued grinning at the older man with a silly, high expression. She raised her hand limply and exclaimed in a slurred speech pattern, "Like, hi, Pops. It's really a gas meeting you."

Daniel Holden rolled his eyes and simply relied disgustedly, "Good Lord."

He composed himself and continued, "I can't say that I'm really surprised Nate. What do you want here?"

Nate threw up his hands up and laughed as he declared, "Hey man, do we have to talk like out here? Can't you at least invite us inside?"

The older man breathed deeply and motioned for them to come inside.

"Now that's more like it," Nate quipped as Sally and he followed the older man into the tastefully furnished Mediterranean-style living room.

Sally looked all around, drinking in the rich tapestry of the plush carpeting and mixture of Spanish and Mediterranean-style rococo furnishings. Her eyes widened, approving of the surroundings she found herself in.

One large tapestry especially caught her attention. It hung on the far wall of the living room and covered most of the area above the mantle of a small wrought iron fireplace grate. The tapestry depicted an elaborate illustration of the various symbolic patterns and signs of the Zodiac as well as depicting symbols connected with Zoroastrian magic.

"Oh wow, far out, Pops! You must really be into this stuff." Her manner positively grated on the older man's nerves.

Daniel Holden breathed deeply again, doing his best to keep his temper in check. He answered her in a controlled modulated southern accent; "The stars have helped me a great deal in my business dealings through the years, young lady. I take it all very seriously. To me… it is a science."

Sally placed a slender hand across her full lips. "O-o-o-w, sorry Pops. I didn't mean to like, ruffle your feathers. I think it's really cool and far out."

Nate inspected the living room and part of the connecting dining room. "Things haven't changed much since I split. It looks exactly the same here as it did when I left."

The older man rolled his eyes again in disgust. "It is exactly the same as when you split from here as you aptly put it. I must say Nate… judging from your appearance and the appearance of your lady friend… you have turned out just exactly the way I predicted you would… good for nothing. You left here a bum and you have returned in a similar manner."

The older man's caustic rebuke set off a short fuse in Nate. Uncle Daniel always knew how to get his back up and exactly how to make him feel like something less than a human being. "Listen here old man… I didn't come back here to get a load full of your bullshit."

Daniel Holden's expression took an amused turn. "Why have you come back Nate?" he asked pointedly.

Nate's eyes flashed with a furious intensity as he screwed up his courage. Sally was somewhat shaken by Nate's angry outburst. She never saw him that angry before. It caught her off guard. She was still feeling loose and high from the joints she had smoked a few minutes earlier. But then, she knew for sometime that there was no love lost between Nate and the older man.

Nate shook his finger at the older man. "All right, Uncle Daniel. I admit that things haven't worked out the way I hoped they would. I admit that I'm tired of living in dirty, little, rat infested, one-room slums and communes. I'm tired of beating my head against closed doors. You want to know why I came back… I want my rightful share of the trucking firm or the money my share would bring if it was sold. I want to live like a well-heeled dude. I want to sleep in a comfortable bed like the one I slept in last night. I want some of the good things in life for Sally. In short, I want what is mine.

The older man began to laugh, obviously more amused than before after hearing Nate's demands.

"Cut it out, uncle. I didn't come here to be laughed at by you or anyone else," Nate yelled.

"Yeah. That ain't very nice, Uncle Daniel. Nate is a real good old man and I don't like to see a square like you puttin' him down," Sally said, her speech slurred from the effects of the potent grass. She reached up and kissed Nate on the lips, provoking another look of disgust from the older man. It was exactly the reaction she hoped to provoke.

"I told you when you left here Nate that you will never see on penny of the company money nor will you ever inherit nay of the real or tangible assets belonging to the company. I would sooner hand the firm over to a charity than let you have any claim to any part of it." Daniel Holden's tone was filled with an ice-cold determination. It stuck in Nate's craw like little daggers dipped in venom. His hatred for the older man seethed over the boiling point.

"I'll get a lawyer. I'll fight you in court. Dad meant for me to have his rightful part of the business when he passed on. Ever since the folks were killed, you have done your best to keep me from what is mine."

"I gave you a choice, Nate. You could have gone on to the university and made something of yourself. And when I finally pass on, every bit of it would have been yours. You didn't honor my wishes in the matter. You will never get one red cent from me or get your hands into the company coffers." There was absolute finality in the older man's tone.

"What gives you the right to call me trash? I've seen you play around with astrology and the occult when you weren't working your ass off like it some big deal. If some of the holy rollers around the boonies here abouts knew the kind of stuff you play around with, man, they would ride your ass out of town on a rail," Nate barked defiantly.

"Get out of here!" the older man barked sharply. "And take that piece of trash you call your old lady with you," the older man shouted with a furious resonance.

Sally suddenly exploded. It was like a silent bomb suddenly went off inside her. She wasn't sure before that she could go through with Nate's plan. But after hearing the old bastard call her trash, she no longer found it difficult at all as she took the long, narrow case from the back pocket of her jeans and withdrew the nearly invisible long and sharp titanium needle from it.

The older man was totally preoccupied with Nate. He did not notice her as she moved around to his backside. An incredible look of amazement and shock etched Daniel Holden's features as she shoved the needle into the back of his neck and up to the base of his brain.

The older man's eyes nearly popped out of their sockets as he made a hideous gurgling sound. Copious amounts of saliva and spittle began to drool from the corners of his mouth.

He tried to reach behind him and pull the long needle out. Before he could do so, his eyes rolled up into his skull. He collapsed like so much dead weight to the floor.

Nate stooped down and checked for a pulse at the neck and wrist of his right hand. There was none.

Sally stood frozen in shocked astonishment. She never thought that she was capable of taking another human life until now. She looked down at the older man's body, feeling as though she could be sick at any moment.

Nate carefully pulled the long needle out of the man's brain and neck. He quickly snatched the case out of Sally's frozen grasp and placed the needle down on the inner lining of the case and closed it tight. He proceeded to place it in the hip pocket of his jeans.

He gently put his arm around Sally's waist. "You did good baby. You did real good," he said soothingly.

The tone of his voice helped bring her partially out of the state of shock she experienced. She looked up at him almost like a frightened little girl, her large brown eyes showing the edge of near hysteria she felt. "I killed a man, Nate. I actually killed somebody."

"Yeah, I know baby. But look at it this way... old Uncle Daniel was one rotten son of a bitch. With him gone, I can probably get the whole firm in time. I've already been in touch with a lawyer up in Jacksonville. He's agreed to contest the old bastard's will after it's read. He's pretty sure we can fight whatever stipulations may be in his will."

He held Sally tight to him as he continued. "We'll finally have nice things. A nice home, good food, lots of bread to spend. We'll be set for a long time to come."

Sally pulled back. She was loosening up and becoming more herself. She gave him a big pot-induced smile, saying, "That really sounds groovy, honey."

He kissed her and told her to wait for him in the bus while he made sure that all the fingerprints they may have made were wiped off around the room and front door. He would make things look like no one had been there.

Sally dutifully responded and went outside to the VW bus. She crawled inside and slumped back against the front passenger seat. She nervously got out another joint of the most potent hashish they had and lit it, sucking in deeply the strong smoke as she put an 8-track tape of Jefferson Airplane music into the tape deck and began to groove on the music, trying to blot out the image of that old man as he died.

Even she was getting stoned again, she could not get it out of her mind that she had just killed another human being.

Chapter 31

SALLY'S EYES GREW big as she sat glued in front of the 19" color TV as the 7:25 newscast began following the first part of the "Today" show with the smiling faces of Hugh Downes and Barbara Walters. The local guy was giving a capsule rendition of the news from around the Jacksonville and northeast Florida area.

She breathed a deep sigh of relief as the newscast came to an end. There was no report on the death of Uncle Daniel.

Nate had gone downstairs to the kitchen of the inn to get some juice, coffee and sweet rolls to bring back to the room along with morning editions of the Jacksonville, Gainesville, and Daytona papers to see if there was any word in the printed media yet on the death of Uncle Daniel.

Sally got up from the chair and went over to the bed. She stretched out across the rumpled sheets as the "Today" show resumed. Frank Blair led off with the usual downers about Vietnam and the aftermath of the Tet offensive and Mai Lai massacre. There was more racial unrest and the latest on the Nixon-Humphrey campaigns for the White House.

She never heard any of it. The only thing she could think about was that she killed a man. She shoved a long, deadly needle into another living being's neck and brain.

Nate had planned it weeks ago and had constantly browbeat her with the smallest details of his plan to day away with dear old Uncle Daniel if he refused Nate's demands while they were held up in the dump back in Fresno. He had it all together before leaving in the VW bus Billy Vargas had turned over to them in exchange for a large catch of high quality hashish Nate was able to hustle for him. Nate told her over and over that she could do it. She had been so sure that she could not right up until the moment she actually did do it.

Daniel Holden was every bit the hard nose, pious bastard Nate had told her he was. A man you could instantly dislike and even come to hate with very little effort. But he was still a flesh and blood human being. She had never before wanted to hurt anyone in her life. But then she would do just about anything Nate would ask of her. She loved him more than life.

She continued to feel cold and numb inside. Taking all the downers in the world wasn't going to change that. She was a murderer. It all seemed so unreal.

The door to the room flew open then and Nate bounced in, dropping a large brown paper sack on top of the small table next to the bed. He took the three papers that were tucked under his left arm and proceeded to hurriedly scan them.

The aroma of hot coffee and inviting fragrance of sweet pastry aroused her enough to make her sit up on the edge of the bed. She got the sack and went over to the large chair by the side of the television and flopped down in it just as Barbara Walters began an interview with Warren Beatty, discussing the sociological implications of the acceptance of violence on the part of the movie going public in his version of Bonnie and Clyde.

She got out one of the large cups of aromatic coffee along with a cup of cold orange juice. She quickly removed the lid of the coffee cup and took a sip, helping to relieve some of that inner cold sensation. She then put the coffee down and repeated the same sequence with the orange juice. She reached into the sack again and got out an apple Danish and quickly ate half of it. She was hungrier than she though she was. But then, when she was really worried or down, eating always seemed to help.

Nate's eyes flashed, betraying his edgy nerves, as he looked over at her and shouted that there wasn't anything in the papers about Uncle Daniel.

Sally cleared her throat and suggested that it was too soon for the papers or TV to get hold of a story on his death. "I mean, like maybe the body hasn't even been discovered yet," she offered as an explanation.

Nate shook his head angrily in protest. "No, no, someone would have checked on him last night. He always headed back to the main office over in Hastings or some other doings. I'm telling you… someone would have checked on him."

Nate nervously began to pace up and down the length and breadth of the room, rubbing the stubble beard on his chin as he did so.

Seeing how nervous he was made Sally as uptight as she was before Nate came back with the morning breakfast. She nervously drank the rest of her coffee and gobbled up the rest of the apple Danish.

"So, what do you think it means, Nate?" she asked groggily. The lack of sleep made her feel as washed out as a dishrag.

"I don't know. I just know that something has gone wrong. We are gonna have to go back here this morning. I have to know what happened." Nate clenched his teeth. His nerves were as tight as a drum.

Sally got out one of the several paper napkins that were in the sack and placed it on the little stand next to the chair and then put the nearly empty coffee and juice cups on the napkin and the sack next to it. She got up and began to shiver. She definitely didn't like the idea of going back to that house again. "I don't know honey. I don't think I can do it. What if someone is there and questions are asked. I don't know whether I can take that kind of scene right now."

Nate lurched at her and grabbed her hard by her soft, white shoulders. It hurt. He never before had hurt her in the time they had been together. His eyes flashed with intense anger and fear. "You gotta Sally. You can stay cool. You can handle it. I know you can. If anybody is around, I'll just introduce myself as the old bastard's nephew. I'm just passing through with my sweet old lady. I just stopped by to see the old fart and say hello."

Sally pulled away from him, turning her back to him. "Yeah, okay. I guess I can do it." She was cool.

Nate's arms entwined around her small waist. He kissed her on the neck. "I knew you could baby. I knew you could," he said.

Chapter 32

THE VW BUS turned slowly into the driveway and pulled up next to a rusty, beat-up looking '59 Chevy. Nate recognized it immediately as belonging to that wrinkled-up old prune, Mrs. Freed. "It's his house cleaning lady's car. Still driving the same old wreck. This must be one of her days to come over and clean the pad." Nate looked all around. Uncle Daniel's pickup truck wasn't in the garage next to the house. The garage door was open and inside of the garage was empty except for a few bins.

Nate looked at Sally. He was in shock. She stared back at him. Her mouth opened wide in astonishment. "Well, one thing is for sure. The cops haven't been called. No sign of anything out of the ordinary," Nate exclaimed as he wondered what the hell was going on.

Nate piled out of the bus and motioned for Sally to get out. She had smoked another joint on the way over from the inn to loosen up. She was still shaken and feeling uptight. She did not want to get out.

Nate hurried around to the passenger side, threw open the door and pulled her out of the vehicle, hoping that she would stay cool and not say anything. The salty sultriness of the muggy overcast morning air didn't help his nerves any as he held tight to her hand and guided her to the large front door under the arched foyer of the front entrance of the house. It was surrounded on all sides by all manner of exotic spiny sea cactus of numerous shapes and sizes.

Nate vigorously rang the chiming doorbell. A few seconds passed by before they heard a click in the lock of the door. The door slowly opened. A tall, skinny woman's head poked out from behind the partially opened door. Her face was a mass of wrinkles. A cigarette dangled from one corner of her mouth. Her hair was pinned up and concealed by a cheap, red scarf. She wore a faded white cotton dress.

She looked first at Nate and then over at Sally suspiciously, "Yeah, whatta you want. If it's a handout you want, I ain't got nothin' to give you."

Nate forced himself to smile. "Mrs. Freed, you don't recognize me?"

The scrawny woman squinted to her dull eyes as a down of recognition began to register with her, judging by her expression. "Oh, it's you, Nate Holden. Where you been keepin' yourself the past few years."

"Been in California," he replied. "Just now came back. This is my girl, Sally Brent.

Sally forced herself to smile when Nate poked her slightly in the side with his elbow. "Hi," was all she could say.

Mrs. Freed cracked a thin smile as she took the cigarette out of her mouth and flicked the ashes outside before they dropped off the tip end of the cylinder. "Hi yourself," she said with a smart-ass cynicism clearly evident.

Nate tried to look past the old woman to see if there was any sign of someone inside. "Is Uncle Daniel here?" Nate asked with a nervous edge.

Mrs. Freed screwed up her badly wrinkled features, showing a great deal of annoyance. "Now you know Mr. Holden goes to work at the crack of dawn, Nate Holden. You ain't been gone that long that you can't remember that."

Nat was now very frightened and very worried although he did his best to conceal his feelings. "He wasn't here when you arrived this morning?"

The scrawny woman's agitation became very obvious. "Now why should Mr. Holden stay here for me? I have my own key. He never has stayed around here for me."

Mrs. Freed's expression turned icy and stern. "Mr. Holden gave me orders that if you ever showed up around here again I wasn't to let you in. So you and your girlfriend better go it you don't want me to call the cops." Her tone was hard and resolute.

"If you want to see your uncle, I suggest that you drive over to the office in Hastings and try and see him there," she clearly shouted as she slammed the door shut and locked it.

Nate seemed to look off into space as they started back to the VW bus. What had happened? The old bastard had to be dead. He had to be. There was no chance of him surviving that long needle when it was shoved up his brain. At least Nate couldn't see how such a thing could be possible. And if Daniel Holden were still alive, surely the fuzz would have busted him by now.

Sally looked frantically up at him. His voice was cold with worry as he told her that he couldn't figure it. But he was for damn sure going to find out.

The close air was suddenly filled with squawking cried as a large flock of seagulls came flying in off of the Atlantic.

Chapter 33

IT TOOK NATE about twenty minutes to get from Seville over to the Holden Trucking Company headquarters, which was just north of the little town of Hastings. It was right off of Interstate 95. Hastings was a quaint little rural community. It's main business was agricultural, growing primarily potatoes, strawberries, and citrus. The primary consignments for the trucking firm was in hauling the various local crops to district warehouses and processing plants.

Nate always harboured suspicions that good old Uncle Daniel had numerous under the table deal son the side with the most powerful farming families and business types in the area. But Nate had only one thing on his mind at the moment. Did the old boy actually survive that needle in his brain or did somebody come along, discover the body and remove it from the house? If so, then for what reason?

Nate pulled into the parking lot practically on two wheels and parked in one of the employee's parking spaces near where the large rigs pulled out from the loading zone when they were ready to hit the road. He was tight as a steel drum as he piled out of the VW bus. His anxiety was written in his troubled features as he breathed in the still, hot summer air that was much drier than it was in Seville. The blazing hot summer sun just added to his ever-growing sense of anxiety and frustration.

Sally was in even worse shape. She had trembled and fretted all the way over. Not even another strong joint helped to calm her down. Her whimpering caused the little bit of mascara she applied that morning to streak as the tears ran down her cheeks.

Sally's continuous whimpering added to his own raw edge nerves. He caught himself several times just before he was ready to haul off and give her a hard wrap across the cheek. It was the first time he had the desire to strike her since they got together. He did not like that sensation.

He looked at her angrily, telling her to stay in the van and to try to get herself together. He would be back just as soon as he knew how the land laid.

He walked quickly across the hot tarmac of the parking lot, heading toward the front entrance of the main office. He opened the large, heavy, glass door and the cool air coming from the main air conditioning vents in the lobby rushed out, offering instant relief from the torrid heat.

The small lobby and reception area was cone in tasteful mahogany wood paneling and decked out with an assortment of potted plants and ferns. Prints of Florida woodlands adorned the walls.

An attractive freckle-faced receptionist with long, flowing locks of flaming red hair sat at a desk close to a door marked "Inner Office." She wore large, black-framed glasses and was busily engaged in the examination of a large stack of official-looking papers.

Nate walked over to her desk and cleared his throat. She looked up at him and frowned, obviously put off by his unshaven, ruffled features and hippie appearance. "What can I do for you?" she asked guardedly.

Nate smiled and tried to appear as agreeable as possible. Inwardly, he had a big desire in his gut to haul off and belt the snotty bitch. "I'm Mr. Holden's nephew. Name is Nate Holden. I just got into town from the coast and came right over here to see how Uncle Daniel has been the last few year." Nate paused and cleared his throat again; his nerves tensing up hard once again. "Is Uncle Daniel in?" he asked, wishing that he could appear much more relaxed than he was able to.

The receptionist smiled uneasily and coolly told him that Mr. Holden wasn't in at the moment. He had not arrived at the office so far this morning. She asked if he would like to leave a message.

"You know when he might arrive?" Nate snapped, his nerves right on the edge. His outburst unnerved the already ill at ease receptionist. She told him firmly that she didn't know when Mr. Holden would arrive. This was the first time since she had come to work here that he had been late coming to the office. She told him that he would have to leave at once, saying that only company employees were allowed on the grounds.

Nate simply nodded in reply and stormed out of the lobby. He practically ran across the parking lot over to the VW bus.

He looked at Sally with a bewildered expression, telling her what that bitch of a receptionist said. Sally became sick with shock. Her voice quivered as she asked "Oh, Nate, what does it mean? He's gotta be dead. He's just gotta."

Nate didn't answer her. He just walked around the bus to the driver's side, opened the door and hopped inside behind the wheel. Sally began to sob. "Shut up and get hold of yourself, you little fool. Somebody might see you." She lowered her head and tried her best to stop crying. She apologized to him like a small girl.

Nate sat hunched over the wheel, trying his best to collect his own thoughts. What happened to the old bastard? If he survived that long, dirty needle in the brain, then where was he and why had he not been to the fuzz? He must have needed medical attention after something like that. A thousand questions popped into his troubled mind.

He was suddenly startled of his speculations by a hard rap on the door of the VW bus. A tall, stocky, middle-aged man dressed in a security guard's uniform stared at him with a mean look all over his craggy, sunburnt features. "No goddamn hippies or anyone else allowed to loiter around here. Only the company personnel. Move out, now," the man barked like a seasoned army drill sergeant.

"All right, I'm going. Okay man, just stay cool," Nate shouted. He gunned the engine and burned rubber, shooting out of the parking lot onto the access road leading to I-95.

He told Sally to get a joint and light him up. He needed one bad. She looked coweringly at him, asked if it was a good idea. "I'm gonna keep it under the speed limit. I noticed that it didn't stop you wanting one. Light me up Sally, and I mean right now," he demanded, a definite threat in his tone.

She hurriedly got one out and lit it, taking a deep drag on the weed so as to get a good burn going. She then handed it over to him. Nate took two deep drags and held it in for as long as he could before expelling the smoke. "Oh, yeah, that's much better."

As he drove along at a relatively steady clip, he began to loosed up and relax slightly as he tried to puzzle out the whole crazy scene in his mind.

He glanced at Sally. She looked like she was stoned. Her eyes were absolutely expressionless. She seemed to be stared off at nothing at all.

"You know what I think babe?" he said with an analytical tone. "I think he probably did survive it… but with a lot of brain damage. He probably stumbled out of the house and wandered into the woods and marshes. There are some close by his pad. He's probably dead now somewhere n those swampy marshes. Maybe snake bit, or he's probably croaked from the needle piercing. Damn needle must be crawling with a million germs. He'll be reported missing. There will be a search and they'll find what's left of the old buzzard bait in another few years. Maybe a week or so at the most.

Sally looked over at him with a mixture of desperation and relief. "You really think that's what happened?"

Nate smiled as he took another drag on the joint. "Yeah, yeah, that's what I think happened. It's the only thing that makes any sense."

Sally suddenly felt a great deal of relief as she thought about Nate's speculation. It did make sense and seemed plausible.

Nate began to feel a sense of hunger then. It was getting on toward the afternoon. Neither of them had eaten since morning. He proceeded to drive into the small business district of Seville and get some chow at the Hideaway Café. It was one of the few good spots in the little own where you could get a tasty meal at fairly cheap prices.

It took him about fifteen minutes form the time he drove off of 95 onto the alternate route which led into the main street of Seville's business district to arrive at the Hideaway Café. He was glad that there wan an available parking place across the street from the diner with a one hour parking zone.

They hurriedly piled out of the vehicle and walked across the street to the diner. They were hot, tired, hungry, and thirsty. The sun baked down on them. The air felt like the temperature was in the upper nineties. A good stiff south easterly breeze gave some much welcomed relief just as Nate opened the door to the diner, allowing Sally to go in ahead of him.

A beefy, middle-age, bleach blond waitress came over as soon as they took a booth close to the large window overlooking the main street of the town. She was decidedly disagreeable. She asked, with a half sneer on her pancake made-up face in a thick country accent, "Whattaya want?" She didn't hand them any of the menus.

Nate was in no mood for an argument. He told her to get them the blue plate special for the day. She yelled out to the man behind the counter, "Swiss steak, mashed potatoes, peas and carrots."

"Yeah, that sounds cool. We'll have a couple of large ice-cold cokes. I also want the largest glass of the coldest ice water you got," he demanded.

The raw-boned hash slinger smiled sarcastically. "I hope you can pay for the food, honey. The boss don't like freeloaders. And he can get real mean when he wants to."

That did it for Nate. He looked up at the floozy and smiled. "Yeah, I can pay for it, fat stuff. Now get me my water and same for my girl."

"Comin' up, hippie freak. Comin' up." The large, raw-boned waitress shuffled back to the counter and returned a minute later with two tall glasses of ice water. She slammed them down on the table, causing a goodly portion of water to splash out of each glass.

She grinned at Nate with a toothy smile. "Anything else I can do for you, honey?"

Nate returned her smile. "No, just your orders when they're ready, honey pot."

Her large, puffy features turned three shades of red as she walked away in a huff.

Nate gulped the ice-cold water down. The liquid instantly relieved the hot and parched sensation in his dry throat. Sally picked up her glass and began to sip from it when she suddenly went deathly pale and let out a sharp scream. The glass fell out of her hand. Water spilled out all over the table.

Nate jumped as a result of her scream and wide-eyed, horrified expression. "What?" he shouted.

Sally pointed a shaking finger at the window. Nate quickly looked outside and cried out in startled shock himself. Uncle Daniel stood just outside, looking at them. He smiled pleasantly and waved just like nothing ever happened.

Nate couldn't believe what his eyes were communicating to him. He was nearly oblivious to his immediate surroundings as the beefy waitress and skinny short order cook ran over to the booth. "Get outta here. We don't want no friggin' hippie bums freakin' out in here," the cook demanded as he got hold of a ketchup bottle and held it threateningly above his head.

It jolted Nate out of the paralysing shock he momentarily felt. He didn't need any prodding as he sprang up and bolted away from the booth with Sally right behind him. Uncle Daniel hurriedly walked away and out of sight of the window.

Nate flung the door open and stepped outside and looked quickly down the street. Uncle Daniel was a block down from the Hideaway Café at the intersection. "The old bastard can really move," Nate hissed under his breath. He began to run down the street with Sally close behind.

The older man raced across the street, displaying an incredible amount of agility, and was instantly on the other side of the street. Nate was startled by the speed with which Daniel Holden could move as he panted for breath.

Nate sprang across the intersection with Sally nearly oblivious to the oncoming traffic. A light, beige Dodge Impala nearly ran into them. The driver leaned out the window and cursed them just as they got to the curb on the other side. They quickly ran into the shop at the corner.

A tall, lanky man with horn-rimmed glasses and curly, close-cropped, grey hair saw them from the rear of the store. He frowned disapprovingly as he started in their direction.

There was a desperate quality in Nate's high-pitched tone, as he demanded to know if the clothing salesman saw an older man come into the store just then. The salesman looked suspiciously at Nate as he replied indignantly that he hadn't had any customers for at least the past fifteen minutes.

"Oh come on, pops. I just saw the man come into this joint," Nate shouted impatiently.

There hasn't been anyone in this establishment for at least fifteen minutes… that is until you came in just now with this girl" The salesman displayed a decidedly tough firmness.

"Come on, man. Don't give me any friggin' bullshit," Nate snorted.

"That does it. You two get out of here right now or I will call the sheriff's office." He started back to the rear of the shop where there was a telephone right next to the cash register.

"Yeah, okay pops, stay cool. I don't want any trouble with the fuzz. I'm going." Nate snapped. He grabbed Sally hard by the wrist and left.

They started back across the street. A Ford station wagon passed slowly by them. Uncle Daniel was at the wheel. He looked straight at them and grinned. Nate lunged forward just as the truck gained speed.

"Come on," Nate yelled. He proceeded at a dead run back down the street to where the VW bus was parked. Sally had to struggle to stay up with him. When they got back to the vehicle, they quickly jumped inside. Nate burned rubber as he pulled out onto the main street, racing for the intersection. He turned the corner on two wheels. There was no sign of the station wagon.

Nate drove around the streets of Seville for more than an hour, trying vainly to spot the blue station wagon. He was weary and badly shaken as he parked the vehicle under a shady live oak. He looked over at Sally. She was badly strung out, looking as though she might collapse at any moment.

"What are we going to do, Nate? He's alive and playing with us like a cat plays with a mouse," she sobbed.

It was a bitter pill for him to swallow, but Sally was right. Through some twist of fate, god old Uncle Daniel survived the needle in the brain. The old fart had won this round.

Nate suddenly felt very tired like some kind of whipped alley cat after a big fight. He sighed exhaustedly, telling Sally they would head back to Warlock Inn and blow this town for the time being until he could think of another way to come at the old buzzard. "I'm comin' back. And when I do come back… I'll get the son of a bitch the next time around," Nate swore under his breath.

He angrily gunned the engine of the VW bus and tore down the street.

Chapter 34

NATE SPED INTO the parking lot of the inn and nearly hit the Chevy Corvair parked in the space next to him. There was a sharp, screeching as the brakes of the VW bus locked into place. They scrambled out of the vehicle and proceeded at a dead run from the parking lot around to the front of the inn, taking the steps up onto the expansive veranda two at a time.

Nate threw both doors open at the front entrance and stormed through the lobby up to the front desk. The tall, balding day man at the desk eyed them with a mixture of contempt and suspicion.

"We're splitting from this mausoleum like right now, pop. Have a bill ready when we come back down," Nate barked.

The day man smiled broadly. "With a considerable pleasure, Mr. Holden. I'll have it ready in five minutes. May I get a bellboy to help you collect your very considerable and fashionable belongings?"

"Forget it," Nate shouted. He stormed over to the stairs with Sally. They flew up the stairs and down the narrow corridor to room 207.

Nate nervously reached into his jeans pocket and pulled out the room key, quickly unlocking the door, he threw it wide open.

Nate's nerves were on the edge of exploding as he rushed over to the closet, opened it, and quickly began to throw their belongings on the bed as Sally closed the door to the room. She proceeded over to the large bureau to get the rest of their things as Nate randomly stuffed the seabag and carpet bag with clothing, pot bags, and other paraphernalia.

A hard rapping knock stopped Nate in his tracks just as he started toward the bathroom. Sally looked at him, betraying of the dread she felt.

Nate shook himself out of his momentary shock of surprise and charged at the door. His heart nearly stopped when he opened it. Uncle Daniel stood at the threshold to the room. A ghoulish triumphant grin was stamped into his features. Mrs. Freed was with him. She wore that same drab cotton dress she had on that morning. A cigarette characteristically dangled from the corner of his mouth. She was always the same.

Nate cringed away from the door as Uncle Daniel and Mrs. Freed entered the room. Sally ran over to Nate and crushed her lithe body against his. She trembled like a fearful child on the verge of soiling panties after being bad.

Nate finally got the courage up to speak. "I — I don't understand. How?" he stuttered. His nerves were almost at the breaking point.

Daniel Holden smiled pleasantly. "You mean why am I alive and standing here talking to you as I am?" He spoke in a nonchalant, matter of fact manner.

Nate could not speak. He answered by nodding as Sally began to sob.

"It's very simple, my boy," Uncle Daniel began. "A few years ago I made a pact with Satan in exchange for his eminence granting me my wish for perpetual life. That is to say that I can live on indefinitely until such time as I may choose to end my earthly existence. But as in all such contracts, the great dragon demanded something from me. In exchange for perpetual existence, I was to present a human sacrifice.

He paused for a moment, appearing to gleefully savor the growing horror that Nate and Sally felt. Sally was almost at the breaking point herself.

"You are my sacrifice, Nate, along with your charming companion. You are my only living relative. You are the ideal choice, according to the master's stipulations."

It seemed like a horrible dream as the older man or whatever he had become continued to speak. "You didn't actually come back here for your own accord Nate Holden. No. I cast a spell of sympathetic magic, making you want something more out of life than just your quaint, hippie lifestyle. I made you want to return and demand your rightful inheritance."

"No, old man. That was me. I wanted it. You didn't have anything to do with it," Nate shouted in a high-pitched, frenzied voice, temporarily shaking himself out of the deadly horror he felt.

Daniel Holden smiled insidiously. "No, no, no, Nate. It was the powerful spell I cast on you using a doll molded in your image. I dressed it in some of your old childhood clothing. You probably would still be in California if the potency of my spell wasn't as powerful as it turned out to be."

He paused for a moment. The smugness of his smile broadened considerable. "You probably didn't realize it yourself when you said it yesterday, but you are right Nate. If the holy rollers here knew the truth, they probably would try to run me out of town on a rail."

Sally stared at the skinny, old crone next to Daniel Holden, wondering why she was here. She screamed out, demanding to know what part the cleaning woman played in this unholy scheme.

Daniel Holden looked over at Mrs. Freed and laughed mockingly as the old crone began to hackle herself, allowing the cigarette butt to fall onto the carpeting. She crushed it with the heel of the sandal of her left foot.

"Oh! This isn't Mrs. Freed. No, I'm afraid Mrs. Freed passed on about a year after you left her Nate," the older man replied with a wicked gleam.

"Well, who the hell is this friggin' bitch?" Nate shouted in a grating tone as the whole room suddenly seemed to come crushing in on him.

"No, not a she Nate, You see Satan gave me a familiar. A pet demon if you like when the bargain was struck and the contact was made. My familiar here has merely assumed the form of the late Mrs. Freed for the time being."

Nate's head was spinning as the older man continued. "You know, Nate… it really is fitting that your sacrifice should take place within these walls. It was the master bedroom of the great Satanist of Seville, Jonas Van Gilder. I much admire the man and what he was able to personally accomplish before the so called "good people" of Seville stopped him."

"Yeah, well, the same thing will happen to you, old man, if you do anything to me or Sally," Nate yelled hysterically.

Daniel Holden's grin widened. "I think not, Nate. Well, I shall take my leave now. Thank you, Nate, for giving me the means of obtaining perpetual life. Goodbye."

Daniel Holden left the room then. Nate started to lunge at him. He found that he could not move.

Nate and Sally looked on in fascination and horror as Mrs. Freed's skinny, wrinkled form melted and the shape changed before their wide, popping eyes.

A mammoth, black, goat like entity standing upright on two legs towered over the. The hideous goat's mouth opened wide. The mouth began to incredibly stretch wider and wider until all they could see was a deep, black abyss. An ear splitting roar like a monstrous beast from hell belched from that black void followed by a jet stream of angry orange and crimson flames.

The horror stricken pair was enveloped in a huge fireball. Their screams of agony merged with the roaring inferno, which rapidly consumed flesh and muscle, leaving charred skeletal remains fused together by searing hellish heat.

The crimson ball of fire vanished instantly as the charred skeletons of the two collapsed onto the floor. A hazy, foul-smelling, bluish wisp of smoke curled up into the air from the charred bones. It was heavy with the pungent aroma of brimstone, pitchblin, and treacle.

A deadly silence fell over the room, as it was suddenly empty of the thing that posed as Mrs. Freed. The charred remains of Nate and Sally vanished and there wasn't the slightest hint of fire or smoke or anything out of the ordinary.

Trance 5
Mama Rosas Sweet Revenge
1973

Chapter 35

IT WAS CLOSE and hot in the small bedroom of Fat Bubba's Bar & Grill. Everett Butler was sweating hard despite the ceiling fan just above his head going at full tilt. His lean black frame was drenched in it, soaking his checkered short-sleeve shirt. The room stank of beer and cigar smoke, which added to his discomfort.

Everett glanced at his Timex wristwatch. It was almost midnight. A lone, wailing voice was belting out a classic B.B. King arrangement from the small bandstand just outside the door in the bar. The lead singer was accompanied by a first rate saxophonist, trumpeter, and guitarist.

Fat Bubba sauntered into the room at the stroke of midnight. He was well named, considering his solid 350 pound, six foot, two inch build. He had a mug that was a tough as any Everett had ever seen. Fat Bubba needed no bouncer for his joint. Whenever any of his customers showed signs of wanting anything more than booze, food or a well done B.B. King rendition by Skinny Higgens and his Blues Boys, Fat Bubba got out his big baseball bat from behind the bar and cracked it just hard enough over the counter to let that boy know that it wasn't cool to mess around in his place.

"Maurice has arrived, Mr. Butler," Fat Bubba announced in that deep, rich, bass voice which many R&B fan listened to back in the late fifties when he was the bass for the Hitchhiker band when they were hot on the charts.

After had brand of blues and rock began to fade, Fat Bubba took his earnings and returned to Seville, his hometown, to open the bar and grill located just on the outskirts.

Everett smiled nervously, telling Fat Bubba to show Maurice in.

"Come on in here, Maurice," Fat bubba's resonant voice barked out. A tall and lanky black young man came through the door. He looked uncomfortably up at Fat Bubba and then over at Everett.

Fat Bubba announced that he had to get back outside and tend the bar. "All right. Thanks," Everett said in a low, intense tone. Fat Bubba closed the door, leaving Everett and the younger man alone in that hot, foul-smelling room.

Everett detected a sense of defiance and seething anger in the young man's eyes. It was a hardness bred of poverty and doing without. An expression that said I'm tired of taking the shit end of life. I'm willing to do anything to crawl out from under.

Everett recognized that look because it was similar to his own twenty years ago when he was poor and just one of six kids in his family. Not one of them, himself included, could mother or father really afford.

He had tasted the shit of the white man when segregation was still the law and the shit of his betters among his own people as well. He had been determined to climb out of the gutter and the daily dose of poverty and violence. Things had gotten as bad as they could back then. Dad came home drunk most of the time and seemed to take great pleasure in beating the hell out of him, always using the excuse that he should tend to his younger brother and sisters better while Momma was playing maid to the honkies.

It was a slow, hard climb out of the black poverty of Seville. He worked his ass off when he could get the work, stole when he couldn't get it, begged, and did anything which would give him the money so he could get through high school and into college. He was fortunate in getting an available scholarship because of his basketball talents.

He worked even harder while attending A&M College, graduating with a BA in business administration. He got a position with one of the top paper mills in Jacksonville and climbed high up the company when segregation began to crumble following the '64 Civil Rights Act.

He met and married Lynette while in management there. Two fine children resulted from their union, his son, Harold and young daughter, Denise.

Everett left the company a few years later when he got the opportunity to start his own business in the Tampa area. He took his savings and got a loan which allowed him to buy out the O'Hanlon Bottling Company which primarily supplied glass bottles and aluminium containers for some of the leading soft drink companies in the nation.

As a result of his prudent business instincts, Everett achieved wealth and a certain amount of prominence. He became heavily involved in local and regional politics within the Democratic party. A number of his supporters were urging him to make a bid for a city council seat in Tampa. He was giving it serious consideration.

One big obstacle stood in his way. It was getting too hot for him to handle. It was the reason why he stood facing that lean, angry copy of his former self.

He visited Seville many times over the years, primarily to see how his brother and sisters and their families were faring along with his father. He was in a nursing home up in St. Augustine suffering from advanced Alzheimer's disease.

There was something about Seville that left Lynette cold. As a result, she never came with him on these trips. On one occasion when he was feeling extremely down and lonely, he went out to a night spot at St. Augustine Beach. A young and exotic black girl was singing that night. She belted out one of the hottest jazzy torch tunes he had ever heard. There was an aura about her. It reached out from the stage and started a fire of desire in his soul. She excited him like no other woman had outside of his early courting days with Lynette. He had to know that sultry vixen and proceeded to pay the manager of the club a sizeable sum to arrange an introduction for him.

The young, black goddess' name was Luana Verneaux. Everett was delighted when she told him that she also was a native of Seville. He offered to drive her back to Seville when the club closed that evening. A friend of Luana usually drove her to the club and back. The friend was conveniently sick that evening. The club manager had gone over to Seville and picked her up and was to have taken her back. She readily accepted Everett's offer.

He drove her back to a little shanty shack near a large swamp where she lived with her elderly grandmother known to the locals as Mama Rosa. The grandmother raised Luana when her mother had her out of wedlock and ran away from home shortly after giving birth to her.

Everett grew more and more excited by Luana's sensual charms. Before she could get out of the car, he was on her; awkwardly lifting her skirt and pulling her lacy panties off and then frantically shedding his own slacks and jock. He put in her right then and there and built to an explosive frenzy. After it was over, h e told her that he wanted her and wanted to be with her every chance he had.

He proceeded to pull out two one hundred dollar bills to reinforce his desires. The expression on her beautiful dark, beguiling features told him that she was agreeable as she took the bills and seductively put them inside her bra before getting out of the car. He watched her every move as she went across the narrow dirt road and entered the shanty.

Things went on like that for over a year. Everett found any excuse he could give to Lynette and the kids in order to get back to Seville for a day or two. He would register at Warlock Inn. When he met with Luana though, they usually headed for a cheap motel over in Hastings. It was one of those seedy places where no questions were asked if the right number of bills went into the owner's waiting hands.

They would indulge in the most passionate encounters he had ever known. They would end with him showering her with hundreds of dollars and expensive jewellery. Some of the money Luana received came from extorting funds from the company's general revenue accounts. Everett always managed to replace those shortages just in time before anyone caught on.

One day, not long ago, Luana announced that she was pregnant. Mama Rosa furthermore had found out about them and was furious. Everett would have to get a divorce or Mama Rosa would do awful things to him. Mama Rosa was a powerful voodoo priestess. She originally hailed from Haiti. She came to the states when she was a young girl with her father. She had brought with her the traditions of Haitian magic. It was said that she could conjure up some of the most powerful loas.

Everett was angry and frightened. He just simply could not leave Lynette for Luana. He would be ruined as far as his reputation was concerned and it would put an end to his political aspirations.

Luana became furious when he told her that marriage was out of the question. "You better marry me, big man. If you don't, Mama Rosa will fix you good. I'll tell your loving Lynette everything. You better give our child a legitimate name or I will fix you good."

Everett tried to arrange a fast settlement, offering her fifty thousand if she would agree to an abortion. Luana replied by spitting in his face, telling him that she would see him in hell first before she did that to her baby.

Everett wasn't going to let all those years of sacrifice and hard work along with his ambitions for the future end on account of a hot ass bitch. He knew Luana meant what she said.

He came to the conclusion that he would have to silence her for good and began asking certain confidants in and around Seville about finding someone capable of putting Luana away permanently. Someone who would be absolutely discreet. The inquiries let to Fat Bubba and his meeting tonight with Maurice.

Everett looked deeply into Maurice's eyes. "You know why you're here?" he asked cautiously.

Maurice smiled broadly. "Yes sir, I know what you want me to do, mister."

Everett got out a fat wallet from his back pocket and pulled out a thousand dollars in one hundred dollar bills. He handed the bills to Maurice. His eyes nearly popped out of their sockets. It had been a little while since he had hustled up that much money.

"I want it to look like an accident. I want it to happen soon. You understand me," Everett hissed. There was a hard nervous edge in his tone.

"Mister… for a thousand, I would kiss your ass or walk into hell and back," the young man stated within unmistakable finality.

Everett was satisfied that he had the right man and smiled. "Just see to it that the bitch is dead soon and don't ever let any association with her death come back on me."

"You got it mister. You're my main man," Maurice proclaimed as he put the ten one hundred dollar bills in his pocket and quickly exited.

Everett took a deep breath as a wave of relief settled in. Luana wouldn't make any more demands on him again or anyone else.

Chapter 36

SUNSET FAST APPROACHED as the swollen crimson sun began to disappear over the tall pines and live oaks off to the west. Maurice sat hunched over the wheel of the late sixties model, rusty, off-white VW Beetle. He was tense with nervous anticipation as he kept watch on the run-down shanty located a block down the narrow dirt road. He was like a lion patiently waiting for the right moment to attack his prey.

He had stolen the bug from a motel just off of I-95 earlier in the day when he spotted it. He watched carefully as the young couple in the car checked into a room. He waited a few minutes, making sure that they would not reappear any time soon. Once he was sure that the coast was clear, he sneaked across the parking lot of the motel over to the bug and jimmied the lock of the door of the driver's side. He quickly hopped inside and hot wired the ignition and casually drove it back to the outskirts of Seville where he replaced the license plate with a fake he had gotten made in case such a job as this one came along.

He had cased the old shack for a week in his beat up Chevy, watching carefully Luana's movements along with the old, wizened, thin woman that the people called Mama Rosa.

Once a week, Luana would leave the shack and walk to the paved road that let to A1A and on into Seville. Ned Struthers would pick her up in his Ford Fairlane and drive her to his farmhouse to baby-sit his two children while he and his wife went out to the weekly Baptist social at their church.

Luana managed to buy an old English Ford Escort but it had broken down on her more than once. She apparently had gotten short on bread. The heap just sat to the rear of the shack. Things had been pretty rough what with the cost of gas going out of sight due to the energy thing.

When she went to the Ocean's Port Club over in St. Augustine to sing, the manager usually picked her ups and brought her home. During the day, she would catch rides with some of Mama Rosa's people, as they were known in Seville. They were the ones who were really into the local voodoo scene.

Luana was one hot mama all right. Maurice thought often about what he could do with an old lady like her. He would get hard when he really started thinking in detail. It was a real shame that a fine lady like that had to be wasted. But she did have to die. There was no turning back now, not with an important dude like Everett Butler behind the purse strings.

Maurice was bothered by Luana being flesh and blood kin to Mama Rosa. He kept saying to himself that he never really took all that voodoo jazz seriously. Mama Rosa was supposed to be a mean mama when she was crossed. But for a thousand big ones, he would risk it.

The sky became a deep, dirty grey as the sun disappeared. It was becoming too damn still. The air did not move at all. Mosquitoes from the nearby swamp began to swarm. Maurice cursed the air as they began to bite.

He pushed the mosquitoes out of his mind when the front door of the shack opened and Luana stepped out onto the small porch. She yelled something to Mama Rosa and closed the door.

She had on a tight pair of hip-hugging jeans and a low-cut, cotton blouse. Maurice sighed. She sure was some fine mama.

When she was well clear of the shack, Maurice hot wired the ignition of the stolen VW Beetle and slowly pulled onto the dirt road. He opened it up wide and zoomed down the road toward Luana, leaving a thick trail of dust in his wake. When she heard the revved-up engine of the car, she whirled around and screamed as the bug bore down on her.

Her scream was instantly cut short as the car plowed into her. Her body went up over the hood like a broken rag doll. It came off the side of the car and fell with a dull thump onto the dirt road and was obscured by the cloud of dust.

She lay there like a broken doll, bleeding profusely from the nose and mouth and ears as Maurice zoomed away, leaving a trail of dust in his wake.

He drove to a secluded area several miles from the scene. After making sure nobody was around, he removed the fake license plate from the car. He got out a large violet handkerchief and dusted the car thoroughly with it, getting rid of fingerprints.

He walked from there back home, satisfied that he had covered himself as best he could.

Chapter 37

THE GREY SHADES of night descended over Seville like a velvet curtain, bringing with it a cooling sea breeze that swept away the remains of the burning afternoon heat. Maurice sped along the highway in the '72 Chrysler Le Baron which he bought from Oatis Carlton with the cool thousand he collected for wasting Luana Verneaux.

The sleek, long lines of the maroon-colored Le Baron had been on his mind for some time. It was all electric with plush velour seats and a stereo that could blow you away. He coveted the wheels more than anything else. He had to have it when Oatis put it up for sale. Now that he had his dream machine, he felt like he was king of the road, sitting on top of the world.

He zipped along with the radio wide open, grooving to one of Sly and the Family Stone's rockin' hits.

He was high, wide, and handsome. His plans for the immediate future included the theft of a couple of car and delivering them to one of his better contacts up in south Georgia. This particular dude would pay premium bucks for the beauties he planned to deliver.

When he got all that green cash, he would get laid and high in the company of some hot mamas he was on friendly terms with up in St. Augustine.

A traffic light up ahead turned red. Maurice quickly applied the brakes. To his horror, the Le Baron did not decelerate, but kept right on going. The speedometer increased rapidly from sixty to seventy to eighty and then past ninety. He frantically pumped the brakes as hard as he could, trying desperately to get the car to respond. The brakes did not.

Maurice went bug-eyed as he zipped and zagged in and around the flow of traffic in a desperate effort to keep from hitting someone or something from being hit.

A concealed state trooper spotted the wild frantic careening of the Chrysler Le Baron and sped onto the highway in hot pursuit. His siren's wailing at an oscillating full tilt.

Maurice's T-shirt and jeans were drenched in his steamy sweat as he continued to frantically bring the car under control without any success. Sweat from his brow poured down into his eyes making it difficult to see properly.

He was zooming toward a big eighteen wheeler. There was no way he could pass the big rig, as a smaller truck was just ahead of it in the passing lane.

The Le Baron careened out of control when Maurice turned the wheels sharply in an effort to avoid rear-ending into the big rig. The car flew off the shoulder of the road and went crashing through a large wire fence directly into a large pine in the adjacent cow pasture.

The Le Baron crashed into the pine with a shattering impact. The front end was completely demolished.

The gas lines ruptured. Fire quickly spread to the engine. Maurice's chest was pinned against the steering column. Blood trickled profusely from his ears, nose, and mouth. He tried to move and found that he could not. There was no feeling. His back was broken.

He realized that he had only moments to live. The fire would soon reach the gas tank. What was left of the Le Baron would blow sky high.

In those last moments of precious time, he saw something in the rear view mirror. It was the face of an old, wizened black woman. The ancient eyes were alive with firs of hate and triumph. There was a broad smile on her thin, dry and cracked lips.

The car exploded in an orange fireball. Thick, black smoke rose up into the hot summer sky.

Chapter 38

EVERETT SPRANG UP from the bed like a bullet, yelling at the top of his lungs. His shaken body was drenched in a cold, clammy sweat. The dreams came to him again much like they had for some time. It was always the same. He vividly was Luana's death through the eyes of Maurice and then Maurice would die in a fiery automobile crash.

He experienced the nightmare now for five consecutive nights. But that was the least of his horrors. He had suffered from those exquisitely agonizing tortures of the body along with the suffering of the spirit. It would end with that abomination when he managed to get to the toilet and excrete or vomit a host of vermin such as scorpions, maggots, spiders, centipedes, and other tiny insects too numerous to relate. His mind would go numb from the horrors that his body would expel. They would disappear almost immediately afterward.

He had lost an appalling amount of weight since it began. He was thin and drawn and looked like hell.

He told Lynette and the kids that he was going to check into the university hospital over in Gainesville to undergo extensive testing. Dr. Faulkner, the family physician, could not pinpoint the problem. He didn't dare tell her about the obscene horrors that came from his body.

Lynette was frightened out of her wits and urged him to have the test at a qualified medical facility. After he told her he was going to Gainesville, he made her promise to stay home and see to the business and the kids while he was to be there. He would let her know something as soon as possible. She was not to even try to call him. He would call her.

He was really going to confront Mama Rosa. During his youth in Seville, he heard the stories the people would tell about Mama Rosa. She was something of a local legend among the blacks and whites alike.

He never took any of it seriously before now. Voodoo hexes, spells, gods such as Damballah Guedo, Baron Samedi, Queen Erzili, and the like were black folks versions of hocus pocus and witchcraft. He had always thought of himself as being too cool to pay attention to that kind of crap.

He wished to God that he had listened more carefully to the stories and believed them. He wished that he had never laid eyes on beautiful Luana. He wished that he had never slept with the hot slut and got her knocked up. He wished most of all that he had not wasted her although there did not seem to be any other solution considering her bitchy demands. It did happen and Mama Rosa knew that he was the one responsible for it. Unfortunately, Mama Rosa was all too real.

That was the reason for him being back in Seville at this time, staying at Warlock Inn during the closing days of September. He was going to see Mama Rosa and try to put an end to his suffering.

He prayed that tonight he would rest peacefully although he knew that it was just a pipe dream on his part. It didn't help much having to stay in the infamous room 207 what with the weird wallpaper designs, paintings, and photographs. He silently cursed the manager when he told him that afternoon room 207 was the only one available at this time. The inn was undergoing extensive renovation.

He planned to confront Mama Rosa tomorrow and admit his guilt. He would get down on his knees and beg her to lift the curse that was on him if he had to. Perhaps fifty thousand that he drew out of a secret checking account from the Fairfax Bank in St. Petersburg might be just the incentive needed to get the old voodoo priestess to remove the curse and forget about Luana.

From what he had been able to determine, the old woman lived in poverty during her entire time in Seville. The kind of money he would offer her might be just the right inducement. It had to be or he just might go completely mad before death mercifully came.

Everett was seized suddenly by intense convulsions. It was beginning again. He tried to hold back the screams of anguish as the pain became overwhelming in the region of his lower intestines. The pain wracked his emaciated body with unbearable intensity as he staggered from the bed across the room to the adjoining bathroom.

His fingers fumbled for the light switch and quickly turned the overhead light on. The pain had spread up his stomach and into the esophagus. He fell to his knees and opened his mouth wide. His eyes bulged as something long and sinewy with beautiful patterns of indigo and violet slowly slithered from between his parted lips in long, thin coils, plopping into the standing water at the bottom of the toilet. The long, thin head of a snake popped up into the air. The serpent's beady little eyes seemed to fix themselves on him. The forked tongue slithered in and out of the venomous slit of a mouth.

Everett's trembling body crashed against the smooth tiles of the wall. He gasped for breath, gulping in large quantities of air as he desperately fought off the encroaching point of hysterical madness that threatened to once again overtake him.

Chapter 39

A COOL, NORTH westerly breeze began to blow though Seville as the clean lines of Everett's Ford LTD came to a slow halt in front of the rural mailbox that was just across the narrow dirt road from the little shanty shack Mama Rosa called home. Everett looked down at the leather-bound valise in the seat next to him and fervently prayed again that the contents of the valise would be persuasive money talk to the shrivelled-up, little old woman inside that brittle, dry wooden hovel.

Swift moving cumulus clouds occasionally obscured the sun in the western sky as the late afternoon merged with the oncoming approach of evening. He opened the door of the LTD and stepped out with his hand gripped tight to the handle of the valise.

He spent most of the morning and early afternoon working up the courage to finally come face to face with his tormenter. He slowly socked away a fifth of bourbon to help bolster his courage.

Everett dreaded and wished again with all his soul that he took more seriously the stories told in his youth about the powerful little voodoo mambo in her home front and her abilities to cast powerful spells and hexes on her friends and enemies with equal ease.

Despite the light cotton knit shirt and thin casual slacks he wore, Everett continued to perspire badly. His body was acting as though it was still summery and in the nineties instead of the low eighties. The last shred of summer swelter hung tenaciously in the air with a cloying sultriness that just didn't want to go away.

Everett breathed deeply and steeled his nerves as he proceeded across the dirt road over to the footpath leading up to the front door of the shanty. He took another deep breath before knocking resoundingly against the brittle wood of the door.

The door opened slowly a few seconds later. The thin, wizened figure of Mama Rosa stood before him. Her appearance was that of a dried-up little hag of a creature. She seemed even more diminutive close up than she had in the brief glimpses he had of her years ago on several occasions. She was barely five feet in height and must have weighed less than ninety pounds. Her hair was as white as wind-driven snow which contrasted sharply from the wrinkled ebony texture of her skin. Her eyes fixed squarely on him. He sensed an unmistakable feeling of tremendous animosity coming from her despite her passive stance.

She wore a grotesquely loose smock with brightly colored floral pattern embroidered profusely all over the garment. A large strand of pearls were draped around her scrawny neck and hung loosely over her flat bosom. A number of metallic rings adorned her long, tapered fingers. The rings were engraved with images of powerful voodoo loas.

Everett cleared this throat. "Mama Rosa, my name is…" She interrupted him in mid-sentence. "You do not have to tell me who you are man. I know who you are." She spit the words like poison dripping from her tongue. She had a remarkably full, throaty voice for a woman of her size.

The total hate which she had for him flashed from her dark eyes. Everett swallowed hard. The blanket of fear, which Mama Rosa immediately aroused in him, caused him to sweat much harder than even a minute ago.

He took in another breath, managing to regain his composure. "Mama Rosa, I must talk to you. Please hear me out." Everett was as forceful in his manner as possible. He had to persuade her. The excruciating horror and pain had to end.

She pursed her thin, cracked lips in a contemptuous smile, "Very well, Mr. Butler. Come in and say what you have to say to me." She raised her talon-like left hand in a gesture of invitation.

Everett breathed deeply once more, smiling nervously. "Thank you." He quickly stepped into the one large room of the shack. The pungent odor inside came from aromatic bottles containing herbs, spices, and incenses. It was a heady mixture in the close air of the shack.

The room was in semi-darkness. What light there was came from numerous small candles under oddly sculpted glass covers. They were placed on small shrines around the room.

The main shrine was to the rear. It was cared with many symbols and effigies representing the powerful pantheon of voodoo gods and goddesses such as Damballah, the king of voodoo.

Mama Rosa closed the door and motioned for him to follow her over to a small, round mahogany table in the center of the room. Four rattan chairs were placed strategically around the table. She told him to be seated and then took the chair across the table from him.

There was a period of silence for a few moments that was strong and deadly in the unbearable tension it produced in Everett. The heavy silence was finally broken by the old voodoo priestess. "What business would you possibly have with me, Mr. Everett Butler," she croaked.

Everett took still another deep breath as he reached down beside him and picked up the valise that he had just sat down on the wooden planking of the floor and placed it on the table in front of him. Mama Rosa frowned as she glared at it. "What is this?" Her voice was pregnant with curiosity and contempt.

Everett barked, "Come on, old woman. Let's drop the pretences. I'm the man who was seeing your granddaughter. We had a fling. She got in a family way and demanded that I divorce my wife and marry her."

"Yes, and you are the man that had my beautiful Luana killed," she barked back at him. "Oh, you didn't do it yourself. No! You go out and you hire one of our poor brothers to do it for blood money. You are too good to do your own dirty work. You are too fine a black gentleman to soil your fine hands with blood."

"All right, old woman. I admit it." Everett screamed out like he could somehow cleanse his conscience by confessing to Mama Rosa. He looked at the mambo with desperation sharply etched in his drawn and haggard features. The wizened old mambo took considerable satisfaction from his obvious desperation.

"Mama Rosa, I've suffered. Do you understand me? I've suffered like on of the damned in hell. I've had enough. I want an end to it."

Everett got out his wallet and took out a small key which he used to open the clasp on the valise. When Mama Rosa saw the contents of the valise, her eyes went wide as she gazed at all the new, green, crisp bills in neat piles within.

"There is fifty thousand dollars in there in denominations of twenties, fifties, and hundred dollar bills. It's all yours to do with as you like. Just end the curse right now. That's all you got to do woman, and it's all yours."

Mama Rosa stood up and crouched over the table. Her wrinkled hands reached inside the valise. She grabbed a fist full of bills. She smiled broadly. Then she began to laugh and laugh and laugh. Everett found the old woman's laughter to be contagious. He began to laugh himself. He could not stop himself from laughing.

She suddenly stopped laughing and proceed to throw the money in his face. Pure venom issued from between those cracked lips. "You think this tainted money can make up for the loss of my beloved Luana? She was more to me than my own daughter was. No, Mr. Everett Butler. You can take your damn money and leave this homefort."

Everett sobbed in desperation. "Let go, old woman. End it here and now. If you won't take the money, then I beg you for death."

Mama Rosa shook in anger. "No, Mr. Everett Butler. I'm not ready for you to die yet. I want you to feel the hideous sting of death in life for a long time and for many, many years you will know the most exquisite agonies I can conjure up for you. When I am truly satisfied, then maybe I will grant you the merciful release of death. In the meantime, at some point down the road, I might decide to do the same to your wife and tow miserable children so that your suffering might grow tenfold."

Everett was filled suddenly with s much hate for the shrivelled mambo as she had for him. "You ever do anything to hurt my wife and kids and I'll find some way to get back at you, old woman, That's a promise. You better kill me now and end it."

A rage was evident in Mama Rosa's wrinkled visage. Everett was seized almost immediately by excruciating abdominal pains that rapidly spread to the stomach. He bolted from the table and doubled over due to the tremendous spasm of sharp pain.

"Take your dirty blood money and get out of here," she ordered.

The pain eased almost immediately after she spoke. Everett reached down with his sweaty, shaking hands and scooped up most of the scattered bills and hastily placed them back inside the valise as Mama Rosa trounced over to the door and threw it open.

Everett shakily closed the valise and quickly walked past the old woman. He looked at her one last time and knew that further argument was useless. She slammed the door shut as soon as he was outside.

What was left of the pain vanished instantly.

Everett stumbled back to the car and crawled into the driver's seat. He sat there for a time as he pondered his predicament. He would have to deal wit Mama Rosa in some other way. There was no doubt of that now.

It took a few minutes for him to steady his nerves enough to drive. He turned the key in the ignition. The engine purred as he slowly drove down the dirt road in the direction of the highway.

Chapter 40

THE RAIN CAME down in a steady downpour out of an ashen grey sky on a sullen mid-October day, as a yellow cab pulled up by the front entrance of the Club Fontaine. Everett was glad that he had his Panama hat and London Fog raincoat with him while he was in New Orleans as he stepped out of the cab into the steady stream of liquid sunshine, as they would say back in Florida.

Before leaving Tampa, he told Lynette that he was going to New Orleans to see a specialist who might be able to pin his illness down. Fortunately, she accepted his story with no questions asked. But deep down, Everett knew by her moods and reactions to all the falsehoods he had told her that she was becoming suspicious of all the frequent trips. He would have to show her some results soon or she would eventually get him up against the wall and demand to know exactly what he was doing to find out what was wrong with him. He did to want to lose her and the kids. He needed them more than ever before.

Everett quickly got his wallet and paid the fare. The cab sped away from the curb down the rain-slick street located in the heart of New Orleans famed French Quarter.

The street was characteristic of the area with a multitude of jazz clubs, bars, and strip joins. The architectural feel reminded him a good deal of the historical downtown district of St. Augustine with old world two-story dwellings with exquisitely carved wrought iron railings decking the balconies.

This particular club had a beautifully decked revolving door at the front entrance. Everett quickly made the circuitous route inside to escape the heavy downpour.

The inside of the club was dark except for the tint of soft orange and amber lights in close proximity of the stage across form the bar and dance floor to the right of he main dining area with its numerous tables stacked with chairs on top. A floor crew busily went about cleaning and getting the club ready for the late afternoon and night time trade.

An enormously bloated black man sat in one of the dining chairs on the stage playing a saxophone. He was belting out a moody blues tune, which fitted in perfectly with the sombre overcast weather.

The musician was enormous. He must have stood at least six foot six and probably weighed more that four hundred pounds Everett judged by his build.

Everett cautiously approached the stage and looked up in guarded awe at the portly musician. "Excuse me, sir. Are you Albert Manness?"

The saxophonist stopped playing and looked down at Everett. He could see a hint of distrust in the small, squinty eyes of the musician. "Yeah, who wants to know?" he replied coldly.

Everett cleared his throat. "I understand that Pappa Jacque Montpellier owns this establishment. A friend of mine in Tamps, Florida said that I would have to go through Albert Manness in order to have a meeting with Pappa Jacque."

"Your friend is right on, mister," the portly saxophonist replied. An unmistakable expression was etched into this dark, beefy features as he stood up and wobbled over to the edge of the stage to the short row of steps leading down to the main floor. He walked over to where Everett stood and towered over him in a menacing manner. "Get your hands high above your head fast, mister." He barked out the orders like a crack drill sergeant in a Marine boot camp.

Everett's arms shot high above his head. The enormous musician proceeded to thoroughly frisk him from head to foot. He got Everett's black leather wallet and opened it, carefully examining the contents. After looking over his driver's license and social security card, he smiled approvingly as he handed the wallet back to Everett.

Everett pulled out the five one hundred dollar bills as his contact in Tampa instructed and handed it to the man mountain.

Albert Manness' smile broadened into a toothy grin, displaying two rows of pearly white teeth. "Solid brother. Follow me."

Everett was right behind the enormous saxophonist as he walked to a door at the rear and side of the stage and opened it, motioning for Everett to follow him. The door opened onto a narrow, connecting corridor. A large ebony door was at the end of the corridor illuminated by several small, incandescent red tear-shaped lights in the ceiling directly above where he stood.

Albert Manness looked down at Everett and told him in no uncertain terms to wait by the door until he returned. His burley form disappeared behind the door. He emerged again a minute later and motioned for Everett to quickly enter.

Everett nervously cleared his throat as he walked inside what appeared to be a handsome cedar wood paneled office. The room even had an air of corporate tidiness about it.

A tall and striking black man in his late sixties sat behind a large, shiny, ebony desk. He had a full head of curly, silver-white hair. His skin texture was as black as night itself. The eyes flashed with a uniquely vivid intensity. His wiry frame was adorned in an expensive light beige business suit.

He smiled pleasantly at Everett and motioned for him to be seated in the large, upholstered chair directly across the desk from him. He stood up as Everett seated himself and then sat back down in the posh swivel chair behind the desk.

Albert Manness firmly gripped Everett by the shoulder and instructed him to do exactly as Pappa Jacque said while he was in there. Everett nodded nervously.

By all appearances, the man he came to New Orleans to see had the look of an executive in some corporate headquarters. He did not look like a man who was called by many the most powerful voodoo priest in all of North America.

He sat back passively, appearing to be sizing Everett as he spoke. A sly smile formed on his thin, sculpted-looking lips. "I've been expecting you, Mr. Butler. I'm a difficult man to obtain an audience with, as you must surely understand. Your contact was very persuasive. He insisted that you have an audience with my person. I believe I know what your particular problem is. But please elaborate the details.

Everett cleared his throat. "Mr. Montpellier, I believe you are the only person who can help me now."

The striking older man raised his left hand which possessed long, tapered fingers such as one would imagine belonging to a fine artist or musician and gestured annoyingly. "No, no, Mr. Butler. Never refer to me as Mr. Montpellier. To the inner circle of my society, I am known simply and tastefully as Pappa Jacque. From here on you will address me as Pappa Jacque."

Everett humbly apologized. The older man smiled approvingly

Everett had made a considerable amount of inquiries among certain knowledgeable associates in an effort to find a papaloi or mambo powerful enough to counteract the hex Mama Rosa had cursed him with. The answers came back from all sources. There was only one person who would do it, Pappa Jacque Montpellier, owner and proprietor of the Club Fontaine in the heart of the French Quarter in New Orleans. A man whose ancestry was also derivative of the most powerful Haitian pantheons and dynasties.

Arrangements were made for this meeting. Everett prayed desperately to the Christian God that this powerful houngan could counter Mama Rosa's spell and make him invincible enough to force back her powerful magic with magic of his own.

Everett was already aware of the power of this man. Mama Rosa's physical and spiritual attacks had ceased the moment he got off the plane at the airport. He took a taxi straight to the Carlton Hotel and checked into his room where he remained until the time approached for the meeting as he was instructed to do before leaving Tampa.

Everett confessed all to Pappa Jacque about Luana. Her pregnancy, her threats to expose him if he didn't divorce his wife and marry her, his hiring a hit man to kill Luana and the subsequent bizarre death of the man he hired before his own personal hell began to take hold, how he tried bribing Mama Rosa without success.

Pappa Jacque smiled when Everett finished. "This young woman Luana, Mama Rosa's granddaughter was an offering to the powerful Loas. She was a key figure in many of Mama Rosa's most powerful rituals, particularly in the ones in which Damballah was honoured and the three key loas of the rada group such as Baron Samedi, Lord of Saturday, Baron Cimeterre, Lord of the Cemeteries, and Baron Crois, Lord of the Crossroads were invoked."

"Luana was the heir apparent to Mama Rosa's society when the old woman passes over to the other side and crosses the great river into the land of the dead."

Pappa Jacque leaned over the desk. "When Luana died, Mama Rosa lost a considerable key element of her power and in her eyes no amount of money can replace that kind of overwhelming loss."

"Can you help me, Pappa Jacque? I beg you to help me." Everett's voice cracked with anguish and desperation.

Pappa Jacque smiled broadly. "But, of course, I can help you, my son and I will. You would not be here now as you are if I could not help you."

"But first," he said with a broad smile as he extended his right hand across the table. It took a moment for the gesture to register with Everett. "Oh," he said excitedly as he nervously reached inside his coat pocket and pulled out a large manila envelope and handed it to the striking older man.

Pappa Jacque's smile changed to a grin as he opened the envelope and pulled out a cashier's check in the amount of fifty thousand dollars.

Pappa Jacque nodded approvingly as he put the check back in the envelope and laid it down on the top of the desk before getting up and walking over to the wall directly in back of him. He pulled back a false wooden panel, revealing a small wall safe and quickly unlocked it. Albert Manness picked up the envelope and dutifully handed it to Pappa Jacque. He speedily put it away in the safe, closed it, and secured the false panel back into position.

Pappa Jacque returned to the desk and reached down underneath, pressing a button located there. An entire section of wall opened up. A large chamber was on the other side.

"Please come with me, Mr. Butler," Pappa Jacque cordially but firmly ordered.

Everett quickly followed the tall, thin man into the secret chamber.

Pappa Jacque ordered Albert Manness to stand watch just outside the door to his office until his business with Everett was concluded. The portly saxophonist dutifully obeyed his master's instructions and stepped outside the office door.

Pappa Jacque pressed another button located on the side wall of the concealed chamber and the false section of wall slid back into place. It all seemed like something out of a James Bond movie. Instead of standing in the sinister headquarters of a master criminal organization, he stood in the homefort on one of the world's most powerful voodoo priest.

An enormously large altar with all the accoutrements and symbols of the various Loas stood against the far wall of the chamber. Etchings and symbols of Pappa Jacque's society adorned every wall. The chamber was lit by hundreds of candles encased in glass of all shaped and sizes much as he found in Mama Rosa's shanty. The strong scent of exotic herbs, incense, and spices were heavy in the close air of the chamber.

The tall, thin man disappeared momentarily just behind the altar and proceeded to disrobe. When he reappeared from behind the voodoo shrine, he worn an enormous, flowing lavender robe, which was profusely illustrated with the Petro and Rada gods and goddesses of the Haitian pantheon.

Pappa Jacque reached inside a niche in the altar and obtained a large, bulbous flask that held a milky-white substance. He secured a small glass beaker and poured a small amount of the solution into it and then looked over at Everett. "Drink this, it will protect your gastrointestinal system from any future assaults invoked as a result of Mama Rosa's death hex attacks."

Everett grabbed the potion and quickly gulped it down, It left a bitter, acrid taste in his mouth and burned slightly as it went down his throat.

Pappa Jacque smiled approvingly as he motioned to Everett to hand back the empty glass as he again reached into the large niche at the base of the altar and obtained a large burlap sack. He reached inside and pulled out a handful of granular, black, powdery substance and threw it straight down on the floor in front of Everett. There was a loud pop followed by a blinding puff of billowy, white smoke. Everett's nostrils burned from the pungent odor of the smoke. As it cleared, he was astounded. A nearly nude powerfully muscular man whose skin was black as the blackest night sat hunched over a large African tribal drum.

Pappa Jacque reached inside the sack again and got out another handful of the powder and threw it on the floor as before. There was the pop and the billowing white smoke. When it cleared, Everett's eyes nearly bulged from their sockets. One of the most beautiful and beguiling black women he had ever seen in his life stood before him. A number of long, silken veils were wrapped around her gorgeously proportioned figure. The veils were thin and nearly transparent. Everett gazed excitedly at this goddess. She indeed put the late and lovely Luana to shame in her radiant sensuality and loveliness.

The powerful black male figure began to play the drum in a compelling syncopating manner. Everett gave himself over to the beat of the haunting musical rhythm as the beguiling goddess began to hum the tune like a sweet bird singing happily. The sound of her voice was lilting and had a rich hypnotic quality.

She slowly swayed and danced to the rhythmic beat of the drum as she teasingly unravelled the numerous veils one by one until her perfect form was totally bare for his eyes to feast upon.

Everett was apprehensive, but his arousal was much stronger than his fears as he felt his phallus stiffen, forming a hard bulge against his pants. He began to sweat profusely.

The tempo of the drumbeat increased rapidly as this goddess of enchantment danced toward him in wild and sensual movements. Everett trembles as her supple body rubbed up against his own. She took his hands into her own and pressed them against her full erect nipples. She guided his hands down the contours of her stomach, abdomen, and finally took them to the lips of her sexual entrance. Everett moaned as his fingers penetrated the warm inner wetness of her walls. He felt the moist sticky fluid ooze from the head of his phallus.

She suddenly broke free from him and stepped back, her arms flung out toward him. The thumbs and forefingers were extended. Everett groaned as he experienced a powerful orgasm and felt the wet stickiness grow exceedingly until his crotch was covered with his semen.

She laughed mockingly as she reached out and took his hands in her own again and guided them around to her full perfectly rounded buttocks. Her eyes opened wide. The index finger of his left hand proceeded to penetrate her anus. His phallus immediately stiffened once again.

She pushed him away suddenly as before and began speaking in a melodious French accent. He was not conversant in French, but he knew that these were the words to a spell being cast as part of the ritual ceremony.

When she finished, there was another pop followed by an even larger cloud of blinding white smoke that before which blurred his nostrils painfully. When it cleared, the beguiling goddess and her accompanying drummer had vanished completely.

Pappa Jacque slowly advanced toward him. He held high above him a glistening, silvery, perforated cylinder suspended from a small chain. A steamy, pungent substance issued from the perforations in the vessel. He began to recite a powerful incantation to the most powerful god Damballah in a booming voice. Mama Rosa's death hex was now nullified. Everett was to be free from all spells and curses invoked against him and was this day onward protected by the great Damballah himself. He then prayed to Baron Samedi and Pappa Legba to look favourable on Everett in his day to day endeavors and to restore him to his former health.

The chamber was suddenly filled with a cacophony of tormented screams and shouts of anguish. It caused the hair on Everett's neck to stand out like the follicles had come into contact with a charge of static electricity. A chillingly cold wind whipped through the camber coming out of nowhere. It all ended in a matter of seconds.

The multitude of candles miraculously continued to burn. Everett was filled instantly with a sense of peace and serenity such as he had not known for quite some time now. He felt more like his old self before all the agony began. His assertiveness and assuredness was suddenly regained.

His tall benefactor grinned broadly as he asked Everett how he felt and told him that he was fully protected as of that moment. Everett laughed and proclaimed that he felt wonderful.

Pappa Jacque chuckled as he reached once more inside the niche in the base of the altar and got out a small baroque, oval-shaped mirror and handed it to Everett. He looked at himself and was deliriously happy. His physical features were fully as they were before the curse was invoked. It was as though it never happened.

He danced and laughed and profusely thanked Pappa Jacque for lifting the hex from him. It was as though he had been freed from an invisible prison. It was his turn now to extract punishment of the ancient hag for all the pain and suffering she had caused him. She would be very sorry that she did not take the fifty grand when she had her chance. She would be very sorry indeed.

Chapter 41

NEARLY TWO WEEKS had passed since Everett's liberating meeting with Pappa Jacque Montpellier in New Orleans. During that interval of time, there had been no further physical or spiritual attacks from Mama Rosa. There were many times when he strongly sensed that she was trying to get at him. Each time she tried met with failure thanks to the invocations of Pappa Jacque. He was fully protected from the power grips of the little mambo.

He looked across the road at the front of the wooden shanty shack as a cool north wind rose and fell with a mournful lonely whistling quality. The curtain of night rapidly descended on the small seaside town of Seville on this early October evening. An early seasonal cold front was just sweeping over the north Florida region.

Everett was determined that before the night was over his problems with the wizened old mambo would end once and for all. He was ready now to confront her and demand that she cease her attempts against him. Is she refused, he would use the total power of the Rada gods against her which Pappa Jacque granted him just before he left the homefort in that jazz club back in New Orleans.

If the old woman refused to capitulate, there would be a contest between them. One would emerge victorious and the loser would most certainly forfeit his or her life and perhaps even his or her very own soul as well.

It seemed appropriate to him that when he signed in at the desk back at Warlock Inn when checking in, he was again given the key to room 207. That room contained the right atmosphere in which to prepare himself for the forthcoming confrontation with the powerful voodoo priestess what with its unique wallpaper design and those grim paintings and tintype photographs, particularly the striking portrait of Jonas Van Gilder which loomed so ominously over the room.

Everett seemed to draw an unusual strength as he slept in that room, concentrating all his thoughts on the coming encounter with the mambo. He felt satisfied in that comfortable feather down bed, knowing that he occupied the bedroom of the evil carpetbagger who in his way was one of the most tyrannical taskmasters toward the people under him and especially his black servants, according to the history he read locally about Van Gilder.

His thoughts returned to Mama Rosa. He had worked his ass off for what he had so far obtained in life. That old bitch and nobody else was going to get in his way now.

He detested having to lie again to Lynette as he had so often about the short trip over to Seville and the reason for it. Lynette was becoming increasingly more suspicious by the day.

She was amazed and happy to see him looking like himself when he returned home from New Orleans It seemed unbelievable that his health had been so fully restored in so short a space of time. He gave her the phony alibi that the team of specialists in New Orleans found that he had a digestive diorder. They gave him a rapid treatment involving newly marketed experimental drugs along with a series of special complex vitamin supplements.

He knew that she did not fully believe him. She did not context his explanation. Every day that passed by, he felt strongly that Lynette believed him less and less. They were furiously fighting most of the time and at each other's throats for no apparent reason. He had to end it tonight before it permanently affected his marriage. It was having a telling affect on the children as well.

Everett steeled himself as he walked across the narrow dirt road and up the path to the front door of the shack. He started to knock when the door suddenly opened wide. Everett jumped back as the wizened old woman stared up at him. Her eyes flashed with fiery hate. An expression of grim determination came from those seemingly all-knowing eyes.

"I'm here tonight to demand, old woman, that your hex on me end once and for all," He tried to show as much determination as she displayed.

She motioned grudgingly for him to enter.

Once inside, he turned and faced her down. "Well, old woman. What's it going to be? I'm not exactly the defenceless man I was when we last met face to face," he noted in a resilient voice.

"I know, Mr. Butler, I know," she replied.

She did not say anything more. She did not have to. Everett already felt an assault silently being conjured up as a cold wind suddenly replaced the north breeze. It blew through the shack with a powerful force of energy that made it difficult for him to stand.

He wondered for a moment if he had made a strategic error in facing the little mambo on her home turf. He began to feel like he was burning up. Faceless, disembodied voices began chanting in rhythmic cadence. It seemed as though the blood in his veins was starting to boil.

He cried out in horror as he reached up and felt his fiery brow. He looked at his hand. It was smeared with blood. Everett began to scream as he realized that his face as dabbled with droplets of hot blood that was seeping from the pores of his skin.

The little mambo rushed over to a large wall pantry where there were all manner of potions in various small glass philtres and jars. She reached up to a large jar and got a huge handful of thick bilious-looking, slimy substance and threw it at him.

Everett cried out in sickening horror as he found himself covered with beetles, roaches, spiders, and maggots. The smell and feel of that crawling filth as it wriggled and danced up and down his body defiled him almost to the point of impending madness.

Everett was nearly at a stage of blind panic. He managed to get hold of himself just as he started to succumb to the horror. He prayed for the assistance of Baron Samedi and Pappa Legba. Pappa Jacque assured him that his patrons would guide him in combat with the mambo. His principal patron, queen Erzili, the voodoo goddess herself that materialized during the ceremony in New Orleans imbued him with her protective essence.

Everett felt her protection and his strength returned as an aura of protection formed around him and embellished him with the essences of the other powerful Loas. The vermin that covered him immediately disappeared. Within seconds, his body was as though the monstrous hoard had never appeared.

His confidence was renewed and a feeling of real fear came from the wrinkled face of the mambo. He felt as though he was gaining the upper hand in the struggle.

He instinctively emulated the arm and hand gestures of Queen Erzili in the final moments of the sensual dance during the New Orleans ritual just before the goddess vanished. He repeated the hand gestures over and over with the thumb and forefinger of each hand extended as he called on Damballah to defeat his enemy.

The force of the wind increased with every passing second. Everett felt like he would be swept off of his feet at any time and would be sent hurtling against the dry, brittle wooden walls.

Be became even more assertive in the powers Pappa Jacque endowed him with as he observed that the little mambo appeared to be gradually weakening. She began to scream and curse him bitterly as she cried out for the protection of her patron saints within the voodoo pantheon of spirits and gods.

The multitude of candles which proliferated about the shack were swept up in the blowing wind and sent flying across the various sectors of the room as Mama Rosa's power and strength suddenly returned. In that instant, Everett felt himself grow weak. He was again on the defensive.

The energy in that ungodly wind proved too much for him He went crashing back against the dry wood of the floor boards. Something enormous hit him in the pit of his stomach and his crotch. The pan coursed its way from his testicles all the way through his body. He laid there totally immobilized by the powerful blows and cried out in agonizing pain for the loas to defeat his enemy.

The wind felt like it was at hurricane strength as the fry timbers of the shack began to buckle. The structure felt like it was giving way as the glass coverings of the candle holders exploded from the intense heat. The flames from the candles somehow continued to burn. Licking threads of flame spread rapidly across the floor and to the walls. Mama Rosa screamed in agony as angry orange and crimson flames licked at the bottom end of her cotton dress. In seconds, her dried-up husk was a raging inferno of fiery death.

The acrid smoke was choking him. Everett passed out as the angry flames approached his inert body.

Chapter 42

SHE SLOWLY OPENED her eyes. A number of her neighbors huddled around her. Henry Turner, who lived two houses down, exclaimed, "You're real lucky, mister. Shack burned down minutes after catching fire. I'm afraid the fire got poor Mama Rosa. Never thought the day would come when that old woman would no longer be around."

Her mind began to clear. She looked down at herself and gasped in shocked amazement as she carefully observed the lower portion of her new body.

The sensations were unusual to say the least as she felt the male penis and scrotum where a short time ago there were the sensations attributed to the female vagina and uterus. Her hands slowly reached up and felt the face. The hands were large and manly. She felt, with an intense curiosity, the strong stubble undergrowth of a man's beard. It had a peculiarly satisfying texture as she felt around the cheeks and jaws.

She then felt the ridge between the much larger nose along the upper lip and was pleased with the neat and trimmed moustache that was there. It itched slightly. That was something she would have to get used to. If it proved too much of annoyance, she would simply shave it off.

It would take some time for her to get used to inhabiting a man's body and assuming his identity. With the guiding effort of the loas and her patron saints, she would get the feel of being a man. In time, she would even begin to think like a man.

She wondered what it would feel like to make love to another woman like Everett Butler's wife. When she finally did, the act would be a great personal victory.

She would eventually become a papaloi. Perhaps some day she would make a journey over to New Orleans and challenge the supremacy of Pappa Jacque Montpellier. That would really be something; to turn the tables on one of the most powerful masters of the religion in this part of the world.

She would probably spare Everett's wife and children and perhaps use them to her own ends.

She had the satisfaction of knowing that his soul was aware and trapped within the blackened bones of her former body and would remain like that until the end of time.

From Edgar Allan Poe's *The Bells*

Hear the loud alarum bells—
Brazen Bells!
What a Tale of Terror, now their turbulency tells!
It the startled ear of night
How they scream out their affright
Too much horrified to speak,
They can only shriek, shriek, shriek, out of tune,
In a clamorous appaling to the mercy of fire,
In a mad expostulation with the deaf and frantic fire
Leaping higher, higher, higher,
With a desperate desire,
And a resolute endeavor
Now — now to sit, or never
By the side of the pale face moon.
What a Tale of Terror tells
of the bells, bells, bells
They are neither man nor woman—
They are Ghouls:
And their king — it is he who tolls;

France Six
Visions of Death
July, 1985

Chapter 43

SHE LAID THERE naked in that small, stifling hot room not able to comprehend how this could have happened to her. She was tied to the bed, painfully bound to the metal head post and footrest. The numbing pain in her half-closed left eye where he hit her following the walloping slap across her right cheek, making a fiery red and purple bruised welt, was almost too much for her to take.

The horror came flooding vividly back to her as she remembered how he had thrown her on the large bed and straddled her. He continuously slapped her about the face, cursed her, and spit on her before he tied her to the bed with those painful lashes of coarse hemp rope. The rope burned into the soft flesh of her wrists and ankles.

She was consumed with panic as she recalled the way he tore her blouse off and cut her jeans away from her lower body with that gleaming razor-sharp knife he had gotten out of the drawer of the little stand next to the bed. She felt utterly humiliated as he cut her brassiere off followed by her panties.

The horror increased tenfold as he assaulted her numerous times, culminating with her mercifully passing out.

She tried to make her mind respond clearly. She kept asking herself how she could have been so wrong about him. He seemed so nice and even tempered when they first met at the little club located in St. Augustine Beach. They had a few drinks and danced till closing time.

She introduced herself as a student at the college in St. Augustine in her sophomore term. He told her that he had stopped of for a week in St. Augustine and would be heading to Tampa next. He was a salesman working for an agricultural firm out of Kansas City, Kansas.

She liked him. An instant chemistry developed between them, or so she thought, almost immediately. They dated every day since that evening right up through that afternoon.

He got her up in his room on the pretence that he wanted to show her some of his photos he had taken while traveling around the country. His hobby was photography. He was supposed to have had an exceptional collection of beautiful American landscape pictures that he wanted her to see.

She could not, for the life of her, detect anything but the most sincere motives in his mannerisms. She met him in the lobby of the small inn. When they went upstairs to the room, he turned into a totally different person once the door was closed and locked.

He started by calling her a slut and a whore and then every kind of vile name imaginable. The shock of it left her stunned and speechless for a few moments. When the effect wore off, she tried to leave. That was when he pounce upon her like a savage animal and began to ferociously hit and slap her. Then he threw her onto the ad and did all those horrible things to her until she passed out.

She was alone now in the stiflingly hot confines of the room. The window overlooking the narrow street was closed shut. He had turned off the thermostatic controls to the air conditioning vents in the room.

The outside temperature was still in the upper eighties, making the small room fell like it was well over a hundred. The room stank from the pungent odor of blood and heavy sweat that came form her aching and bruised and cut body. Together with the lingering scent of his strong manly sweat made her wretch and gag.

She was sick again, wanting desperately to throw up. A large piece of surgical tape covered her lips. She fought desperately to keep from doing so, realizing that she could drown in her own puke.

The sheets beneath her were awash in her sweat and his. The sheets clung cloyingly to her back and buttocks and the underside of her legs.

She began to struggle, causing the twin lashes of coarse hemp to bite deeper into the tender flesh of her small wrists and ankles. It felt like burning fire as she vainly struggled to somehow find a way to free herself.

She looked over at the door that opened onto the bathroom. It was slightly ajar. The bathroom light was on. It was the only light coming through the otherwise darkened room. A faint light could be seen at the window that came from a small wrought iron street lamp just outside at the corner intersection where the inn was located.

She stiffened as she heard the sound of running water and the regurgitating noise of a toilet being flushed. He was still there in the bathroom.

The door to the bathroom was thrown wide open. He sauntered back into the room, wearing only his bikini-style jocks. He swaggered over to the side of the bed and looked down into her terrified eyes.

She could not see his face. It was dark in there. He gently began to caress her bruised and swollen features. Then he slapped her viciously across her swollen cheek again and cursed her under his breath, again calling her a whore like all the rest of the women he had known. He had encountered many as he went around the country in the past few years. They were all whores just like his mother had been a whore all during her adult life.

He paused for a dreadful few seconds. Then he told her in an almost reverential tone that he was going to end her whoredom just as he did for all the other sluts before her. She would be one less stinking whore to spread death among innocent men like his mother had when she got syphilis for years ago and infected his father. Both of them were dead now. His father had gone to be with the Lord and his mother now burned in hell along with the devil's other sluts… not to mention the faggots and junkies who helped contribute in the vile illnesses of the world.

He reached over to the little stand and picked up the long, sharp piece of cutlery and began to make painfully tiny pinpricking cuts about her breasts, stomach, and thighs, The pain was excruciating.

The stillness of that oven-like room was shattered suddenly. There was shouting and knocking at the door of the room. She prayed that the torture she endured was nearly over. He leaped across the room and unlocked the door.

The door burst open. She nearly passed out again as she heard voices and the beginning of a fierce struggle. There was another woman's voice as well as his own.

She heard other voices coming from the hallway. Another man's voice was shouting along with his as someone rushed to her side and began to free her from the painful bindings of the bed.

She felt herself being helped out of that soaked bed. It took a few moments for the blood to again flow properly through her numb limbs.

She started to hobble across the room with the aid of her benefactor when he fell full force against her. She was propelled off of her feet and went smashing against the window of the room. The glass exploded from the impact of her body which went straight through the opening and went hurtling downward to the hard pavement below.

She hit the pavement with a sickening thump.

Her neck was twisted and broken, as was her back. Her life's blood flowed freely from her nose, ears, and mouth as the merciful veils of darkness, which was death, began to descend over her.

"Wake up, Ramona, Come on baby… wake up," Rob said as he gently tugged on her shoulder.

"Wha-a-a-t," she said with a start as her eyes fluttered open.

She was having one hell of a nightmare and started screaming in her sleep. "It must have been a real doozy what with the way you were carrying on," he said softly as he looked down at her.

She took a deep breath and was now wide awake. "Oh yeah, worse goddamn nightmare I ever had." She shuddered as she remembered the events of the vivid dream that was still fully impressed upon her conscious mind.

"You okay now?" Rob asked, showing a great deal of concern.

She smiled and nodded as he got the half-empty pack of Pall Malls from the stand next to the bed and offered her one. She took it. He proceeded to light her up with his yellow Bic lighter. She took two deep drags and slowly expelled the smoke after each one.

He slowly brushed her hair back from her damp brow and asked if she felt better now.

"Much better," she affirmed.

"Want to tell me about that bad ole dream?" he asked.

After two years of living with Rob, Ramona knew she could not put him off. Besides, she was still shaky from that horrible dream.

Ramona waited for a moment to get herself fully composed and then related the sequence of events in the dream: she was another woman. A younger woman and she was residing in St. Augustine. She met this nice guy, or so she thought. They dated every day for a week. He invited her up to his room in the small inn he was staying at in St. Augustine's historical downtown district on the pretense of wanting her to see a collection of landscape photographs he had taken during his travels around the country.

When she got up to the room, he turned on he like a wild animal and began to beat and violate her repeatedly after lashing her to the bed. He beat her and cut her for an interminable length of time. She finally passed out. When she came to, he brutalized her all over again. It was interrupted suddenly from sounds just outside the door in the hallway. He unlocked the door. It burst open and another man began struggling with her tormentor as a woman came to the bed and freed her. She was helped up and started out of the room when he fell against her, causing her to crash through the window to her death on the street below.

Rob became deeply disturbed by her vivid recounting of the nightmare. He proceeded to light a cigarette for himself and took a deep drag, expelling a steady stream of hazy smoke from his nostrils and mouth. "Wow, that is one hell of a humdinger."

They remained silent for a short while. Then Rob shouted. "You know what it is, Ramona? It's this goddamn room they put us in. That's what caused you to have such a damned nightmare. The minute we came into this friggin' room… I should have gone straight downstairs and demanded they give us another one or refund the room rent rather than stay here."

She looked at him attentively as she took another deep drag on her cigarette.

She vigorously shook her head. "No, I don't think it's this room, honey. Despite how different it is, I'm sure it's not the room which triggered the dream."

Rob kissed her on the cheek and asked if she felt better now. She snuggled up close to him, receiving some sense of security as she pressed hard against his lean, solid body.

"Think you can get any more shut eye tonight? Fourth of July parade is tomorrow in St. Augustine. If we want to get a good parking place, we better leave early in the morning," he reasoned as he looked at the digital display on his watch. It was now 3:30 a.m.

"Yeah, I think so," she said in a whisper.

"Good," he said as he kidded her teasingly behind the earlobe.

He held her close in his arms. Her sense of security grew although the vivid details of that hideous dream continued to parade before her mind's eye.

Chapter 44

RAMONA EXAMINED HERSELF in the medicine cabinet mirror above the lavatory basin and frowned while splashing some cold water in her face. It was nearly six. They wanted to get away early. They knew from their experiences in the past few days since arriving from Ithaca that the little historical district of St. Augustine would be filled with tourists and natives alike; ready to take in the local fourth of July festivities. Most of the parking lots and parking spaces would be filled up during the early morning hours.

She tried her best to put that horrible nightmare out of her mind in the past few hours. She found it nearly impossible to do so. The images of that young woman and sadist continued to flash in front of her.

She tried to conceal her inner turmoil from Rob. He, after all, did have a lot on his mind these days what with his imminent transfer by the Simpson Photo Labs coming sometime in the year from the Ithaca plant down to Jacksonville, Florida which was just due north of St. Augustine and Seville.

Rob loved Ithaca. Their families and friends all resided in the general vicinity of Ithaca. But his work and position within the company was just as important to him. He had a lot of job security built up in the company along with quite a few fringe benefits, and with the coming move came an additional two grand a year increase in his basic salary.

During the two years they had been together since their meeting at her art show where she had several of her best abstract metal statues on display, they had developed a loving rapport. The attracting between the two of them was almost immediate. They had so much in common. Everything seemed so right.

They did have some basic differences. For instance. They were on opposite ends of the political spectrum. Rob was a great deal more conservative that she was. They never let their differences get in the way of what they had together.

After dating for several months, Rob asked her to move in with him to see how they liked the arrangement. She was eager. She soon settled into his place nicely. Rob even let her use the living room of his four-room apartment for her working studio.

Just before coming down to Florida in time for the fourth of July holiday, they had an additional week in which to scout around the Jacksonville area for the right living accommodations, Rob popped the question to her, asking her to tie the knot. He wanted the wedding to take place in Ithaca just before they had to leave for down there. Ramona didn't have to think about it. Rob was the man for her. She gave him an enthusiastic "yes."

She loved Rob Lyman more than any man she had ever known. And she had known a few jocks along with some real nerds before Rob came along.

After the proposal, they quickly packed and came straight down on I-95 until they hit St. Augustine. They were taken back when they found that every place in the St. Augustine area was full. Rob figured it wrong, thinking that all the big doings would be going on south of St. Augustine down state in places like Disney World, Busch Gardens in Tampa and the Miami area.

While St. Augustine was no big place and certainly didn't go in for the big, splashy things like the more renowned spots in Florida, the oldest city still managed to pack the tourist and the locals in on the major holidays of the year.

When it became painfully obvious that they would have to seek accommodations somewhere other than St. Augustine, they headed south along the old coast highway of A1A, enjoying the occasional view of the ocean between the sand dunes and the numerous beach houses and condos, observing flights of seagulls or pelicans as they hugged the coastline or veered slightly inland off of the Atlantic.

Upon arriving in Seville, they stopped at a Texaco station and asked the attendant if there were any good motels in the area with available occupancy. The agreeable, stocky, middle-age man told them about Warlock Inn. It was the best place by far in Seville and the rates were fairly reasonable.

Rob thanked him and followed his directions carefully. It took them only a few minutes drive to find the large, rambling, old house on the scenic expanse of lovely grounds surrounding the old, quaint inn, which, on appearances, looked to be as good as any that could be found around home and upper New England.

When they checked in at the front desk, they considered themselves extremely fortunate as there was only one room left. The inn was pretty full up with tourists either headed down to Daytona or up to St. Augustine for the fourth.

The room was number 207. When the bellboy unlocked the door and showed them inside; it proved to be startling, to say the least, what with all the paintings and old photographs depicting all sorts of disasters and tragedies and the weird wallpaper design on all of the walls in the room.

The bellboy did not help either as he went on to tell them something of the history of the place with great relish, going into some detail about the man who built the house after the Civil War, a practitioner of the black arts. He was supposed to have murdered a number of virgin girls and children, offering them up to the devil as human sacrifices in far out religious ceremonies. The room was, in fact, the master bedroom where the perverted murderer slept and plotted his evil deeds.

Rob wanted to leave right then and there. She urged him to think about it since it would probably be next to impossible to find a really good motel. They were both really wrung out form the sweltering heat and steamy humidity. They would only be staying for a few days at the most, after all. After the fourth, they would pack up and head for Jacksonville during the rest of his leave time while he got a feel for that city before heading back up north.

Ramona loved him deeply. She did hate the idea of having to give up her friends and family.

She just had to face it, Rob would be down here for at least five or six years; maybe a great deal longer. If they were going to make it permanent thing, then she would have to move with him. She knew that she had a great deal of adjusting to do; perhaps sun, sand and surf were preferable to shovelling snow in the winter. She would certainly have to get used to the strong Florida sun.

Ramona shook off the reflective mood she was in and quickly changed into her tennis shorts and bikini halter and finished by coating her exposed skin with a generous amount of sunscreen lotion and coconut butter tanning oil.

When she finished, they proceeded downstairs to the much more agreeable pleasant dining room and had a tasty breakfast that consisted of grapefruit portions, poached, eggs, toast, juice, and a small urn filled with freshly brewed coffee. The food helped her outlook and disposition considerably.

It seemed easier following the breakfast for her to get more into a festive mood for the day ahead. But try as she might, she could not totally erase the vivid images of that terrible dream from her mind. Rob could detect the trouble beneath the surface and asked if there was anything he could do.

Ramona smiled pleasantly, saying she was fine. She realized though that he knew better than that. They had been together too long now for her to hide her feelings from him

His frustration returned; he again blamed the damn dream on the crazy room they were stuck in. He went on an angry tangent about the goofy decorative scheme of the room. It was the work of a real nut ball. The owners of the damn inn ought to be taken to task for having a room in such a state, despite what the man at the desk this morning made along with the bellboy yesterday in relating the history of the inn, saying that the room was a read drawing card for a lot of the patrons they had as guests through the years. Rob was almost shouting. Some of the other guests in the dining room stopped and began to look their way.

When he realized the way people were looking at him, he became momentarily embarrassed by the attention he was getting and stopped. He continued in a much lower tone. "Selling point, my ass. Probably just a bunch of sickos that like getting their kicks by staying in that room and this place because of the weird history and the fruity decorative scheme of the room and the fact that the pervert slept in there just like what the bellboy said yesterday."

Rob continued to fuss as they left the inn and went around to the parking lot toward the back. Ramona was relieved when they climbed into the late model, light beige Firebird and got under way.

It took about ten minutes for them to get back into St. Augustine from Seville and another fifteen for them to crawl across the bridge of lions into the historic heart of the ancient city. The town was filling up fast even though it wasn't yet 8 a.m.

Ramona tried to focus on the skyline of the old historic area. No matter what she did to get it out of her mind, the sights of that nightmare continued to parade across her mind.

She shuddered as the image of the brutal attack against the girl tied to that bed at the mercy of the sadistic brute came back again and again. The gleaming razor-sharp blade of the wicked knife making pricks and cuts in the girl's soft, white skin. The vivid streaks of scarlet seeping from those little wounds. The unidentifiable man and woman breaking into the room; mere figures concealed in deep shadows. The violent struggle between the girl's tormentor and the unseen man as the woman freed her from her painful restraints. And that final ironic horror as the girl's tormentor crashes into her, sending her smashing through the window to her death on the pavement below.

The girl of her dream was so pretty. The sadistic bastard that did those horrible things to her appeared to be so normal and nice; almost like the proverbial good-looking boy next door.

Ramona continued to shiver as more images flashed across her mind. Images of the sadistic brute and numerous young women and teenage girls. Images of him raping, strangling, stabbing, and even dismembering some among the number of his female victims.

The monster in her mind had killed them all over a period of four of five years as he went around the country from the Canadian border to Texas and up through the Midwest, cutting across country through the New England states and then making his bloody way south.

Rob felt Ramona's inner anxiety. He asked if there was anything the matter as he turned off San Marco, the main thoroughfare leading into the historic downtown section, and slowly drove parallel to the scenic Matanzas Bay.

Ramona smiled thinly, telling him that she was all right. But again, it was obvious that he did not believe her. He did not pursue it as he turned off of San Marco into a small parking lot across the street from the historic fort overlooking the entrance of Matanzas Bay, the Castilla de San Marco. The old fortress had stood on the sight since the earliest Spanish period.

After paying the parking attendant, a sprightly old fellow dressed in a colourful Spanish costume of the late 1500's, Rob carefully parked the Firebird in one of the few remaining spaces left in the small lot.

Ramona continued to appear edgy. Rob cursed the inn again under his breath and was totally convinced that damn room had everything to do with her state of mind. If she didn't snap out of it soon, he was going to see his attorney when he got back to Ithaca and see if there were any grounds to launch a suit against the owners of the place on grounds of mental duress or something. He would force then to do something about that room. They would pay dearly for Ramona's nightmare. He would see to it.

He managed to get his mind off that and was glad that he decided to wear his white cotton walking shorts and light, loose knit shirt for the day. Even though the morning was still early, it was already hot as the devil and very close.

He proceeded to get out and go around to the trunk and open it, getting out his large canvas bag. He proceeded to sling the straps under his arms. The bag held his Sharp camcorder as well as the plastic bags of sunscreen lotion and coconut tanning butter plus a can of Woodcutter's Insect Repellent in case they ran into many mosquitoes or mites. He was hoping to get some good footage of the parade scheduled for the noon hour to show the folks back home.

"All ready, honey?" he asked.

Ramona tried to appear as relaxed as she could as she smiled nervously. "All ready," She answered.

They proceeded from the parking lot down the main tourist area along St. George street, giving all appearances of a typical tourist couple. The images of the nightmare continued to blot out any carefree attitude for Ramona.

Chapter 45

THE HOT NOON day sun was almost directly overhead as they stood shoulder to shoulder along the curb side of San Marco. The parade was just getting started. The heat had been unbearable through most of the morning. Finally, a moderate breeze began to blow in off of the Atlantic across the bay and into the downtown district, giving them some much needed relief from the nearly stifling heat.

They spent most of the morning taking in the arts and crafts show in the little park one block west of the old coquina stone pavilion within view of the bridge of lions which ran across the bay. The edifice was the sight of slave auctions in the antebellum days prior to the Civil War much like the one in Charleston, South Carolina, according to an old gentleman they talked with briefly. He was a spry character and something of a local historian and had been a resident of the old city for over thirty years.

The twang of banjos generating the rhythm of folksy bluegrass music was in the air as young and old alike ate, drank, and frolicked around the various exhibits.

They went from the little park over to Lightner's Museum located in the grand Moorish designed building built by O.C. Lightner, taking in the impressive collection of authentic antiques and artefacts of old Europe and the orient as well as curios from the other four corners of the world that were elegantly displayed on the three floors of the section of the huge building which housed the museum.

They finished up the morning with an early seafood lunch on the marina pier overlooking the bay. Rob feasted on lobster and cracked crab while she had an order of steamed oysters and clams. She finished the meal with several ice-cold Cokes while Rob downed a tall, cold bottle of Miller Lite.

Ramona continued to try her best to concentrate on the holiday festivities and keep her mind focused on the here and now. She still could not erase the details of the nightmare from her mind.

Always, the image of the naked girl tied to the bed and the sharp knife pricking her flesh just enough to bring up nasty red whelps which oozed little streams of scarlet and looking almost like strawberry pop was with her.

Rob knew it to, which did not help his disposition any, despite his trying not to show it. Ramona felt remorse at spoiling the festive mood for him. It was obvious that he was doing a slow burn about it although he didn't mention it during the morning.

She was grateful when the sea breeze kicked in off of the Atlantic as they made their way along San Marco back toward the old fort for a good view of the parade when it got started. The relief from the heat helped him cool off emotionally as well. She found that she could relax a little better also.

She hoped Rob was right about the dream. This it was the result of staying in that awful room.

It was certainly the most absurdly decorated place she had ever slept in. She felt a disturbance inside her from the first moment they sat foot in the room. But that feeling she had that dream was due to more than just the bizarre nature of their room continued to stay with her. She never before had experienced a dream in such exacting detail. It was like watching a horrendous drama being had experienced a dream in such an exacting detail. It was like watching a horrendous drama being played out on a TV screen except that the screen was in her mind and it was continually being replayed.

The parade got under way as local civic and political figures began to pass by working the crowd with waves and kisses from the various demonstrator cars they rode in. They were followed by a platoon of National Guardsmen n parade dress and naval personnel in the rear proudly displaying old glory and several naval pennants.

A small group of clowns were next, performing various acrobatic manoeuvres and bits of slight of hand magic for the amusement of the children as they handed out chocolate kisses, candy canes, and lollipops.

She asked Rob to let her have the camcorder so she could get the shot she wanted of a colourful group of mounted police riding gorgeous white Arabian stallions. The horses were among the most beautiful she had ever seen. She loved horses more than any other animal since childhood.

Rob passed the camcorder to her. She immediately hoisted it up and looked through the viewer to line up the best shot. She froze. The young woman of the nightmare and her tormentor stood right across the street.

Rob glanced at her and was struck immediately by the look of stark shock etched in her attractive features. “What is it, Ramona? What’s the matter?”

She stood in silence for a moment with the camcorder deadlocked on the girl and her companion. Rob tugged on her arm, snapping her out of the momentary paralysis she was in the grip of so suddenly. She looked up at him with one of the most incredible expressions of disbelief he had ever seen displayed by another human being.

“Rob, I saw them. The girl and the man in my nightmare. They’re right across the street,” Her voice almost faltered as she spoke.

“What!” he shouted, not able to comprehend what Ramona had just told him.

“I tell you, it’s them Rob. I’m not hallucinating or anything like that. The pretty brunette in the tattered denim shorts and tank top halter and the slender man in the jeans and cut away T-shirt… they are just across the street. I’m not hallucinating Rob. They are the people in my nightmare. I spotted them while lining up the shot.” The urgency with which Ramona spoke readily communicated to him her absolute sincerity.

He grabbed the camcorder from Ramona and looked through the viewer directly across the street and spotted them. The girl and the man with her did fit the description Ramona gave him of the main characters in her dream when she got up.

Despite the heat and humidity, Rob felt a chill creep through him. It gave him a feeling that seemed as cold as a winter’s wind emotionally. “You’re absolutely sure Ramona?” he demanded.

“Yes, I am, Rob,” she snapped as the tension she felt continued to build. “They are the people in my dream, goddamnit.”

Despite his own unsettled feelings, he wanted to get Ramona to calm down and to let her know that he was supportive of her for the time being. “Okay, I believe you. What do you think it all means?” Ramona trembled slightly. “I don’t know. Rob… we have to follow them wherever they go. This means something. I can’t explain it. I just know that something bad is going to happen and maybe my dream might help to prevent whatever it is from coming to pass.”

Rob protested, “This is crazy as hell, Ramona. I don’t like it one bit.”

A flash of anger sparked in her eyes as she snapped at him. “How do you think I feel? I don’t like it one goddamn bit either, mister. But I can’t just pretend that I didn’t have the dream and the people in that dream aren’t standing in the flesh just across the street from us this very moment. I’m going to follow them whether you come with me or not.”

Rob had never seen her this upset and genuinely frightened before. He was worried and frightened himself. For the time being, he would humor her and go along with her wishes. It was that or face her wrath and anger for a long time to come. He prayed to himself that this was all some kind of bizarre coincidence and fervently hoped the whole thing would pass quietly and Ramona would get it out of her system.

The good time plans for the day were shot to hell anyway.

Chapter 46

THE SEA BREEZE died shortly after the parade ended. The afternoon heat was stifling as the temperature soared well past ninety. The crowd slowly broke up. It took some considerable effort for them to elbow their way across the street in time to stay within sight of the girl and her companion as they walked slowly south along San Marco in the direction of the central core of St. Augustine's historic district.

Rob's concern for Ramona increased. The strain on her emotions became considerable and very obvious with every passing minute. His own inner frustrations were becoming more apparent as well. Ramona's inner self was at war emotionally. He hoped this experience didn't leave her with any long lasting emotional scars.

As Ramona strolled along, her eyes firmly fixed on the girl and the man; new images flashed shockingly before her. Images of a crazed mother preaching about the whoredom of all women to a frightened little boy, telling him that all women were worthless sluts. The whole lot of them. Womankind was the beast of burden to man ever since Eve tempted Adam with the forbidden fruit.

The boy became a teen and feared all girls he came into contact with. He was jeering and taunted by his classmates in school.

His suppressed sexuality became increasingly confused and upsetting. Finally, his inner psyche cracked wide open.

The teenage boy was now a man. The horrible images of little girls, pretty teenage girls, and attractive young women again were viciously assaulted, tortured, and then either strangled or horribly stabbed to death. The images continued to flash before her; one right after the other.

Ramona was more afraid now than she had ever been. Despite that sickening anxiety, she was driven by some inner compulsion she could not avoid. The images in her mind were telepathically coming from the inner consciousness of the male companion. They were scenes from his boyhood right up to and including the present day.

Between the mental strain and the oppressive heat, Ramona began to feel slightly light-headed and queasy in the stomach as the girl and the man turned off of San Marco onto one of the small side streets. They headed in the direction of St. George Street, which was the main tourist Mecca of the ancient city.

Ramona wanted desperately to stop and reset. She could not allow herself any relief. She had to stay with them no matter what.

They stayed behind the girl and the man at a safe distance so as not to be noticed by them.

Rob was becoming extremely anxious for her as they turned into St. George Street. He maintained his cool.

They passed a squad of men from the national park service dressed in the uniforms of 17th century soldiers representing Spain, France, and England as they walked south along St. George Street. Ramona stopped him as the girl and the man went inside a small bar about a half block from where they were.

Rob got out the monogrammed white handkerchief from his back pocket and wiped the sticky sweat from his brow. "Man, I'm glad those two went inside that joint. I could use a cold beer about now."

Ramona smiled uneasily. She was as glad as Rob was to get inside someplace with air conditioning and get something cold to drink. She was beginning to get a sinus headache and was feeling slightly queasy.

They slowly walked down the street and went into the semi dark, small confines of the bar that was lit in low key amber and orange lighting. There was just enough to see by.

They got a couple of seats toward the end of the bar. Ramona looked all around, spotting the girl and the man as they sat at a small table in the corner of the room. The walls around them were festively mounted with stuffed swordfish and sharks. In addition, there was a collection of shark's teeth and fishermen's nets.

A classic fifties jukebox stood near the front of the bar. A standard Juice Newton tune from the early eighties filled the small bar with mellow country sounds while Rob ordered an ice-cold Bud for himself and a Coke for her. The smiling gent tending bar yelled, "Comin' right up folks."

Ramona tried to be as inconspicuous as possible while keeping an eye trained on the girl and the man. She prayed that she would not be noticed.

The bartender returned with a tall, foaming glass of beer and a large sixteen ounce bottle of Coke. Rob quickly paid him and slid the bottle of Coke over to her. She quickly gulped down three large slips. She felt instantly relieved as the ice-cold pop went down her throat, rapidly cooling down her internal body heat.

The girl began to giggle along with her companion. They laughed heartily, at some joke, no doubt, as they each finished drinking two glasses of what looked like champagne. The man reached over and kissed her lightly on the lips. They got up after finishing their drinks and walked over to the cash register at the other end of the counter and paid their tab. They then left the bat.

Ramona nudged Rob hard in the ribs. He glanced at her with a look of anger. "They just left. Come on," she snapped.

They got up and quickly went outside. Ramona spotted the girl as she headed in one direction while Rob watched the man disappear, turning off of St. George a block down from the bar.

"You follow him and I'll follow the girl. I'll meet you in the park near the old pavilion in about an hour."

"Oh, for Christ's sakes, Ramona," Rob snapped.

"Do it Rob, or our relationship is in real jeopardy," she snapped back with an anger which he had never before seen in her.

"It's that important," he said, still hardly believing the sequence of events that had transpired from the time of the parade.

She nodded a silent yes.

"All right. I just hope this isn't all for nothing, or maybe I better say I hope it is," he quipped before jogging down the street in an effort to catch up with the man.

She silently prayed to herself that it really meant nothing as well. She knew in her heart that a life just might be saved on this fourth of July as well as countless others lives.

Chapter 47

RAMONA DIDN'T KNOW whether it was the close heat and strong afternoon sun or the throngs of people passing her that made her feel confused and light-headed. A sinking sensation began to sweep through her as she looked frantically about her for the girl. Suddenly, she was nowhere to be seen.

Ramona made her way through the clusters of Americans, Latinos, Europeans, and Japanese tourists. Her eyes roved all about in an effort to spot the girl. She sighed a breath of relief when she saw the girl looking in the window of a costume jewellery and dress shop just south of where she stood. The girl stood looking in the display window for several minutes and then went inside.

Ramona breathed deeply as she walked in the direction of the front door of the shop. She had to go inside. She had to talk to the girl. She had to know her name, where she lived, and hopefully learn something about him.

A strong sensation came over her. The horrors of that nightmare would happen soon, maybe even tonight.

She breathed deeply again as she opened the door and stepped inside the little shop. She spotted the girl over by the jewellery counter looking at several display cases. A pleasantly appearing stocky sales lady was talking with her and pointing to an elegant pendant necklace in one of the cases as well as a number of other pieces of handsome imitation jewellery.

Ramona tried to appear as casual as possible. She pretended to look over a rack of summer dress wear and jogging suits.

A skinny sales girl came over and asked if she could be of assistance. Ramona smiled pleasantly, telling the girl that she was just browsing. The girl smiled back. In a heavy cracker accent, she told Ramona to take her time. If she found anything she liked, just let her know and she would be of service.

Ramona smiled and thanked her. The girl then walked over to a couple just entering the store. Ramona's attention again focused on the girl of her dream as she continued to converse with the stocky sales lady.

The sales woman left after a few more minutes, disappearing into a back room at the rear to the shop. Ramona swallowed hard. This was her chance to get the girl's attention.

She breathed deeply again and slowly walked over to the jewellery counter, standing right next to the girl.

"My, but that is a lovely necklace," she said casually.

The girl looked at her and smiled. She answered in a pleasantly low modulated voice. "That it is. I would like to buy it. But the price is too high for my budget right now."

"That always seems to be the way of it. The most desirable things come along when you can least afford them," Ramona quipped jokingly.

The girl laughed as she heartily agreed with her. Ramona steeled herself, pretending to be a casual tourist. "Didn't I see you with a good-looking guy at the parade across from the Castilla de San Marco?" while reaching out to shake her hand and introduce herself to the girl.

The girl's name was Shirley Fargo. She was from Flint, Michigan and down in St. Augustine as a student majoring in commercial art at the local college. She decided to stay on in the St. Augustine area for the summer so that she could take advantage of some courses in sculpting that were being offered at the St. Augustine Art Institute.

Her folks back home were in the middle of a messy divorce. She had no desire to get into the middle of an emotional scene like that at the present time. She was still very close to both parents.

"I'm sorry to hear that," Ramona said. "I can understand where you are coming from. My aunt and uncle recently went through an unpleasant divorce. You might say that we are sisters under the skin. It so happens that I am a commercial artist and do a little sculpting in metal on the side."

The girl immediately warmed up to her. They continued to talk enthusiastically about their common vocation. Once a rapport developed between the girl and herself, Ramona began to probe her about him.

'Have a boyfriend down her?" Ramona asked politely.

Shirley told her in glowing terms about having dated a few of he boys in her class, but there was no one special until just this past week.

"Oh," Ramona commented, trying her best to constrain her inner feelings. "I imagine you are referring to your handsome friend I saw you with at the parade."

The girl smiled and nodded shyly. His name was Jerry Tanner. They met at a dance club over on St. Augustine Beach and hit it off right from the beginning. He was originally from Lexington, Kentucky and was a travelling salesman for a company out of Kansas City, Kansas the specialized in heavy duty machinery for agricultural and forestry products and agri-business. He was down here to conclude a large deal for harvesting equipment with a farming consortium out of Hastings, a little town southwest of St. Augustine. They had been dating every night since they met. She really liked him and things seemed to be getting serious between them very fast.

Shirley asked about Ramona. She related the essentials. How Rob was down her on a working vacation of sorts. They had plans to look over the Jacksonville area. His company would be relocating there sometime next year.

Shirley glanced at a wall clock after she had finished telling her the particulars about herself, saying that she had to go. She had a lot to do before meeting with Jerry for the fireworks display later on in the evening.

"Maybe I'll see you and Rob there," she quipped before departing the shop.

"Maybe," Ramona called out as she left. Ramona now had a case of the jitters which was nearly impossible to hide.

She quickly left the shop and followed discreetly behind Shirley, walking along St. George Street until coming to the intersection close to the old inner city cathedral that was just across the street from the little park.

A fairly large crowd strolled about the park as a smaller cluster of people huddled around the little gazebo-like band shell which was across from one of the large obelisk-shaped memorials dedicated to the memory of the fallen in the Civil War. A trio of Dixieland musicians were belting out an old ragtime tune.

As soon as the street light changed, Ramona hurried across and frantically made her way through the crowd in the direction of the pavilion. She spotted Rob sitting on a bench next to the narrow walkway by the pavilion. The bag containing the camcorder was tucked under his arm next to him.

She hurried over to the bench and quickly sat next to him. She saw instantly that his mood had not changed since departing on St. George street. His feelings of anxiety and frustration were even more apparent than before.

"Did you stay with him?" she asked anxiously.

"Yes," he answered in a miffed tone. He had followed Jerry Tanner over to the south end of the old city district to a small inn, which was just off of San Marco close to where the Florida National guard headquarters was located, by the bay. He went inside the small inn. Rob followed discreetly behind as he went upstairs to his room on the second floor.

"did you get the room number?" she demanded frantically.

"Yeah, number eight," he replied coldly. "The inn is called the Monk's Habit." He waited around in the lobby for a short time waiting to see if the man was going to come back downstairs. After fifteen minutes, he left and came back to the park and waited for her to return.

Ramona told him what she was able to learn while talking to the girl.

Rob's features were suddenly flushed with anger. All his pent-up frustration erupted. "Ramona, you had one hell of a bad dream last night. You saw those tow standing across the street during the parade and they looked something like the characters in the God awful dream. But honey… it was coincidence. You have let this thing get way out of control. I'm really starting to get worried about you."

Ramona exploded then. All her inner feelings spewed forth. "No, no, no. It was more than just any dream, Rob Lyman. I don't know how or why it came to me, but it did. And I can't let go of it."

"Rob, that guy who calls himself Jerry Tanner is a serial killer. He's killed countless numbers of girls and women. He's going to kill Shirley Fargo… maybe this evening. I can't ignore it. You and I might be the only people in this world to keep that from happening."

Rob turned livid with anger. "Christ woman. What are we supposed to do? What do you think the cops would say if I went and said my girl had this dream last night. This dream involved a Miss Shirley Fargo and a Mr. Jerry Tanner. It seemed that Mr. Tanner is gonna kill Ms. Fargo and it's all gonna happen just the way my girl dreamed it. Now — would you be good enough and go arrest Mr. Tanner so my girl can have some peace of mind."

Ramona sat cold and stony-eyed for a moment. "Rob, we've got to stop him," she exclaimed as a feeling of total helplessness sat in and pervaded her spirit.

Rob blew up, "I'll tell you what I'm gonna do. I'm going back to that little bar and maybe get loaded. If you come to your goddamn senses, then come on over and join me."

He bolted from the bench and slung the pack straps over his shoulder and went off in a huff.

Ramona sat there for a long period of time in a daze, hardly believing that this could really be happening. She was afraid and hurt. She knew only one thing, whatever Rob was thinking, whatever this might mean s far as their relationship was concerned, she had to try and stop that man from killing Shirley Fargo no matter what the consequences might be to her personally.

Chapter 48

RAMONA PACED BACK and forth along the walk in front of the narrow cobblestone street. She was increasingly disturbed as she closely watched the front entrance of the small, two-story, white façade, old world style, Spanish inn. A large brown sign erected just about the entrance proudly announced in large, bold, amber Gothic lettering that the establishment was the Monk's Habit. A comical caricature of a 17th century monk of the Franciscan order painted in bold strokes was next to the name.

She had stood watch for several hours, finding this place easily as she followed Rob's directions after the blow up in the park.

She was exhausted, hot and thirsty. She hadn't eaten anything since the late morning. The sickening sensation of fear and raw nerves along with the painful tightness that squeezed her stomach all the way into her bowels was almost too much for her to bare.

She had no clear idea on what to do or how should she hope to convince the authorities when they were needed. She had only a half-baked idea on how to stop the heinous crime from happening before Shirley Fargo was brutally murdered by the man who called himself Jerry Tanner. She could not even be sure that it would happen tonight although her gut instinct told her that it might very well occur this evening.

There had been no sign of his coming or going or anything else. If he was in his room, then he probably hadn't left the inn since Rob followed him there earlier.

Ramona was thankful that a late afternoon sea breeze came in off of the ocean as it did earlier after enduring the brutal heat during most of the late afternoon. The sun almost became too much for her several times in the intervening hours.

Ramona glanced at her watch. The passage of time had gotten on top of her. It was now 8:09. The brilliant yellowish orb, which was the sun, was in the distant western horizon. The light was becoming much softer. It was starting to fade much faster as sundown approached.

She was nearly ready to throw in the towel when she saw Shirley come around the corner and approach the front entrance of the inn.

Ramona quickly concealed herself as best she could in the doorway of the little coquina shell building across from the inn and watched intently as Shirley went inside. She had changed into a light, loose-fitting, white cotton dress with bare shoulders since their encounter in the shop that afternoon.

Ramona began to feel real helplessness after Shirley disappeared inside the inn. She just did not know how to prevent the girl's death now that the dream seemed so close to becoming reality.

A middle-age couple passing by saw how distressed she was. The man, a rather distinguished-looking person with silver white hair and an iron grey moustache, asked if she was all right.

For a second, she thought about telling them of her predicament, but the feeling of helplessness was too strong as she realized how it would sound to them.

She smiled and thanked them for their concern. There really wasn't anything that they could do.

"All right miss," he said, smiling uneasily as they walked away. The couple soon disappeared from view as they went around the corner at the other end of the block.

Ramona fretted with herself in silence for another fifteen minutes, realizing that it might already be too late to do anything for Shirley. As the sky took on deeper hues of grey, orange, and an pinkish fringe tint with the oncoming sunset, she knew she had to act.

She went across the street and quickly entered the lobby. It had a strong feel of old Spain about it and was cast in soft amber lighting which came from ornate candle-shaped lights that were in uniform rows on all the walls.

Ramona composed herself as best she could and casually strolled up to the front desk when a slightly built, balding, little man stood. He had a thick half-smoked, smelly, cigar tucked firmly in the right corner of his small mouth. He looked up at her and took the stogie out of his mouth, laying it in a tarnished brass ashtray on the counter in front of him.

He smiled pleasantly as he asked if there was anything he could do for her. Ramona forced a smile as she said to him that she was a friend of Mr. Tanner. She wondered if he was in his room at the present time.

The little man frowned slightly, saying that Mr. Tanner was in, but he had another lady friend visiting with him at the present time.

The little man frowned slightly, saying that Mr. Tanner was in, but he had another lady friend visiting with him at the present time.

Ramona's nerves tingled as she told him that she was a friend of the lady visiting with Mr. Tanner. They were all going to meet here and go out for the evening together.

The little man grimaced slightly and then smiled forcefully. "Well, in that case, you can go up. Its room number eighth. Just turn right at the top of the stairs. The room is down the hall on the left.

"Thank you," she said pleasantly.

He forced another smile and then picked up the stogie and popped it back in the corner of his mouth.

Ramona slowly walked over to the narrow stairs. Little knots formed in her stomach and the tightness in her bowels increased significantly as she braced herself and proceeded to climb up the stairs, holding tightly to the solid walnut wooden rail until she was at the top.

Her heart raced faster as she walked down the narrow shadowy hallway until she got to her room number eight.

She froze in front of the door and listened intently for any sound coming from inside. There was some movement in there. It sounded like someone was trying to frantically move about, but was being prevented from doing so because of restraints.

All of Ramona's frustration and horror became too much for her. She pounded on the demanding the he stop doing the horrible things he must be doing to poor Shirley right now. The jig was up. The cops were on the ay. He had better give himself up.

The door suddenly burst open. He grabbed her by the arm and threw viciously inside the room. Ramona almost fell form the violent jerking action.

At first, she was dazed and sick from the affects of her ever-growing fear along with the toll that the daytime heat had taken on her. Her vision swiftly became acclimated to the darkness of the room. She became even sicker as the strong stench of blood and urine assailed her.

Her eyes almost bulged from their sockets when she saw him standing nearly nude before her except for a pair of male bikini-style jocks. The large bulge at his crotch could clearly be seen. He held the long, wicked knife she saw in the dream threateningly in his right hand. She could not take her eyes off of the long, gleaming blade of the stiletto. It was stained with scarlet blemishes.

She glanced over at the brass bed where Shirley lay spread eagle. She was totally naked. Her wrists and ankles were lashed by heavy hemp lines securely to the head post and foot rail of the bed. Her soft white flesh was blemished with numerous pricking wounds. They oozed little streams of sticky red blood. Some of the wounds had dried and the blood had coagulated and crusted over.

Her face was badly swollen and bruised. The girl's eyes nearly popped from their sockets as she stared at Ramona. Those eyes cried out in horror and helplessness. A large adhesive bandage covered her mouth, preventing her from crying out.

"Who the hell are you? How did you know about me?" he demanded.

Ramona stood frozen in horror and shock. She found it impossible to speak or react in any way.

A wicked gleam appeared in his truly evil eyes. "What's a matter, lady. Cat got your fucking tongue? Since you're here… you might as well stay for the party. I'll have the pleasure of slicing up two motherfuckin' sluts tonight.

Just as he pounced upon Ramona, the door to the room burst open. Rob came charging inside. Tanner whirled around to see who the intruder was. The knife swished through the air several times. Rob was nearly cut the second time, but he managed to duck out of the way and grab hold of Tanner's arm. A terrific battle ensued between them.

Ramona leaped over to the side of the bed and went about undoing the painful skin-burning knots of coarse hemp from Shirley's tender wrists and ankles which kept her pinned to the bloody urine and vomit saturated mattress.

Ramona carefully peeled the heavy adhesive bandage away from the girl's cracked and parched lips as the battle between Rob and the sadistic monster continued to rage about the room.

The girl convulsed and sobbed, "Oh! Thank God. Sweet merciful Jesus in heaven. Thank you."

Ramona helped her to her feet. They started toward the door when Rob dealt the bastard a hard blow to the solar plexus which sent the madman crashing against Shirley. Glass exploded everywhere as she went sailing through the gaping hole in the window.

Ramona heard a sickening thump from outside. There was screams and shouts from passers-by on the street below and the noise of a car's brakes being applied suddenly. The vehicle came to a screeching stop.

In spite of everything, it had ended just like in the nightmare with poor Shirley Fargo falling to her death in the street.

Rob caught Ramona in his arms as she mercifully fainted.

Chapter 49

RAMONA GRADUALLY REGAINED consciousness. She had been in a near comatose state for several hours. She was dressed in a white, regulation hospital gown, lying in a regulation-size hospital bed in a small, off-white room.

Rob stood over her. He smiled as he asked how she felt. She was groggy and woozy. Other than that, she felt as well as possible considering everything.

"Did Shirley Fargo survive the fall?" she asked urgently. Rob frowned as he shook his head, signalling that the girl did not make it.

Two other men walked over to the side of her bed from out of the corner shadows of the small room. One of the men was a police officer, judging by the uniform he wore. The other was probably an attending doctor on call. He wore a white linen jacket.

The police officer introduced himself as Sergeant Lee Philips of the St. Johns County Sheriff's Office. He was a weather-beaten, slack-jawed, angular man in his late forties. The sergeant told her that she had a very close call. Thanks to Rob, she was saved from that murdering monster she knew as Jerry Tanner, but unfortunately Miss Shirley Fargo was killed.

Ramona was confused and distraught, despite the strong sedative that she had been given. The doctor asked her to stay calm and quiet. She had suffered a strong shock and was suffering some trauma as a result of her experience.

Rob tried to reassure her once again while holding tight to her hand. He told the sergeant that they met Shirley and Terry Bradley at the parade, although Bradley called himself Jerry Tanner. They became friendly and agreed to all meet at the Monk's Habit and go out together that evening to watch the fireworks display. He had a problem with the car. So, Ramona came on ahead to the inn to meet Shirley and him.

Ramona went up to the room and found Shirley tied to the bed and horribly cut. Tanner came out of the bathroom and tried to attach her with a knife. That's when he arrived. When he saw what was happening, he tried to stop Tanner. There was a fight. In the struggle, Tanner fell against Shirley after she was freed from the bed and on her feet. The impact caused her to fall through the window of the room to her death. "It was one of those bizarre tragic things that happen sometimes," Rob concluded solemnly.

"Is that right, Ms. Wyzconski? That's the way it happened?" the sergeant asked in a quiet but firm voice.

Ramona looked into Rob's eyes. She answered, "Yes, yes. That's the way it happened officer."

Rob breathed a deep sigh of relief. He was glad that she realized his false explanation was for the best. The truth about the vision in the dream just simply would not be believed by a typical hard nose cop. There would probably be months of legal hassles, examinations, and cross examinations by a battery of cops and legal people. It would just not be worth it and the police would never fully accept the truth.

Ramona asked for a drink of water. Her throat was scratchy and dry.

Rob reached over and got the pitcher on the little table by the bed, pouring out a medium amount of cool water in a clear, plastic glass. He got one of several clear straws on the small tray where the pitcher of water sat and put it in the glass. He smiled at her as the sergeant helped to prop up her pillow. Rob gave her the glass of water. She emptied it in a second.

Ramona looked up at Sergeant Philips and asked "Who is he really?"

The detective studied her drawn features for a moment. Then he told her that the killer's real name is Terence Spencer Bradley, twenty-six years of age. After putting out a make on him with the FBI and other law enforcement agencies around the country, they had him pretty well fingered as the serial killer responsible for the brutal murders of at least twenty young girls and women spanning a period of some two to three years. Since his arrest, he had confessed to at lest three of the murders that he was suspected of during that period of time. "The bastard almost bragged about the way he killed those poor kids" the sergeant stated. His southern drawl was heavy with disgust and revulsion.

Rob then asked the sergeant how long they would have to remain in the St. Augustine area, telling him that he was due back to work in another week.

Sergeant Philips nodded understandingly, saying that they would have to make statements and give depositions. But after a few days or so, they should be able to leave, although they would have to return to give testimony at the trial when the time was set in the future for a specific date.

Ramona smiled uneasily as the doctor told her she was doing fine and would be able to leave the hospital around noon the next day. Sergeant Philips told them that would be all for the time being and thanked them. He would see them in the morning before Ramona was released from the hospital.

The doctor told Rob it was time to leave. He had to make his rounds and Ramona needed her rest.

Rob asked to speak with Ramona for a few minutes. The doctor agreed and left the room along with the sergeant.

Despite her medication, Ramona broke down and began to sob once they were alone. "Oh Rob, that poor girl. After all I tried to do to save her, she died just like in that horrible dream."

Rob took her clammy hand in his again and squeezed it reassuringly as he kissed her on the damp brow. "I know baby. I'm just sorry I got so mad at you and left you alone like that. If I hadn't cooled down, you might be in the morgue along with that poor kid instead in here in a hospital bed."

He looked deep into her eyes. "I love you Ramona, more than anything. Just as soon as we get back home, I want us to get married."

She smiled as he bent down and crushed his lips against her own. "Yes, oh yes. That sounds like haven to me," she said.

Ramona became passive as she thought about the terrifying events of the past day. "Do you suppose that it was meant to be, Rob? Poor Shirley dying the was she did?"

"I don't know honey," he said. "Why not think of it this way… you probably have saved any number of girls from that murdering scumbag."

He looked at his watch. "I better go now. See you first thing in the morning," he bent down and kissed her again and then left.

A nurse came in just as he left. She poured out a small paper cup full of water and gave her two Demerol capsules. Ramona quickly popped them in her mouth and washed them down with the water.

It wasn't long before she fell asleep.

The girl lay strapped to the bed all cut about and oozing blood. Ramona enters the room. His face looms over her like a wild animal snarling and ready to pounce on its prey.

The door burst open. A fight ensues as Ramona frees the girl from the bondage of the bed. The girl had wicked bruises and whelps on her wrists and ankles where the coarse rope burned deep into he soft, white flesh. She starts across the room when he falls against her. She screams in horror as she is sent crashing through the window.

Ramona springs up in the bed. Her heart is pounding. She is drenched in a cold sweat. She nudges against something solid that is next to her. She looks down. The lacerated, broken body of Shirley Fargo is next to her. The body is grotesquely twisted.

The skull is caved in. The neck is broken. The eyes are alive and staring at her. Those eyes almost pop from their sockets. There is a wild look of insanity in those eyes, which are alive in death.

Shirley's mutilated features grin. A horrible laugh echoes in the close spaces of the room. That awful mocking laughter begins to pound its way inside Ramona's head.

She screams and scrams and screams. Several nurses and orderlies run into the room to see what is the matter. Ramona continues to scream even as they try to comfort and reassure her that everything is all right.

Nightmare/Parrott

How different? one might ask. In this: That the thing invoked is a thing of a different nature; however, it may put on a human appearance or indulge in its servants' human appetites. It is cold, it is hungry, it is violent, and it is illusory. The warm blood of children and the intercourse at the Sabbath do not satisfy it. It wants something more and other; it wants obedience, it wants souls, and yet it pines for matter. It never was, and yet, it always is.

Charles Williams,
Witchcraft

The gates of hell are open night and day; smooth the decent, and easy is the way.

Virgil,
Aeneid

Chapter 50

AGAIN, MIRANDA'S ASTRAL spirit left its host and floated freely in the peaceful void of black space. It proved to be a unique experience as she felt Mama Rosa's spirit gain ascendancy over Everett's newly found powers. There was an exhilaration brought on by release of spiritual energy as his soul left that dried shell and took possession of Everett's younger and stronger male body.

Miranda hoped with all of her karma Mama Rosa had failed ultimately in her scheme to dominate and subjugate Everett's wife and children. Everett was a hypocritical bastard in life, but Lynette and the children did not deserve the suffering Mama Rosa must have planned for them as part of her revenge.

For some reason, Miranda felt more at peace following this out of body trance than she did in the aftermath of her experiences than she did following the previous ones. She was becoming more assured as she moved through the peaceful void of space.

Following a short interval of time, she felt the veils of darkness left. Again, she could see her physical self in the chair. John hovered over her anxiously.

She sucked in a deep breath when her astral spirit merged with the material body. Her eyes slowly fluttered open. Moments later, the eyes focused sharply.

She looked up at him and winked, smiling sweetly as she did so. "It was much easier this time. I don't feel nearly as drained

John gently rubbed her left cheek with the palm of his right hand. "I'm certainly glad to hear that. I don't mind telling you that it continues to worry the hell out of me when I'm not able to discern a proper pulse. Your skin becomes very dry and unusually cool until the spirit and flesh are once again joined.

Then it's like you just came out of a steam bath or something similar."

"Speaking of something wet, I could really use another cup of water." Her throat was dry and felt like parched sandpaper. That part of the trans channel state remained very much the same and no wonder, considering the enormous expenditure of psychokinetic energy expended during the deepest phase of the trance state.

"Another cup of water coming up my lady," John cheerfully quipped as he moved across the room and disappeared momentarily into the adjoining bathroom.

Miranda listened to the pleasantly lulling sound of running water coming from the lavatory tap. John re-emerged with a cup full of cool tap water and quickly handed it to her.

Miranda gulped it down. The water immediately eased the parched sensation in her throat.

Chapter 51

"ARE YOU ALL right? Snap out of it, Miranda," she faintly heard him say as her spirit reunited with her physical body and a state of unconsciousness was once more achieved.

Her eyes slowly opened. It took a few minutes for them to properly focus. She looked into the spiralling bands of the scope while coming fully out of the deep trance state. The visual stimulus helped her to become fully aware in much the same way that it helped her to go into the trans channel state of hypnosis and transmigration.

This last trance was the most stressful of any for her. Her head throbbed with a dull, pulsating pain that was painfully acute around the temples. Her heart action had accelerated to a potentially dangerous level, beating well over a hundred times per minutes.

She was drenched all over in a cold and clammy sweat. The pupils of her eyes dilated. More than several minutes passed before they returned to normal. The pit of her stomach was tight and sore. She felt slightly nauseous and her mouth was as dry as sandpaper. In addition, her tongue felt thick and coated. There was an awful bitter taste in her mouth.

She looked up into his eyes and began to cough and gag slightly as the nausea quickly began to subside. He took her hand in his. "Hey, are you all right?" he reiterated.

She swallowed hard and got some saliva going in her mouth before she attempted to answer him. "Yeah, I'm okay John," she said in a confident but weak tone.

Her eyes locked onto his in a pleading fashion. She flatly stated that she could not go through another transmigration of the astral spirit any more at this time.

He smiled as he brushed the damp hair from her face. She felt a great relief when he told her that this last session was the final one. According to all the data he had been able to gather on the history of the house and this room in particular, there was no further unusual or bizarre manifestations or phenomenon beyond what they explored during the night.

Miranda gulped hard. She began to relax and breathe easier as her pulse arte rapidly returned to a normal state, "Thank God for that," she said wearily.

He went over to the table and got the bottle of Jim Beam along with a Dixie cup and measured out a small amount of the whiskey and handed the cup to her. "Here, have another snort. You've earned it, lady," he said forcefully.

She raised the cup to her dry lips and took a large sip. It went coursing down her throat and esophagus, immediately warming her up. The cold, clammy sensation was quickly replaced with a warm, tingly feeling.

She asked what time it was. He looked at his watch and announced that it was approaching four in the morning.

"Did you get it all on tape like before?" she asked with a note of urgency.

"Everything," he replied with a grin.

"I would like to hear it tomorrow," she said. He squeezed her hand, replying that he would give her a command performance to this evening's very successful endeavor.

Miranda handed him the cup after emptying it of the contents. He placed it on the table by the spiralscope and metronome as she told him to turn the instruments off. He did so immediately.

She was even more exhausted than she realized and slumped back against the straight back chair as best she could, taking an additional few moments to regain some of her strength.

"I hope the taping went excellently, John Nash. I tell you now that I will never again do anything more like we did here tonight in this place." She shuddered as she tried to blot out the numerous horrors of the past few hours from her still stimulated mind. She had never experienced such an overwhelming feeling of evil before this past night.

In her minds, she still saw the chilling visage of Jonas Van Gilder on the wall of the room. She felt tremendous malice and hate wail up in her bosom as the black, cancerous evil of that man impressed itself more acutely upon her state of mind. "The portrait of the evil man who built his abomination would be taken out somewhere and burned. If the owners of this place really wanted to do what was right, they would rip out everything in this room that had any connection at all with him and have a priest perform an exorcism and then have this room sealed off from the outside world for all time."

He was taken back by the intensity of her conviction. This place had its affect on her.

"I doubt that will happen any time in the foreseeable future, Miranda. This room has been a pretty big draw for the inn over the years," he commented while giving her a hand up. She still felt somewhat weak in the knees

"The almighty dollar once more takes precedent over the right thing to do," she said bitterly as he helped her into the adjoining bathroom. She opened the cold water tap wide in the lavatory and rapidly splashed a generous amount of cool water in her face, which aided her considerably in her recovery.

She looked over at him and grinned. "Oh! That's much better," she squealed. Beads of water dripped down over her drawn, attractive features in tiny rivulets.

He handed her one of the soft fuchsia-colored hand towels. She carefully dried her face.

She asked him for an aspirin then and he dutifully opened the door to the medicine cabinet, getting out a small bottle of Anacin. He hurriedly opened it. She got two and popped them into her mouth as he handed her another Dixie cup filled with tap water. She took the cup and quickly washed the aspirins down.

She felt even better almost immediately after swallowing them as she followed him back into the room. She sat back down this time on the edge of the bed. He sat next to her. "All better now?" he asked.

She looked over into his eyes and nodded yes. It was at that moment she picked up on his innermost thoughts. Her sense of relief was immediately gone. He had not yet gotten the house out of his system. He had not come to grips with the house and its neurotic obsession centering around it.

Miranda shuddered. She was more afraid for him now than ever before. He had lied to her. She sensed his overwhelming determination to go downstairs and to the back of the house. He was determined to penetrate the evil darkness of the closed away cellar where Jonas Van Gilder and his female accomplices practiced their blasphemous rites and murdered so many of the innocent.

She was very frightened for him. Her sixth sense told her that something which was the total embodiment of all that was Jonas Van Gilder's perverted personality which was left behind after his demise dwelled in that cellar.

Her thoughts turned to the horrible episode, which took place at the close of the roaring twenties when that pathetic transsexual psychotic gained access to the cellar along with the Cuban rum runner during the hurricane that hit the area at that time. The transsexual was almost immediately possessed by the demoniac atmosphere of the place. She was sickened again as she saw in her find the way he sliced the Cuban's throat and held the head until it was hacked completely off. Chills went up and down her spine as she again saw the reverent manner in which the transsexual approached the well and dropped the head down into the dark seemingly bottomless realm beneath the earth of the inn. She clearly heard the eerie growl of satisfaction over and over in her mind as the thing began to feed on the head, taking sustenance from the brain.

In that split second, she came to the realization that she was in love with John Nash. She now was prepared to give herself fully to him. She would do anything she could to keep him from harms way.

Her eyes caught his in a deep, passionate embrace. Tears rolled down her cheeks as she stood up over him. He stood up and she threw her arms around his neck, burying her head against his chest. "I love you, John Nash. And I'll be damned if I will let this place bring harm to you. Forget Warlock Inn. I want you. I need you.

He pulled gently back and looked deep in her large, wide eyes. He read the desire and the need in those eyes as he crushed her to him. Their lips met in a long deep and passionate kiss. It felt so good for him to feel her body cling tight to his own.

He had wanted her this way for what seemed like an eternity of time. He thought this day might never arrive. Perhaps it was the intensity of this night and the experiences she had endured for him which caused her to realize her true feelings for him, whatever it was that finally made the difference, he was ecstatically grateful.

She whispered to him in an earthy tone, telling him to quickly gather up the tools of her work and put the smaller cups back in the valise. He smiled and answered dutifully, "I hear and obey."

As he hurriedly went about the task of gathering up the tuning fork, metronome, spiralscope, and crystal brandy glass and placing the smaller items carefully in the valise, Miranda quickly turned down the covers of the bed and got out of her clothes.

When he turned and saw her standing gloriously naked before him, he swallowed hard. He wanted her so much. It took the events of the past few hours to finally make it happen.

His heart raced faster as he felt the blood rush to his shaft, causing it to become nearly erect. It bulged noticeably against his crotch.

He quickly pulled off his slacks and jocks after tossing his shoes and socks in a corner and climbed into the large bed next to her. He crushed her soft, warm body against him and smothered her face and neck with kisses.

"I love you, Miranda. I have ever since we met in college," he whispered just before he darted his tongue in and out of the deep, warm recessed of her yielding mouth.

He then kissed and bit her lightly on the earlobe and neck and then worked his way down to the swell of her breasts, gently licking and sucking on her taut, erect nipples, sending waves of warm excitement through her body.

She responded with a feverish intensity of her own. One which she never knew herself capable of before now. It was as though all the repressed passion and sensuality she had hidden inside her erupted all at once. They petted in a mounting frenzy for some period of time, their bodies were washed in warm perspiration due to the sexual energy of their ever increasing lovemaking.

Miranda went wild after John mounted her and fully penetrated the deep inner recesses of her sexuality with his long, thick shaft. He began to move in and out at an ever increasing pace. She managed to keep up with him as the pace quickened to a furious level of absolute ecstasy. She screamed and squealed with delight as she experienced a wonderfully powerful orgasm just as she felt him explode inside her.

They laid very still in each other's arms for several minutes after they climaxed together at virtually the same moment. She was limp and exhausted.

Between the passion of lovemaking and the tremendous amount of energy expended while she was undergoing the trans channel experience, she was drained totally. In a short period of minutes, she was fast asleep.

He watched her lovingly as she slept and stayed very still for a while, making sure she was fast asleep. Once he was sure she was, he slowly untangled his arms from around her and slipped out of bed.

He hurriedly put his clothes on and tiptoed over to the closet. He carefully opened the closet door, keeping the noise down to a minimum so as not to wake her, and got down a small crowbar and a large halogen lamp from the upper shelf. He looked back at her. She was still fast asleep.

He proceeded to tiptoe over to the door of the room and open it. He looked back at her sleeping form, blowing her a silent kiss. He went out into the hallway and quietly closed the door behind him.

The dim, amber glow of the lights in the corridor produced a soft, shadowy affect. It gave him a slightly creepy feeling of total solitude as he moved down the hallway to the staris.

He breathed a little easier as there was no sign of anyone around. He hoped to conceal himself from the night man on duty downstairs as well as from any of the other staff who might be around. It would be hard indeed to explain the high beam light and crowbar he had with him.

His intentions were to quietly get downstairs and to the back hallway of the inn where the door to the cellar was located. He would use the crowbar to pry off the large padlock on the door and gain access into the underbelly of Warlock Inn. He was determined to finally explore that legendary hell hole as some of the local residents referred to the cellar.

He had learned a good deal this night during Miranda's retrogressive transmigrations. The house was heavily scarred by Van Gilder's monstrous personality with particular emphasis on the infamous room 2-7 which was the satanic warlock's master bedroom during his years of residence in the house. Somehow, the malignant atmosphere of the house and that room in particular drew those evil or ill-fated souls to the inn through the years. Those who died as a result deserved their fates. Those souls, which survived their ordeal, gained tremendous if scarring insight about themselves that would probably serve them for the rest of their days.

All through the night, the aura of the cellar reached up into room 207 urging him down there to come face to face with whatever secrets it held just as it had since his youth.

He hated to go against his promise to Miranda, but his was something he had to do no matter what the consequences might be. He simply knew that he would never be able to rest well until he had come fully to terms with everything connected with the inn including the cellar.

If Miranda did indeed love him, she would forgive him and come to accept his need to conquer his fear and fascination with the house. He would do everything he could to earn her forgiveness after this was all over.

When he reached the narrow landing by the stairs, he stopped and made sure that no one else was about in the lobby below. He slowly made his way down the stairs, careful not to make any sound that would alert anyone to his presence. He concealed himself in the shadows as much as was possible. When he was finally at the bottom of the stairs, he breathed considerably easier and tiptoed over to the other side of the lobby as so to peek in the direction of the front desk.

The night man on duty was hunched over the desk totally engrossed in an article he was reading in one of the current issues of "Time."

He looked all about again and was satisfied that he was the only one around besides the night man at the front desk and slowly moved in the direction of the narrow corridor that led to the rear of the inn.

His nerves tightened as he slowly made his way down the corridor until he was about halfway between the front of the inn and the back, stopping at the massive door which opened onto the cellar.

A thrill of nervous anticipation went through him as he turned on the high beams of the lamp and looked down at his watch. He blinked several times and squinted his eyes so as to see the time clearly. It was not 4:55. After turning the light off, he glanced all about and took the crowbar, wedging the tip end of the flange in between the metal collar and the wooden frame.

It took all his strength along with three powerful jerks on the crowbar before the heavy screws that secured the hasp to the wall were loosened. One more tremendous expenditure of energy on his part forcefully freed the lock from the door.

He did his best to keep the noise down to a bare minimum with a certain amount of success. His brow was beaded with heavy perspiration, which he quickly wiped away with the back of his left hand.

A thrill of fear and wonder went through him. After all the years of waiting, he would finally have his chance to really explore the core of the house. The ungodly chamber where Jonas Van Gilder slaughtered so many during his reign of black terror more than a century ago. He was going to at last come face to face with whatever force of entity that had haunted him for so much of his life.

His adrenaline surged as he laid the crowbar down along with the light and reached out for the doorknob with a trembling hand. It took a considerable effort just to open the massive door. The large iron hinges were badly corroded from years of neglect. He very slowly inched the door open. The hinges squealed and squeaked in such a was as to send the hairs on the back of his neck bristling form the grating noise.

His heart began to race as he opened the door wide and reached down to pick up the large light. If he was discovered now, Stavolous would probably have him thrown out and barred from ever again stepping foot in the house.

A foul-smelling stench came rushing out into the narrow hallway. The odor was a disgusting mixture of mold, mildew, fungusoid bacteria, and rat droppings. The stink was so pungent that it made him slightly queasy for a few moments.

As the awful aroma began to abate, he stiffened his resolve and overcame his basic fear as much as he could. He would have to close the door once he was inside to keep from being discovered.

With the crowbar in hand, he switched on the light as he placed the crowbar down on the top step of the narrow wooden stairs that led down into that unholy chamber. He hurriedly forced the door to shut tight. The hinges made the same excruciatingly dreadful grating noise as before.

The powerful halogen beam of light from the lamp revealed the gloomy dimensions of the place as he slowly descended down into the heart of the cellar. The thick, coquina, stone walls were covered in black grime and mildew. Sickening green fungus bred slime, which sprouted along the damp walls. Gigantic spider webs and sotags streamed like gossamer threads from the heavy support beams and crossties of the ceiling. The silken threads fell neatly down to the pitted stone flagging of the floors.

His skin crawled as he was consumed with disgust. The floor undulated with numerous fat hairy rats. Some had dirty brown fur while others were a motley grey. Swollen roaches and spiders danced about the floor and wills of the horrid chamber.

He played the light around until it fell on the large satanic altar at the rear of the pesthole. This was the damn site were the warlock and his female counterparts took many innocent lives. Close to the back wall slightly off to the side of the damn thing was the large cistern well.

He was again consumed with a sense of loathing disgust, but he was determined to see it through until he was finally satisfied.

The large rats began to squeal and scamper for hiding places as he moved about. There wasn't a sign of the filthy vermin within a few seconds. He breathes easier as the sight of those filth-ridden vermin was making him sick.

His skin continued to crawl nevertheless. The overwhelming sense of evil down in the ungodly place simply could not be denied.

His attention was suddenly captured by what seemed like a low, muffled grunt coming from the area of the well. He swallowed hard as he braced himself. He literally had to force himself o advance in the direction of the well.

No matter what it was he heard, he had to know everything there was about this place. He had to.

His back stiffened as he slowly moved over to the large stone cistern and hovered over it.

He was soon covered with a cold sweat as that ominous grunting noise continued. The light trembled unsteadily in his shaking hand. He held it high and aimed the powerful beam straight down into the well.

It seemed incredible, but there did not seem to be any bottom to the well. Where was no water, no solid earth or solid stone foundation… just an empty black hole that seemed to go on forever.

Something suddenly sprang up out of the blackness. He screamed once as he never had before as a monstrous thing pounced upon him before he fully knew what was happening.

It had the shape of a man. It was huge and muscular. The flesh was like scaly, grey, reptilian hide. The face seemed human and the features resembled the likeness of the man in that troubling portrait up in room 207, Jonas Van Gilder.

He was paralysed in a state of heart-stopping terror as the beast growled triumphantly as it raised its talon-like left hand that ended in long, razor-sharp claws. It slashed at his face repeatedly until one could not even recognize him as having been human.

It took his lifeless body and slung it across its massive shoulders and leapt back down into the seemingly limitless black void of the well.

It continued to growl with a deep sense of satisfaction as it munched on his braid after having ripped off the top of his skull.

Chapter 52

MIRANDA TOSSED RESTLESSLY on the mattress, groaning and sobbing as she slept; vividly reliving her experiences while in the various retrogressive transmigratory trances. It was as though all those tragically frightening episodes blurred and melded together in one very frightening mosaic.

She was pursued first by Frank in female dress. He was a grotesque parody of a gaudy flapper girl.

He lingered menacingly in shadows while pursuing her through the various rooms and corridors of the inn, brandishing that wicked-looking skewering knife that he used to kill the Cuban. Frank was almost upon her. The knife was held high, ready to strike as she reached room 207 and threw open the door. She ran inside and slammed the door shut, crying out when she hard the blade of the knife as it was embedded in the wooden panel of the door.

Her heart pounded She was covered in a chillingly cold sweat. A heavy silence followed the near fatal attack.

When she was certain the dreadful figure of the transsexual was gone, she braced herself while again opening the door. She was greeted with more shock. Nate and Sally stood in the hallway. Nate grinned at her. He had the long, nearly invisible, needle-sharp, steel probe. Sally smiled sheepishly. She was glassy-eyed and looked like she was stoned out of her mind.

"See this babe? It's a real gas. This'll kill you," Nate said. His speech slurred so badly she had trouble understanding him.

Nate handed Sally the long, thin needle and told her to put it to the bitch just as she did it to dear old Uncle Daniel. Sally held onto it between the thumb and fingers of the right hand. She began to giggle stupidly while moving threateningly in Miranda's direction.

Miranda slowly backed away from the girl. Suddenly, she heard something that sounded like a goat baaaing and whirled around. She screamed. A monstrosity in the form of a black goat standing upright on tow large legs loomed before her. Its eyes were two slits that burned with the scarlet flames of hellfire.

The monstrosity opened its mouth wide. The jet trail of flames spewed from that obscene mouth and again Nate and Sally were consumed in a fiery inferno.

Miranda continued to scream hysterically as their bodies melted away and disappeared followed by the goat monstrosity.

She was alone again and trying desperately to fight off the feeling that at any moment she might lose her mind.

A struggling sound got her attention then. It came from the bed. With a sense of trepidations, she walked over to the bed and cried out. The horror nearly overwhelmed her. Poor Shirley Fargo lay naked. She was stretched out on the bed with her wrists and ankles painfully slashed to the head and bottom rest of the bed; her mouth painfully taped, preventing speech.

The serial killer stood over her with the large razor-sharp knife in hand. He proceeded to inflict tiny nick and gashes in her soft white flesh, creating red whelps that oozed little streams or red.

Despite her near hysteria, Miranda ran toward the serial killer with the intention of somehow stopping him from tormenting the poor girl. She cried out when she went right through him and fell across the bed straight through what appeared to be the girl's mutilated body.

She continued screaming while fleeing from the room in a near panic. Her heart was racing faster. Her head throbbed from an intense feeling of aching pressure.

She stopped just short of the stairs. The frightened figure of Bobby Sailor stood by the stairs. The boy began to pleas with her, screaming for her help. He was lost and didn't know what had happened to his parents.

She ran over to the frightened boy and tried to hold him close and comfort him. He may have been a spectral figure also. But she took great comfort as he put his arms around her neck. She held him tight.

Miranda closed her eyes and promised the child she would do all she could to help him.

The boy suddenly felt different. She opened her eyes and nearly fainted. Mama Rosa stood before her. The old crone began to cackle like a crazed loon. Her dried-up, little mouth opened wide. A number of tiny serpents wriggled out of her mouth and spilled out onto the floor. They wiggled obscenely about at her feel and then slithered away.

She fled down the stairs as that insane cackle reverberated throughout every nook and cranny of the inn.

She looked all around. The immediate area of the lobby was totally devoid of human presence. Moreover, there was a remarkable physical change. The wallpaper was stained black with mold. It was yellowing with mildew. Spider webs hung from every arch and column in sight.

Miranda jumped back in disgust as a vicious, large, grey rat with hungry eyes pranced close by and began to squeal annoyingly at her presence.

Her attention was further arrested as the lilting sounds of "Moonlight Serenade" filtered into the lobby from the ballroom. She slowly walked toward the double doors, which opened onto the ballroom. She opened them wide. She was back in the era at the height of the second World War.

The small stage was filled with a big band orchestra. They were performing a melodious arrangement while shadowy figures of young men and women danced cheek to cheek on the small dance floor.

She carefully moved around the parameters of the room. It was very dark. She was stopped by a new horror. A large, oak wood coffin stood in one corner of the dance floor. One of the small, humanoid creatures that was not of this earth stood on one side of the casket. Tom Sanchez stood on the other side. He beckoned to Miranda. She started forward as the alien creatures opened the transom of the coffin lie.

Miranda looked down and screamed hysterically in a dreadful cry of horror. Her body lay within the confines of the oblong box.

Miranda fled from the ballroom back into the hallway. She cried out with an overwhelming sense of relief. John stood close to the front desk. His arms stretched out to her. She ran to him and crushed her body against his and smothered him with kisses of relief.

He held her tight and whispered in her ear, telling her that he had something very important to show her.

He slipped his arm around her waist and guided her through the connecting corridor leading to the rear of the inn. He stopped in front of the open door to the cellar.

She pulled back. "I'm frightened. I don't want to go down there," she pleaded.

He smiled reassuringly, telling her not to be afraid. He was with her. He would protect her.

He reached out for her. She reluctantly took his hand. He let her down the narrow steps into the dark realm of the cellar. She was nearly overcome with the vile stench that hung heavily in the close air.

She wanted to pull away from him and flee. He held tight and promised that no harm would come to her as he led her past the ruins of the blasphemous altar over to the ominous well.

Her fear became more than she could bear, strongly sensing the presence of something which was down there in the confines of the old cistern. It was the ultimate embodiment of the evil that haunted the house since it was built in the last century.

An insane laughter followed by a tormented wailing reverberated within the dark prison of the cellar. The underbelly of the inn was instantaneously populated with all the spectral figures from the visions encountered during her transmigratory episodes.

Rob and Ramona, Shirley and her tormentor, Nate and Sally along with Uncle Daniel and Mama Rosa were closest to her. Marisa Stohler held Bobby Sailor's left hand. Tom Sanchez held the boy's right hand as they led up the rear of that ghastly procession.

They advanced slowly in her direction with expressions of total madness etched on each and every one of them.

She looked up at John and knew the ultimate horror. He was not there. The figure, which held her hand in a vise like grip so tight that she thought the bones might be crushed, was none other than Jonas Van Gilder.

The apparition smiled as a scream froze in her paralysed throat. He proceeded to sweep her off her feet, holding her tight in his powerful arms.

He then jumped down into the dark confines of the well with her. It felt as though she would go on falling forever through some black void that had no bottom.

Her eyes flew open. She ached from head to toe. It took a few moments before she realized that she had fallen out of the bed onto the floor. Fortunately, the rich, soft weave of the fabric cushioned the fall, preventing any injury to her.

She slowly got to her feet and managed to stifle a scream when she looked at the bed and saw that it was empty.

She trembled while crying out, "you in the bathroom, John?"

There was no answer.

She ran to the bathroom and threw open the door. It was empty.

A cold, sinking feeling swept over her as she saw that his clothes were no longer mixed on the floor with her own.

She hurriedly dressed, praying that he was all right as she ran to the door of the room and threw it open. She did not take the time to close it.

She ran down the darkened hallway to the stairs and rapidly descended them. When she was at the bottom, she looked all around. There was no sign of John. The feeling of rising anxiety and panic grew much stronger as she approached the front desk.

Nick Stavolous was behind the desk busily examining the registry. He looked up and smiled. Miranda anxiously asked if he had seen John. He observed her anxiety and showed his concern as he observed her ruffled appearance. "Why no, I haven't Ms. Spencer. Is there anything the matter?"

She was near tears and did not try to conceal it from him. "Are you sure, Mr. Stavolous?" she asked urgently.

"Yes, Ms. Spencer, I am. However, it's possible that some of the early morning staff might have seen Mr. Nash. Many of our employees have gotten to know him in the past several weeks. Just a second. I will ring the bell." He proceeded to tap the little bell next to the registry hard with the palm of his right hand.

One of the bellboys appeared moments later along with a white-haired, middle-age lady dressed in one of the maid service uniforms. They observed her tousled look and obvious anxiety. "Bobby, Mrs. Saunders, have you seen the gentleman who is doing the articles about the inn? Ms. Spencer is looking for him."

"No, haven't seen Mr. Nash since yesterday," the bellboy replied. The downstairs maid replied in like manner.

Nick Stavolous smiled uneasily and thanked them before sending them back to their duties.

He expressed his regrets to Miranda." Would you like for me to tell Mr. Nash that you are looking for him if I should see him?" he inquired.

Miranda seemed to stare off into empty space. A cold and all-consuming feeling of great loss settled upon her.

"Ms. Spencer, would you like me to tell Mr. Nash that you are looking for him if I should see him?" he asked with a growing sense of concern for her.

Miranda snapped out of it. Again, she fought back the tears, replying that it would not be necessary.

Nick Stavolous compassionately asked if there was anything he might do for her. "Forgive me, Ms. Spencer, but you seem very distraught."

She forced herself to smile, replying, "No, there is nothing you can do, Mr. Stavolous. Thank you all the same."

He smiled uneasily in return and wished her a good morning as she walked away from the front desk and quickly went around the narrow connecting corridor leading to the back of the inn. Her fear increased significantly when she stopped halfway down the hall in front of the door, which she instinctively knew opened onto the cellar.

She cried out bitterly, "Oh, dear God, no!" The padlock had been pried loose. She reached out with a trembling hand and tried the doorknob. The door opened.

Tears streamed down her cheeks. Her darkest fear was not confirmed. Her overwhelming loss flooded in upon her. She cried in wracking sobs for more than a minute. When she was able to regain her composure, all she could think of was to collect her belongings and get out of that house of death and horror known formally as Warlock Inn just as soon as she could.

She ran frantically back to the lobby and upstairs to her room and then to room 207. In something approaching panic, she busily went about gathering up her things in both rooms and furiously packed. She hated the house more than anything she had ever before encountered in her life and wanted to be out of there for good.

She stuffed the tools of her trade in the valise and overnight bag and fled down the hall to the stairs, taking the steps two at a time and ran over to the desk.

Nick Stavolous looked at her in shock. He asked again if there was anything the matter. She nodded negatively, saying that she had urgent business to attend to back home. She had just learned about it and had to leave at once.

"This is so sudden, Ms. Spencer. I was given to understand that you would be staying wit us for several additional day," he said.

"I'm sorry, Mr. Stavolous. But I must leave now. If there are any expenses, please make out a bill immediately.

"Oh no, Mrs. Spencer. The arrangements Mr. Nash's publishers made with the inn covered fully your expensed as well as his own. I'm sorry you have to leave like this. I hope your short stay was a pleasant one."

Her lips trembled. She tried to smile. "Everyone had been most gracious and kind. Thank you."

She turned and hurried toward the large double doors at the front entrance.

"Do you want me to relay any messages to Mr. Nash when I see him?" he called out.

Fresh tears rolled down her cheeks, noticeable streaking them. "No, no messages. Thank you." She put down the overnight bag long enough to open one of the doors wide. One of the bellboys ran over to her and offered to carry her things out to the car. She responded politely but firmly that it would not be necessary and proceeded across the veranda. She rapidly descended the steps down to the walk. The bellboy frowned as she disappeared from view and went back inside.

The End

www.ingramcontent.com/pod-product-compliance
Ingram Content Group UK Ltd.
Pitfield, Milton Keynes, MK11 3LW, UK
UKHW020144250726
13967UKWH00002B/852

9 781425 150532